No Cream In The Middle

A novel by

Carlos Harleaux

NO CREAM IN THE MIDDLE

Copyright ©2017 by Carlos Harleaux.

Published by 7th Sign Publishing

(www.PeauxeticExpressions.com)

ISBN 978-0-692-85589-8

Book Cover Design and Illustration by Jeremy Biggers

Photography by Mr Fotobooth (Chris Booth)

Also By Carlos Harleaux

Poetry & Prose
Blurred Vision
Hindsight 20/20
Honesty Box
Stingrays

Novels
Fortune Cookie

Look out for the upcoming poetry book, *Commissioned To Love*, as well as the final installment of the *Fortune Cookie* series.

PROLOGUE

His mortality flashed before his eyes on his way down. There didn't seem to be any time to think between when the SUV smashed into the barricade several times and ultimately being ejected from the vehicle. All he knew was this was not how his life was supposed to end. If he ever had the chance, he would seek revenge by taking matters into his own hands. He would make sure they both suffered long, slow deaths. But as he accelerated towards the water, his plan seemed doomed; so did his life.

Boom! His body slapped the surface of the water as large shards of glass grazed across his skin. As he plunged into the water, he could feel the sting of the cuts. His chest and back immediately felt sore from the forceful impact of falling from the bridge and into the water. Despite his pain and fatigue, the adrenaline of the moment helped him push his way back to the surface of the water. The surrounding areas were desolate and he could barely see any stars. He looked up and saw the road lights on the bridge, but they were of no help to him down there.

That's when everything went black and it wasn't just from the darkness outside. He could still comprehend everything that was happening but his body was paralyzed. He didn't see a way out of this one and his energy was quickly waning. He must have been losing consciousness. There was nothing he could do now other than accept his fate.

After what seemed like an eternity, he finally found some semblance of dry land. There was a faint light looming over his head. It was just before dawn. When he finally came to, he could faintly make out a woman kneeling over him. Her hands were moving towards his chest: she looked just like Cookie. Was it her coming to finish him off? He wasn't going to let that happen. With a jolt of energy resembling an electric shock, he reached out and began choking her. He squeezed harder and harder as Cookie kicked, screamed and shouted to break free. That's when he got a really close look. It wasn't Cookie after all. Just a woman that looked eerily similar to her. He then loosened the grip on her neck.

The woman hacked up from the back of her throat and spit in his face and then slapped him. "How dare you?! You crazy bastard! I found you out here and was just trying to see if you were still alive," the woman screamed. Brandon apologized, but she was too far gone and frazzled at this point. Still coughing and gasping, she decided to call the police.

"Wait. Wait. I'm very sorry. There's no need to do that. I'm Jason by the way. I just thought you were someone else. I got into a horrible accident last night. I know it sounds crazy, but I'd rather not get the police involved. Nothing they can really do now anyway at this point, you know," he said.

"I understand. Well, I probably should go then. I hope you find the help you need," the woman responded. She was clearly out for a morning run, judging by her attire. Ironically, there weren't any other people out around them. As Brandon stood up, he did see a man far in the distance. He just wasn't sure if he was heading their way. "You know you really look like you need some medical attention. Let me at least call and get you some help, okay?

Brandon stared at her as he watched her dial 911. He couldn't believe that she completely disobeyed his command. He had to think quickly, while there was still no one around them. He slammed the phone to the ground with one hand and grabbed the back of her head with the other. He dragged her by her hair until they reached the edge of the water again. Brandon held her underneath the shallow water just long enough for her to stop breathing. Once she became as limp as a ragdoll, he whispered softly in her ear, "Maybe next time when I tell you to do something, you'll just follow instructions."

CHAPTER ONE

They say it takes 21 days to break a bad habit. Isn't it funny how it only takes a moment to form one though? You spend the rest of your days chasing that initial thrill. You never reach it, but the chance of even getting close to it is what draws you in. Chelsea stuffed her package deep inside the side pocket of her long trench coat. She looked around to make sure no one was watching her get into the car, as she crossed the street.

The pavement was damp and slippery. So she walked swiftly, but cautiously, as not to fall. More importantly, she didn't want anyone to see what was in her hand. The night's brisk chill was highly unusual for a summer night like this. All the way home, her hands were shaking on the steering wheel. A myriad of thoughts began racing through her mind.

When she came to a stop at a red light, she looked inside the window at the car next to her. The woman sitting on the driver's side stared back at her intently. Someone rose out of the backseat, but she couldn't make out their facial features. Her heart started beating faster. Did she know? Who was that lying in the backseat and why were they just now getting up? She was just paranoid. That was it. After all, it was after 11:00 pm on a week night; the roads were very thin with traffic. Chelsea brushed it off as she continued her path on the way home. As she pulled into her garage and let the door down, she exhaled and let out a deeply relieving sigh.

She started to hear rain drops falling on her roof. They were light at first, and then they started pouring down faster and harder. "Thank goodness," she thought. She made it home just in time before the hard rain. Ever since the car accident with

Cookie and Brandon, she always felt uncomfortable driving at night. Just as she removed her key from the ignition, she heard a knocking sound on her garage door. The rain was coming down hard, but it couldn't have been hailing that quickly. Plus, the sound had too much of a rhythm. It sounded forceful; human. If there was someone out there, they would have to come in to get her. There was no way she was going to open her garage door. At times like these, she was glad she had a door to enter her house through the garage.

Chelsea sat her keys down on the kitchen counter and poured herself a small glass of lemonade. She took the package out of her coat and placed it on the counter. There was no one in the house but her, but she looked around to make sure she wasn't being watched. The knocking came back again. This time she was sure it was not rain. It was a person knocking at her door with considerable strength. Whoever it was must have seen her pull into the garage. She removed her trench coat, making sure her package was still in its pocket, before hanging it on the rack. The knocking stopped for a moment and then started up again. "I know you're in there! Open the door, please!" a husky, raspy voice yelled on the other side of the door.

This was way too much excitement for one night. She had good reason to be nervous, as she tip-toed along the side of the wall. Her front door was made of wood and several glass panels. So it was easy to see light, shadows and movement from the outside. Whoever was outside must have been getting drenched out there. She hoped the man wasn't in trouble or injured. But she couldn't risk opening her door. Within the next 30 seconds, the knocking came to an abrupt stop. The man never uttered another word. Relieved, yet still nervous about this strange man knocking at her door, she moved quietly upstairs. Chelsea decided to leave the kitchen light on downstairs to be able to quickly see any shadows coming from downstairs. She then pulled her gun, a Bersa Thunder 380, out of her bedroom closet, to sleep with it under her pillow.

Chelsea expected the knocking to pick back up and continue throughout the night, but it never did. She didn't remember falling asleep at all. The sunlight peered through the window and woke her up naturally before her alarm was set to go off. She opened her eyes, somewhat discombobulated from last night as she looked around the room. The gun was still under her pillow and everything seemed to be intact. She got out of bed and started to get dressed for work.

Chelsea checked her coat before leaving to make sure the package was still there. She gathered her things for the day and cranked up her car as she let the garage door up. She backed out slowly and pushed the button to let her garage door back down. Before pulling all the way out of the driveway, she saw some distinctive mud prints on the door. She looked closer and realized that they read, "I KNOW". The sun wasn't fully out yet, but she could still make out the letters distinctly. Maybe this was some kid playing late night jokes in the neighborhood. But the man that was at her door last night sounded grown, even elderly.

There was nothing she could do about it. She just still couldn't shake the nervous feeling that someone was watching her. She opened her bottle of green tea, but the cap fell out of her hand and onto the floor underneath her foot. She waited until she pulled up at the stop sign to reach down to pick it up. Just as she was raising her head back up, she heard a loud thud hit her windshield. She looked up quickly and saw a dingy looking old man slapping his hands on her window. She screamed at the man to get off her window. She took her foot off the brake and proceeded to drive off, forcing the man to hop back quickly from the moving car. "I know! I know! I know!" he screamed, as she drove off. He just stood there in the middle of the street with a piercing, stoic stare as she drove away.

Chelsea picked up her phone and dialed Mel. He would know just the right thing to say to calm her down. She and Mel had been dating for about eight months. She finally started to feel like she could give her heart to someone. Before Mel, Chelsea hadn't been in a serious relationship in a while. She was always guarded; afraid to let anyone get close to her heart, much like Cookie. When it came to men, Chelsea talked a good game, but it was a different story when turbulence hit her own love life.

She smiled when she saw the picture of Mel saved in her phone. His attractive physical appearance helped win her heart over, if she must be honest. Mel had a dominating presence that made Chelsea like putty in his hands. He wasn't a man of very large stature in terms of his stockiness. He was slim and tall, with a muscular build. But you wouldn't guess it in his clothes. He had the gentlest green eyes and a smile that gave him a sexy 'bad boy' mystique. He had one single tattoo of an eagle that started at the back of his left shoulder and wrapped around his chest. Chelsea got excited just thinking about him. For a moment, she even forgot she was calling him to report the strange man that jumped in front of her car.

Mel's phone rang five times before he answered. He was an early riser, so Chelsea was surprised she was about to miss him. When the phone finally picked up, Chelsea beat him saying hello. "Hey babe! I'm so glad I caught you. You won't believe what happened to me this morning while I was leaving for work." There was dead silence on the other end. Chelsea looked at her phone to make sure her reception was fully available. All bars were up, but still no sound from Mel. "Mel, baby? Are you there? Hello???" Chelsea asked.

"Ooh baby, yes right there. Hell yeah! That's how I like it. Move it just like that," Mel said. His statement was followed by several loud slaps of flesh. She could hear a woman whimpering in pleasure in the background. "Yes, deeper! Deeper Daddy! Spank it! Oooh...right there. Bite it! Suck it! Don't stop! I'm about to...." the woman screamed.

"What?" Chelsea whispered in fury, with clenched teeth. Now her curiosity set in and she held the line to see just how long it would take to for Mel to realize that he accidentally picked up the phone. She couldn't believe it. She trusted this scumbag. Chelsea could have kicked herself for even believing Mel was the man she could see herself marrying. She didn't want to believe it was true. But the proof was right there. She was hearing it first-hand.

"Oh, shit. Be quiet. Be quiet!" Mel said, as he hung up the phone. Chelsea smiled deviously as she looked at the phone after Mel hung up. She already had an early start to her morning and she could spare about 30 minutes before arriving at work. She made a detour and decided to head to Mel's house. Surely, she wouldn't find him there. Certainly, he at least had the decency to not bring the tramp he was screwing to his own house. She at least gave him that much credit. Chelsea and Mel lived about 20 minutes apart from each other and her job was another 15 minutes, in the opposite direction.

Chelsea drove like a race car driver, quickly watching for the police in her side and rearview mirrors. Before she knew it, she arrived at Mel's house. She parked on the curb and got out of her car, just as the woman she heard on the phone was walking out. Chelsea immediately charged forward to greet her.

"Well, hello. I'm Chelsea. Mel's girlfriend. And you are?" Chelsea interrogated the woman. She didn't look familiar, so at least she was grateful for that. There would have truly been some tables flipped if he was messing around with one of her friends or someone close to her.

"Um, I'm Rhonda. Girlfriend? You're Mel's girlfriend?" Rhonda asked with a very puzzled look on her face.

"Yes, mam. Let me guess. He didn't mention me, did he? If you'll excuse me, I just need to go have a word with him for a moment. Nice meeting you sweetie!" Chelsea smiled, while waving goodbye to Rhonda as she walked forward to open the front door of Mel's house.

"Um, have a nice day," Rhonda said, as she walked quickly towards her car. She didn't want to get caught in any unnecessary drama. "That bastard. He told me he was single," she whispered, shaking her head and pulling out of his driveway.

"Hey baby! Look at you, getting all fresh and clean. Mmmh hmmm," Chelsea said, walking in on Mel washing away his sex residue in the shower. "I really wish I had time to jump in and get a little wet with you. But I have a meeting this morning for work. Did you enjoy your little slut? Don't answer that. I'm sure you did," she sneered, putting her finger over his lips, as she turned to walk away.

"Huh? Baby, I would never do anything to hurt you. I'm so sorry. I didn't want you to find out like this. I just had a few drinks last night and things got out of hand, that's all," Mel said, running after her naked from the shower.

"Find out like this, huh? No explanation needed babe," Chelsea said calmly. On her way out of the bedroom, she smashed his nightstand lamp on the floor. Then she walked into the living room and ripped his exquisite 'Peacock in the Forest' painting in half. "Awh, so sorry! Maybe you can get another one of those," she pouted.

"What the hell are you doing? You are crazy! Get out of here right now!" Mel shouted.

"Get out? Ok, sure. I'll leave." Chelsea stared Mel in his eyes coldly as she stormed out of his front door. She pulled a pocket knife out of her purse and keyed the passenger side of his car from the right headlight, straight back to the right tail light.

Chelsea laughed all the way to her car and drove off to work as if nothing happened. Mel stood by his front door in disbelief. She was a woman scorned and he knew there was no way to get her back.

CHAPTER TWO

Sunday morning arrived quicker than anticipated. Ken woke up swinging as he felt something tickling his nose. He tried to brush it off, but in a couple minutes it was back again. He was so tired that he could barely open his eyes. But he had to see what was agitating him in his sleep. Of course, it was Cookie.

"Go on now, woman," Ken laughed, grabbing Cookie's wrist. "I knew I should have let you go to sleep first. Always being a prankster".

"Whatever. It's time to wake up anyway, Sleepyhead. We just landed. I can't wait to get off this plane. My legs are so stiff. I need to stretch," she said. She and Ken had just returned from Beliz for their third wedding anniversary. It was a trip they planned for and a place they both wanted to visit for years. "How about I stretch you out again later?" Ken whispered in Cookie's ear, kissing her on the cheek.

"Mmmm, I don't know about that Mister," Cookie said, pausing and waiting for the disappointed look on Ken's face before she continued. "There's only one condition. How about we start in the kitchen this time?" she said, flashing a mischievous grin back at him.

"I like the way you think. See, now that's why I married you," Ken replied, with a million dollar smile.

"Oh really now? So now we're getting to the truth about it. I see how it is," she laughed. As they made their way off the plane, Ken hugged Cookie around her waist. She loved how affectionate and attentive he was. She never told him, but she had just recently gotten to the point that she believed he was really the one. Even right after they got married, she was always afraid that something would happen to tear them apart. Now, she believed that they really would last forever. The dark days of her past were finally laid to rest and she was relieved.

"Oh no, Chelsea's been blowing up my phone. I hope she's okay," Cookie said. She picked up her phone to let Chelsea know they landed. Chelsea insisted on picking them up from their trip, since she was in town a few days for business. They really were okay with just leaving their car at the terminal, but thought it was a nice gesture that Chelsea volunteered to pick them up. "Hold on baby, let me call her and find out what's going on. Please don't let anything be wrong with this girl," she said as she dialed her sister's number.

"Hello? Cookie, is that you?" Chelsea asked. "I have the craziest news to tell you. But first, how was your trip? I know you both must have had a blast. I can't wait to see the pictures!"

"Well, we actually just landed. We're walking towards the gate now. We had an amazing time and took plenty of pictures too" Cookie replied, as she reminisced about their amazing getaway.

"Great, I love it. I'm about 5 minutes away. Now, get this," Chelsea interrupted as Cookie just looked at the phone and shook her head. "I wake up Friday morning and call Mel on my way in to work. Didn't want anything special, just to shoot the breeze and say good morning. So the phone rings about four times before he answers," Chelsea paused to catch her breath.

"Ok...and what did he say?" Cookie asked, while Ken looked concerned. She switched the phone to her other ear as she prepared for a lengthy conversation.

"That's just it. He didn't say anything. He answered by mistake. I hear him moaning and groaning. Then I hear some slut saying "Give it to me Daddy," in the background. His dumb ass finally figures out that he answered the call and then hangs up. So you know I couldn't just let that slide. So I show up at his house. Her car is parked in the driveway. She comes outside. I keep my calm and let her know who I am as she drives away in her little Hyundai".

"That's when I went to his bedroom. He was in the shower by then. I was acting seductive like I was about to join him. Then I let him have it. I told him I knew about the girl and knocked down his lamp, knocked some pictures off the wall and ripped that painting he loves so much," Chelsea said, finally coming up for air.

"Cookie. Are you still there?" she asked said.

"Yes, I'm right here. I didn't know you were done. I was just letting you finish. Honestly, I'm speechless," Cookie replied, shaking her head at Ken and rolling her eyes to signal that she had an earful to tell him about the situation later. But as loud as Chelsea was talking, he could practically hear every word she was saying on his own.

"I just can't believe it. He's such a bastard, Cookie. This is some bullshit. You finally give in to your feelings to somebody and then this happens. Be glad you have true love. It's really hard out here," Chelsea responded, her voice quivering. Cookie could tell she was trying to hold back her tears. "But um, I'm sorry girl. I'm pulling in now. I'll see you and Ken in a minute".

"Ok sweetie. We'll be here. Don't you worry about Mel; that's his loss. I'll even help you key his car if that makes you feel better," she laughed, as she turned to Ken. He gave her a stern, yet confused expression that let her know he wasn't too hot on her idea.

"You are a fool, but I love it. You know I already did that. But, hey, I might just take you up on that depending on how I feel this week," she laughed. "Ok, I just pulled up".

"Cool, I see you now. Here we come," Cookie responded, before hanging up the phone. Cookie didn't have time to fill Ken in on the whole story, but she let him know quickly that she would tell him later.

"Ah, look at my love birds. I am loving these tans you came back with too. Nice. Well, somebody is glowing," Chelsea said, giving Cookie and Ken a hug.

"Ah, thank you. We did get a chance to soak up some sun while we were there. It's good to see you Chelsea. Thanks so much again for picking us up, especially during your business trip," Ken replied.

"Oh, sure thing brother. I figured it was the least I could do since I was in town anyway. I fly out on Tuesday morning, so this works out perfectly. The rest of my time here will be pretty relaxing," Chelsea responded.

"Well, maybe we can grab lunch tomorrow while you're still here. We need to get some time on the calendar soon too. I'm due for another visit home anyway. Maybe I can get some quality time in with my sister. Ken, maybe you can come too?" Cookie smiled and looked over at Ken nervously in the backseat. She didn't mean to volunteer him for an obligatory trip. He just rubbed her back and replied, "Sure, baby. That would be nice. I'll let you know when it might be best for me with work," he said. Ken didn't necessarily need to or want to go on the trip, but he knew it would make Cookie happy. He was pleased to do it, for that reason alone.

"That sounds really nice. I'm looking forward to it. We'll have to see when is best, but let's do it soon. I love you Cookie and sorry to talk your ear off earlier girl," Chelsea laughed.

"That is okay. You needed to get that off your chest. I just still can't believe it," Cookie responded.

Neither can I sis. Neither can I," Chelsea said. The ride from the airport to Cookie and Ken's house wasn't too far. They talked lightheartedly the rest of the way home. They both thanked Chelsea again for picking them up. Chelsea expressed to Cookie that she was looking forward to their lunch date tomorrow. Everyone said their goodbyes as Cookie and Ken loaded their bags towards the front door.

"So, is everything okay with your sister?" Ken asked.

"I don't know if she is now, but she will be. I'm sure you heard most of it but long story short, she broke up with Mel today. Caught him cheating on her," Chelsea said, with a disappointing tone. "I thought he was really nice too. Just goes to show I guess you never know people like you think you do. People always have a way of surprising you. And oh, I wasn't trying to volunteer you for a trip. I was just trying to think on the fly to cheer her up," Chelsea added.

"Baby, you don't have to apologize. Besides, you haven't been home in a while anyway. I think it will be good for us to go," Ken said as he pulled their luggage through the front door. "Baby, why don't you just relax a bit. I know that was a lot to take in with Chelsea. I'll bring the rest of the bags up".

"You don't mind?" Cookie asked, hoping he wouldn't change his mind.

"Of course not. I love you baby," Ken said, kissing Cookie before grabbing the rest of their things.

"Ok, well I think I just might take you up on that," she responded.

Cookie walked to the kitchen to pour herself a glass of water. She started to feel dizzy suddenly, but she wasn't sure why. After she finished her water, Cookie walked into the bedroom and laid across the bed. As soon as she started to get comfortable, a wave of excruciating pain started in her stomach. She rubbed her stomach softly, hoping the uncomfortable feeling would subside.

Ken walked upstairs after getting all their luggage inside. He found Cookie lying on the bed, curled up in pain. "Baby, are you alright?" Ken he asked, seeing the painful expression on her face.

"Oh yeah....I'll...um. I'll be alright baby. Guess I just have a strong cramp. Thanks for checking on me," Cookie replied, managing to give him a slight smile through her pain.

"Hmmm, if you say so. You stay right there. Let me go get you some more water. Maybe that will help," he said.

Ken was only gone a couple of minutes before he saw the horrific sight back in their bedroom. "The baby! Cookie, what's wrong?" he screamed. Cookie hadn't looked down yet, but now realized why Ken was in such a frantic state. She was bleeding through her shorts and onto the bedspread.

"Ken! No. No. It will be ok. It's fine. It's just something else. It's something else. This can't be it," Cookie said, dazed and crushed by the devastating blow. She felt it in her spirit that this was going to be detrimental. Ken grabbed some towels and helped Cookie get off the bed. She turned on the shower and stared at herself in the mirror before taking off her clothes. The mirror started to steam up and Ken stood there in disbelief. He was probably even more excited than Cookie was about her being pregnant. He could do with or without having kids, but he was so excited at the possibility of parenting with Cookie. Now, he may not be able to get that chance.

After Cookie and Ken stood there awkwardly for what seemed like an eternity, Ken helped Cookie take off her clothes before getting in the shower. He took the comforter off the bed and then got in the shower with Cookie. He held her and put her head on his chest. Cookie cried hysterically and he could feel her shaking uncontrollably. Tears streamed down his face as he could do nothing but hold his wife. There was nothing he could do at that moment to take her pain away, or even his for that matter.

Once Cookie finished showering, Ken helped her out and they both laid across the bed with their towels. "Maybe it's something else. We should set a doctor's appointment. Even if it's not what we want, we'll just try again. You're going to be a wonderful mother. It's just may not be our time right now. We have to wait until God says so. At least we didn't tell anybody yet," Ken said.

"Yeah you're right. That is a good point. Thank you babe. I know you're going to be a great father too. Just can't believe this is happening again. I mean, is there something wrong with me? I just don't know," Cookie said.

"Baby, there is nothing in the world wrong with you. You are beautiful. Wait a minute. What do you mean 'again'? What other time did this happen? Was it with me and you didn't tell me?" Ken asked, with concern but a brewing of angst in his voice as well.

Cookie knew she had messed up now. She couldn't believe there was yet another part of her life that she hadn't shared with Ken. She honestly thought she told him, but apparently, she hadn't. He looked at her piercingly, waiting for her to explain her statement.

"Um, Ken, I must not have told you this. I'm sorry. So sorry. I really am. But I've had a miscarriage before. It was before Brandon and I got married. Of course, it worked out for the best. The doctor just ruled it out as stress and didn't really know what caused it. But with this being the second time now, I'm really concerned. I really want this baby," Cookie responded cautiously.

"Well, let's call the doctor tomorrow. In God's time it will happen. I'm sure of it," Ken said, with a stoic look in his eyes.

"Yeah, it will. I just....Wait. You're not mad at me for what I just told you?" Cookie asked, looking puzzled.

"Surprised? Yes. Upset? Mmmh...maybe it just hasn't set in yet but I wouldn't use that word to describe how I'm feeling right now. Besides, Brandon was in your past and I'm here now," Ken smiled and kissed Cookie on her forehead.

Deep down, Ken was feeling uneasy. Ever since they got married, he kept finding out little things about Cookie's past that seemed to have been conveniently left out. He was really starting to feel unsure if Cookie had really divulged all the major secrets in her life. Only time would tell. Ken just hoped he would be able to stick around long enough to see the truth.

CHAPTER THREE

Things remained tense the rest of the week until Thursday morning. Ken had to leave early that morning to travel to North Carolina for work. Usually they both couldn't stand to be apart from each other long. Now, they both secretly were glad to get a break from each other after the miscarriage and its subsequent awkward moment of Cookie revealing that she suffered a miscarriage with Brandon as well.

Later that Saturday afternoon, Cookie decided to give Ken a call. He was scheduled to be back in town Tuesday morning, but she was hoping their time apart had cooled his mind down. However, she was in a particularly good mood, as she was getting dressed to celebrate Sheila being honored at a Dallas awards banquet. Things were really looking up for Sheila. Her business was booming stronger than ever before. Plus, she had been in a steady relationship with a very handsome and doting man named Sean for the past nine months.

"Hello," Ken answered, panting like he was out of breath. "Hey babe, how are you?" Cookie was a little uneasy about talking to Ken and the way he answered the phone didn't help. Although he was very expressive in his communication towards her, he really wasn't one to argue. So, it made it that much harder for her to decipher when his anger was at a slow warm up or a raging boil.

"Hey, I was getting ready for Sheila's event tonight but just was giving you a call to see how your day was going. I know yesterday was a long day for you. Did I catch you at a bad time?" Cookie asked. He better not say it was a bad time. What was all that heavy breathing for anyway? He must have been working out. That's had to be it. After all, he was still the fine, physically fit man he was when they met almost four years ago. Cookie hated when she had conflicting thoughts like this. Even as a married woman, it made her feel so insecure and desperate.

"Yeah, yesterday was a beast. But it's ok. Closing this deal will really help me get that promotion. But today is a little more relaxed. The weather is beautiful here. You would love it. I just finished a run outside. Hate I can't be there with you tonight for Sheila's award. I know she's got to be really excited," Ken responded.

"That's great you were able to get a run in. Yeah, she's really excited. I'm truly happy for her. Wish you were here with me too. But duty calls, right? I'll send you a picture of me before I head out. How about that?" Cookie asked, in a much better, cheerful tone.

"I would so love that, beautiful. Don't forget. I love you babe," Ken responded.

"I love you too baby. And hey, I know it's all water under the bridge now but I really am sorry about earlier this week. I don't want you to ever feel like you can't trust me or I'm hiding something from you. I promise to always be honest with you and thanks for always being so honest with me too," Cookie added.

"I can't lie, it stung a bit. But we'll get through it together. I'm all about moving forward. Let me know when you make it to the event tonight," he said.

"Ok, sure thing handsome. Love you and talk to you later," she said, before hanging up the phone. Cookie's hair and makeup were complete and she was about to slip her dress on, but decided to take a picture of herself in just her bra and panties. She sent that one to Ken, along with another picture of her fully dressed in their full-length mirror right before she walked out the door. Cookie looked damn good and she knew it. But as she looked deeper into the mirror at her reflection, she felt empty. Even though it was a God-send that she never had children with Brandon, she now thought something was seriously wrong with her after having a miscarriage with Ken's baby as well. Her head began to feel light and her knees were weak. For the first time in a few years, she contemplated thoughts of no longer being alive.

****

Meanwhile, Ken decided to go to a local bar in Charlotte, North Carolina with his coworker Charles. He really didn't feel like getting out. He was content in his hotel room. But Charles was one of those guys who always had to be out on the scene. He wouldn't rest until Ken finally agreed to join him for a couple beers at one of the bars downtown.

"You know, this bar is really not jumping enough for me. Let's try the one up the street," Charles said. He could see the look of frustration on Ken's face.

"Are you serious? We just got here. The beer is nice, good food and the DJ isn't half bad either," Ken rebutted.

"Spoken like a true married man. You have your queen at home already man. I'm just trying to find a freak of the night in the meantime, if you know what I mean. This place is dead. Not one bad chick in here. Not one," Charles responded.

Ken quickly surveyed the bar and had to admit with a laugh, "Yeah I guess you do have a good point. Not much to look at here at all. Just saw one I thought you might be into. But then she turned around and that face ruined everything. Alright then, let's get out of here," Ken said.

The next bar that Ken and Charles arrived at was a complete 360 degree turn from the previous one. Ken even felt slightly uncomfortable with all the beautiful women around. Cookie was still a stunning knockout, no doubt. But several of the women inside that bar could give her a run for her money, at least looks wise.

They hadn't even been in the bar ten minutes when a sexy caramel colored woman gracefully glided her way towards the bartender to order a cranberry and vodka. She smiled and winked, focusing her on attention on both Ken and Charles, but mainly on Ken. "Now what brings you two handsome men here tonight?" she asked.

"My friend and I are just checking out a bit of the nightlife here. We're only here this week on business," Charles answered before Ken could get a word in.

"Yeah, we'll actually be leaving here in a couple days. What about you? Are you local?" Ken asked. Charles shot him a confused look, as he really didn't expect him to give her any special attention. He sensed that he must have really liked the woman and smirked while nudging him on the shoulder.

"I guess you could kinda say I'm local. I just really needed a release from the week, you know? I've been to this spot a couple times. It's one of the best ones downtown. No riff-raff. Great drinks and just a really good time." She smiled and slid her hand down Ken's shoulder. At this point it was clear that while she may have found both men attractive, Ken was the one she was after. "Excuse me. Let me get one more of whatever this gentleman is having," she smiled and slid him her business card. Cynthia Wilcox. "Now what's a married man as handsome as yourself doing out this late? Wait let me guess. Is your friend dragging you out against your will?" she pouted.

"Not exactly, Cynthia," Ken laughed. Now Charles was a bit concerned. He was beginning to think Ken forgot all about is wife at home. Just then, a text alert flashed across his home screen on his cell phone. It was Cookie. He glanced at the phone, but remained engaged in Cynthia.

"Well, I know enough about married men to know that's a trap I refuse to fall into again. But if you ever find yourself single and I'm still available, give me a ring," she smiled. Cynthia then placed both of her hands on Ken's chest from behind and gripped tightly before letting go. Ken exhaled deeply as he took the last gulp of his drink, hoping it would somehow cool his hormones down. It didn't. "You boys take care, alright?" Cynthia waved, as she slithered her way back into the crowd.

"Man, do you know what you just passed up? I must admit, I'm a little jealous. You had that in the bag and you just let her walk away? Dude, what were you thinking?" Charles exclaimed.

"Well I was thinking that I'm a happily married man who has a beautiful wife back home in Dallas that I don't want to step out on. How about that?" Ken responded, with a wave of weakness in his eyes.

"Hmmm…ok. Hey, you're a stronger man than me. The flesh is weak and He knows my heart," Charles laughed.

"Boy, you are a fool. I'm not letting you get me into trouble," Ken said, shaking his head.

"She almost got you, huh?" Charles asked jokingly.

"Yeah she really did. Man let's get out of here before I end up in a situation I shouldn't be in," Ken replied.

****

Cookie checked her phone to see if Ken had responded to her text, but he hadn't yet. She sent him a picture of herself with Sheila right after she won her award. She was the toast of the evening, having received the night's highest honor: Businesswoman of the Year. Her catering business was flourishing like never before, so much so that she opened up her own café called SHIELA'S last year. In just a few months, it was one of the most popular spots in Dallas to dine at. Although the event was honoring women, SHEILA'S was arguably the fastest growing restaurant of its kind period, whether owned by male or female.

Even though Cookie was extremely happy for her friend, she couldn't shake an eerie feeling she had for most of the night. She tried to shake it off as paranoia. But there was something that just didn't feel right. Lately, she couldn't stop remembering something Sheila tried to tell her on her wedding day. Their schedules were so busy that they didn't get to meet for workouts or dinner much anymore. Cookie didn't want to dampen Sheila's big night, but her curiosity was eating away at her. Deep down, Cookie couldn't bear to hear what Sheila had to say because she knew it would be something bad. She wanted to live in her own make believe abyss, if only for a few moments, without any more tragic interruptions.

She decided to wait until Sheila completed her congratulatory hugs and pictures before she even gave any indication that she wanted to pick her brain.

"Girl, thank you so much for coming. You always have my back. It really means the world that you're here. I hate Ken couldn't make it out tonight, but I understand he has to make that money," Sheila said, reaching out to give Cookie another hug.

"Really, it's my pleasure and I wouldn't have missed this for the world. I'm so proud of you. Love you girl," Cookie replied, while hugging her back. As soon as she let go, Sheila noticed a sudden change in her friend's face. Her expression was almost frightening almost.

"Cookie, is everything ok? You look so flushed. What's wrong?" Sheila asked, concerned.

"Oh nothing, just um...Why is Sean getting up on the stage right now?" Cookie had a hunch of what was about to happen, but tried to push her own selfish thoughts to the back of her mind. She was just going to see what happened and not think the worst. After all, he could be up there for anything.

"Excuse me everyone, I do have one more announcement to make for our honoree tonight," Sean said, motioning for Sheila to come forward. She walked towards him with a smile, not fully knowing what to expect. Cookie gave her friend an approving smile to help ease her nervousness. After all, at this point, Cookie didn't think Sean would do anything to harm Sheila.

"Sean, what in the world are you doing up there?" Sheila smiled at him lovingly.

"Sheila, I'm so proud of you. I love your ambition, your drive and your persistence. All the blood, sweat and tears you've put into your work and now you finally get to enjoy all the fruit of your labor with such a prestigious and deserving award. I do have one question to ask you though. Depending on your answer, you'll make me a winner for life. Sheila, would you do me the honor of being my wife?" Sean asked.

He stepped down off the platform of the stage, while Sheila was already making her way closer towards him in excitement. He knelt on one knee and revealed a beautiful diamond ring from the black velvet box. "Will you please do me the honor of being my wife, Sheila?" Sheila replied, "YES! YES! I would be so honored to be your wife". The room was filled with thunderous applause, while tears streamed down Sheila's face. Sean couldn't look more elated.

Cookie blended in with the rest of the crowd and gave her friend a tight squeeze. "Congratulations girl! Yes, this is your night two times over! I'm so happy for you. I love you. And Sean, I know you'll treat her right. Congratulations!" Cookie's plastered smile was in full effect. However, she couldn't help wondering how in the world she was going to ever get the opportunity to interrogate Sheila about information she was so ready to give on her wedding day. Maybe it just wasn't meant to be. After all, it couldn't have been that big of a deal. Sheila wouldn't have kept something serious from her for this long.

"Well, I will let you two love birds continue this celebration for then night. Sheila, I'm truly so excited for you girl," Cookie exclaimed.

"Thank you so much again Cookie," as tears welled up in her eyes again. "You've been such an amazing friend to me. I'm truly grateful you were here to share this night with me. I'll be talking to my Matron of Honor this week. We have some planning to do now," she said with a gleaming smile.

"Yes, we do. It would be my honor. Just let me know and I'm there. Have a good night sweetie," Cookie replied cheerfully. She followed a group of people outside to the parking garage, so she wouldn't have to walk completely alone. She checked her cell phone before starting her car, expecting to see a text back from Ken... still no response.

CHAPTER FOUR

"Hey babe, I have a couple dresses I need to take to the cleaners. I know you have an early day tomorrow morning. Do you want me to take anything for you?" Cookie asked Ken, as she cleared the table. The couple just finished eating dinner that Cookie prepared: chicken parmesan, fresh green beans and garlic mashed potatoes.

"You really outdid yourself tonight. Dinner was so delicious, baby. Another one of the reasons I married you. A woman that knows the way to my heart," Ken joked. "On the clothes, I do have a pair of jeans and my suits from the trip that I could take. Thank you honey," he added, kissing Cookie on the cheek.

"First it was just for my sex. Now, you're only here for my cooking," Cookie laughed. "So glad you enjoyed dinner tonight. I tried something a little different with the chicken parmesan. I'm just experimenting with some new things for my baby. It's not like you're an amateur in the kitchen yourself you know. You can really throw down too," she smiled.

"You just really know how to make a man feel good, huh? Speaking of feeling good, I know Sheila has got to be ecstatic about the engagement. I know you're happy for her. Now you don't have to listen to her talk about how there are no good men out there," Ken laughed.

"Yes, she always has been quite the pessimist. It was cute the way he did it too. I'm happy for her. I'm sure she'll be calling me tomorrow with details already for the wedding."

"I texted you a couple pictures from last night, but I'm not sure if you got them or not. I forgot to mention it this morning too when we talked," Cookie responded. Although she was very happy her husband was back at home, they hadn't really had a long conversation since the miscarriage. Cookie tried to block it out of her head and take things one step at a time. However, she would be lying if she said she didn't feel insecure when Ken failed to respond to her texts. But the timing was an hour ahead there. Maybe he didn't even get it. Whatever the case, she couldn't spend time worrying about it.

"Oh no baby, I'm sorry I didn't get them. But if you have them on your phone still, I would love to see them. Charles drug me out to a bar last night. Could have been bad reception in there or something," Ken said. He could tell by the tone in Cookie's voice that she felt uneasy and somewhat bothered about him not returning her texts. He remembered now. He saw a text from her when he was sitting at the bar, but he never responded to it. Damn. He really wasn't up for an argument tonight and was hoping to avoid the conversation taking an ugly turn.

"It's no biggie babe. Sure, I can show them to you later. Yeah it probably was just the reception. I don't even have to ask if you had a good time with Charles. That boy is such a fool. I knew when you told me that he was coming along on the trip, there would be trouble," Cookie laughed.

"Yeah you know him. He was a real hoot, crazy as ever. We had a good time," Ken answered curtly. Although he didn't want to hurt Cookie's feelings, he refused to play a ring-around-the-roses guilt trip game with her too. There was an awkward moment of silence before Cookie told him she was about to get her clothes ready for work tomorrow.

Ken finished washing the plates from dinner, while Cookie gathered the clothes for the cleaners in the bedroom. He got in the shower after he finished cleaning the kitchen. Cookie could see the steam coming out of the bathroom as Ken was just starting to remove his underwear to get inside the shower. Damn. Even after three years of being together, just the sight of him still turned her on. It also helped that he was now standing there butt naked.

"Oh, I didn't know I was getting a private show after dinner," Cookie said playfully, flashing a sexy smile at Ken.

"Well there's still room on the stage for you to join me. Come on in when you're ready," Ken responded, with a hungry, lustful look in his eyes. He stood there long enough to tease her before fully stepping into the shower.

"That sounds like an offer I'd be more than willing to take you up on, sir. I'll be right in!" Cookie said.

Cookie quickly gathered the few items she was taking to the cleaners, along with Ken's dress shirts and suits from his business trip. Then she realized there was a pair of jeans in the same stack that she missed. She always checked the pockets to make sure she didn't leave anything valuable in there. It was a habit she started forming years ago after having jewelry and money that she knew she left in her pockets come up missing from the cleaners. As she flipped Ken's jeans to check the back pockets, a business card was sticking out of the top. She pulled it out and it was for a lady named Cynthia Wilcox, who apparently was a hair stylist.

She thought it was odd that Ken would keep a business card from another woman who clearly had nothing to do with his line of work. Cookie figured there wasn't any harm in asking Ken about the card. After all, they kept no secrets from each other and she had no reason to believe he was a liar.

"Um, this water's going to get cold soon baby. I need you in here to heat it back up," Ken smiled, peaking from inside the shower curtain, biting his lower lip.

"I'm on my way baby; just had to gather these clothes for the cleaners. Give me 60 seconds and I'm all yours baby," she replied. Although Cookie did feel uneasy about finding the business card in Ken's pocket, she missed her husband. She missed his kisses, his warmth, his hugs and him being inside of her. She knew if she brought up whoever the hell Cynthia Wilcox is tonight, she would regret it and possibly miss out on a great orgasm. She weighed her options and placed the card inside of the drawer of her nightstand.

As Cookie walked into the shower, Ken took a moment to really admire her body. She was still as beautiful (if not more) as the day they first met. Although she gained just a tad bit of weight, it was in all the right places. Her legs were a little thicker and so was her behind. Ken shook his head in amazement and said, "Is all of this for me? You are just too beautiful. Do you know that?"

"Well I'm glad you think so. I must be the luckiest woman in the world to have such a handsome, strong and sexy husband like you. I love you baby," Cookie responded, as she moved in closer to kiss Ken. He kissed her back firmly with passion as he wrapped her inside of his bulging biceps. There was no safer place that she could be at that very moment. She could feel him rising, stiff as cement against her navel.

Suddenly, Ken backed up against the wall of the shower and told Cookie, "Come here". She walked towards him slowly and before she could make another move, he picked her up and wrapped her legs around his back. "I missed being inside you," he whispered in her ear. "I missed you more. Can you feel how wet I've been or you?" Cookie replied, barely able to talk from the immense pleasure she was feeling.

Ken then placed her feet on the ground and turned Cookie away from him as he entered her love from behind, with one hand pulling her hair and one hand on the small of her back. He switched up between slow, long and forceful thrusts, as her moistness drove him wild. Both were so overwhelmed with passion that they couldn't last much longer. As they both climaxed in unison, Cookie's body fell limp as Ken held her up with what little strength he had left. "Damn, you got my knees weak," Ken barely uttered, breathing heavily on her back.

"Who are you telling? I can barely hold my head up. Damn." Cookie could feel his heartbeat pounding against her back. Whoever the hell Cynthia Wilcox was must be sad at home knowing she wasn't getting a piece of this. Ken dried Cookie off first and then himself as they stepped out of the shower together. They decided to just sleep naked in bed (something they often did).

"I have something to tell you baby," Ken whispered in her ear, with his hands wrapped around her midsection in a spooning position behind her.

"Oh yeah? Sure, what's that?" she answered, surprisingly.

"I want you to know that I'm not going anywhere. I'm here forever. I didn't forget about last week. I just got a little caught up in my feelings. I guess when you said you had the miscarriage with Brandon too. But I love you. I'm here. We're going to get through this together. We'll have another baby together. I can feel it. I know it's going to happen," Ken said, squeezing her tighter.

"You just made my heart melt. I was so afraid that you were still mad at me about that. I swear I thought I told you. I guess I've tried to block that out of my mind for so long that I fooled myself into thinking I mentioned it to you. You have no idea how relieved I feel," Cookie responded, with tears running down her face.

"Don't cry baby. It's going to be alright. I promise, it will, "Ken said, trying to console Cookie.

"I know. I know it will. It just hurts. All of that just put me back in a bad place. Just didn't think that when I was ready to have kids by a man whom I wholeheartedly believe will be a great father that my chance would be taken away from me. But you're right. We'll get through it," she sighed.

Ken hated seeing Cookie hurting and tears now began to stream down his face as well. "We will baby. It's me and you forever, no matter what."

"Yes, no matter what," Cookie smiled. It was the last thing she remembered before falling asleep.

About two hours later, there was a knock at the door. The knock didn't come from the front door though. It was from the bedroom door. Ken looked over and Cookie was still asleep. Maybe he was just hearing things. He closed his eyes and laid his head back down on the pillow again. At almost that same instant, he heard the knocking again. This time it was louder; more persistent. He eased out of the bed to see who was there. It was the lady he met at that bar in North Carolina, Cynthia. What was she doing here? How did she find out where he lived?

Cynthia stood there staring back at him, with a sinister grin on her face. Her hair was long and fell just above her breasts. She was wearing a long, black trench coat. There was one single button fastened in the middle of the coat, which revealed a metallic silver, lace bra that pushed her breasts up beautifully towards the top of the collar of the coat. He could see her midriff, revealing her washboard stomach and the top of a matching metallic silver pair of boy shorts. She touched his face and stepped closer towards him and whispered, "Now that's no way to greet your fantasy is it? Aren't you going to invite me in?" Cynthia said.

Ken looked at Cynthia and then back at Cookie. By this time she was awake and she was laying there taking it all in, smiling. "How did you get here?" Ken asked, looking dazed and confused. He was so turned on, yet so nervous that he literally didn't know what to do.

"Never mind that, sugar," Cynthia said, wrapping one leg around his waist, resting her the heel of her laced up stiletto boot right at the crack of Ken's behind. "Let's just enjoy the moment, shall we?" she smiled.

"It's okay baby," Cookie said. "Go ahead. I already know you want to. It actually turns me on too," she said, grazing her nipples with her fingertips.

Cynthia grabbed Ken's face and kissed him hard on the lips, while she dug her nails into his back. Cookie got up from the bed and stood behind Ken while he was still kissing Cynthia. She began to lick his back and squeeze her hands forcefully on his ass. Ken was feeling overwhelmed with an anxious passion he never felt before. This could not be happening. Two beautiful women all over him, one of whom was his wife and she was co-signing the idea of a threesome. He turned around and started kissing Cookie as Cynthia fell to her knees. Cookie then took Ken by the hand and led him to the bed. "I want you to taste her, while I watch you," she said.

"Or better yet, how about I taste you instead, while he watches?" Cynthia suggested to Cookie, with a seductive and devious smile.

CHAPTER FIVE

Ken woke up in a cold sweat. He looked over and Cookie was still in the bed. Did that really just happen? It must have been a dream. But why did it feel so real? Although the thought turned him on, he was uneasy about having such a vivid dream about another woman. He checked his phone to see what time it was. 6:03 am. His alarm was about to go off soon anyway, so he decided to get up. He made himself a smoothie, took a quick shower and got dressed for work. By this time, Cookie was just waking up. Ken kissed her on the forehead before walking out the door. "Bye baby. Hope you have a great day. I love you."

"I love you too. I feel like a piece of lead. Thanks to you last night," she smiled. "You have a good day too baby".

Even after a great ending to the night with Ken, Cookie still woke up feeling troubled in her spirit. Cynthia popped up in her head again. She decided not to pursue a conversation with Ken about her, but there was one way that she could get more information on who this woman was; social media. She logged into Facebook and searched for the name Cynthia Wilcox. There were about 12 people that came up on the list. Just great. Then she filtered by state and there were 2 women in North Carolina with that name. However, there was only one that owned a salon there. Supreme Cuts Unlimited. Yep, that was the same name listed on the business card.

This had to be her. The pictures on her profile didn't help much. She had most of her information blocked from the general public. Plus, the majority of her pictures were either with clients or with other groups of people. Ugh! This was a waste of time. She was upset at herself for even stooping so low as to look through this woman's profile. She couldn't get a grip on what it was about her that made her feel so insecure. It was a foreign feeling and the first time she felt this strongly, with regards to another woman and Ken.

After she got ready for work, Cookie decided to give her dad a call on the way in. He always made her and Chelsea feel like Daddy's little girl. Even now, she still felt so safe and secure in his presence. He didn't answer, so she left him a voicemail. "Hey Daddy. Guess who? I didn't want anything. Just wanted to hear your voice. Hope everything is okay with you and mom. I love you. Talk to you soon," she said.

As soon as Cookie put her phone down, it rang. It was her dad calling back. She smiled as she answered the phone. "Well hello there Mr. Brighton? How are you, Daddy?" Cookie asked gleefully.

"Hey there, baby girl. How's my Candy doing? I just barely missed you. I was out here building a shelf for your mom. We were in that big furniture mart close to downtown. She kept going on and on about this shelf she liked there. I looked at the price tag and told her, "Not on my watch". So I'm proving to her that I can make one even better than the one she saw in the store."

"Well I don't have to ask if you've been busy lately. That is hilarious. How is it coming along? I would love to see it," she replied.

"It actually looks pretty amazing if I do say so myself. I'll send you a picture of it once I finish sanding it down and painting it," he responded boastfully. "But forgive me sweetheart. You called me. How are you and my son doing?"

Cookie's heart melted every time she heard her dad call Ken his son. She never thought she would see the day when he liked a man that she was in a relationship with, let alone ever calling him his son. "He's doing well. Busy as ever with his job. I couldn't ask for a better husband", she replied. At that moment, she was so glad she didn't tell anyone about her pregnancy. Now there was no need to even mention that she had a miscarriage and repeatedly relive that pain over again.

"Well I'm glad to hear that. Sounds like you all are doing well. I wish I could say the same for your sister though. Your mother and I really worried about her," he said.

"Really? Oh no what's going on with her? I just talked to her a few days ago", Cookie responded. She assumed he was talking about her dramatic break up with Mel. However, she didn't want to spill the beans about her sister's business. She prayed to God that it wasn't something else besides that.

"All of this stuff going on with Mel. As bad as I feel for her, you know I always said something wasn't right about that boy. I just could never put my finger on it. Besides that though, she's just been acting strange lately. Something's wrong with her, although I don't think it's the drugs again. At least I really hope not," Bill replied.

"Yeah she did tell me about Mel. I just told her that it was his loss and it's a good thing they weren't married or had any kids. That would have been a disaster trying to deal with that on top of him cheating. I thought he was a good guy for her. Guess he had me fooled. But exactly what has she been doing that's strange lately? I'll give her a call today too and see if I can find out what's going on," Cookie said, expressing genuine concern for the mental well-being of her sister.

"I don't know. She just has such bitterness. She's been angry and irritable the last few times your mother and I have talked to her. But if she sounds better with you, then that's a good thing. I just hope she's ok. I never want anything to be wrong with my girls. We've never had to worry about you, but your sister....that baby girl is a different story," he said, with a hint of sadness in his voice.

"Well I really should get better about talking to her more often and checking on her. Come to think of it, the last few times I've talked to her we have dealt with crises she had going on. We haven't had a decent, normal conversation in a few weeks. I must do better. I feel like a horrible big sister," Cookie replied.

"Ha....well, uh. You are fabulous. Yeah, you know I think I will take a nap after a while. Baby, yep. What were you saying there baby girl?" Bill slurred.

"Dad? What's wrong? Why are you talking like this? Is everything ok?" Cookie asked in fear.

"Bill!" Cookie heard her mother scream as the sound of her father falling to the floor echoed through the phone. She was so shocked and paralyzed. She didn't know what to do but call out to her mom in hopes she would hear her.

"Mom! Mom! Is he okay? Please say something," Cookie pleaded.

"Baby, I'm calling 911. It's me. I'm here. I think your dad just got over worked," Lisa said. Cookie could hear her mother talking to the 911 operator, telling them what happened. Thankfully, her mom left her dad's phone on so she could hear what was going on. Cookie sat in a frozen silence waiting to hear what was happening on the other end with her father. She could hear her mother sobbing in the background.

"Mom? It's going to be ok. He's going to be ok. I know it. Are you there?" By now, Cookie could tell her mother was off the phone with the paramedics. Honestly, she was very afraid for her father and his health. Nonetheless, now wasn't the time to show her sadness. She had to be strong for her mother.

"I should have made him go to the doctor when he first told me he had chest pains last week. I just feel so bad. You're right. He's going to be ok. I have him sitting up on the couch now. He's awake but listless. Go ahead and call your sister if you don't mind. I'm going to get ready before the paramedics arrive," Lisa responded.

"Ok mom, I'll be there too. I'll talk it over with Ken and hopefully we'll be there by tomorrow. I love you. I'll call you back in a little bit, ok?" Cookie said.

"Sounds good baby. They're here now. Talk to you soon," Lisa responded more calmly than Cookie expected, considering what was happening. Now it was time to call Chelsea. She hadn't talked with her sister since her breakup with Mel, so she didn't quite know what to expect.

"Cookie? Well what do I owe the pleasure of this phone call from my big sister?" Chelsea answered the phone sarcastically.

Cookie figured there was no better way than to just jump straight into it.

"Hey sis, I have some not so good news. I was just on the phone with dad and he passed out. We don't know what's wrong, but mom mentioned he had chest pains last week. Mom's on the way to the hospital with him now," Cookie said.

"What! Oh wow. What happened? I don't remember him looking or feeling bad. I was just over there last week!" Chelsea exclaimed. Both sisters paused on the phone for a moment before saying anything. Bill was the rock of their family and the thought of losing him made Cookie and Chelsea sick to their stomachs.

"Yeah, I really don't know. We were just talking and his speech started getting really slurred. I could tell something was wrong because his words weren't making any sense. He fell right after that. I'm going to talk to Ken here soon and make my way there by tomorrow. Hey, I love you Chelsea. You know that, right?"

"Okay, that sounds good. I'm sure mom and dad will really be happy to see you, especially during a time like this. I love you too Cookie. Of course, sis. I do know it. Hope you know I love you too. Now, enough with all the mushy shit. Let me go find out where dad is so I can head up to the hospital. See you tomorrow," Chelsea responded.

"Ok, see you tomorrow then. Keep me posted if you hear anything in the meantime. Talk to you later," Cookie said, hanging up the phone. She replayed the conversation in her head and wondered why Chelsea said mom and dad would be happy to see her. Would she not be happy to see her? In the whole scheme of things going on now, it was a petty thought. But she would be lying if she said her feelings weren't a little hurt by it. There was no time to waste on further analysis of that situation. She had to call Ken and fill him in.

"Hello? Hey baby. This is a nice surprise. I usually don't hear from you this early in the day. Wait….is everything ok?" Ken asked. He could tell before he even asked the question that something was wrong with his wife.

"Not really baby. I just got to work, but I was talking to my dad on the way in. He passed out and my mom called the paramedics to come get him. I really want to fly out and see him. Just to be close to him, you know? I understand if you can't make it because of work, but hopefully you can come with me", Cookie said. Although she left it open for Ken to decide whether he could come with her, deep down there was no option. She needed him by her side.

"Wow, I'm so sorry baby. I hate to hear that. Of course, I'm going with you. Let me just wrap up some things here. I may have to stay late tonight to make up for some things tomorrow, but I'll make it work. Keep me posted on what you find out," Ken responded.

"Ok, thank you so much for coming with me. It really means a lot. I'll let you get back to it babe. I love you," Cookie replied, with a sigh of relief.

"And I love you back. See you tonight," Ken replied.

Cookie hung up with Ken and took a deep breath before checking on her mother. She may be still on the phone with

Chelsea anyway. She also said a prayer for her father. Although she knew her parents were getting older, it was still a shock to know her father was so ill. He barely even had a cold when she and Chelsea were growing up.

Cookie gave her mom a call back to find out how her dad was doing. Lisa answered the phone and sounded much calmer than earlier. That was at least a sigh of relief for Cookie. "Hello baby. I just got off the phone with your sister. She's on her way up here now. I'm just sitting in the room with your father now. I've always loved him, but you don't really realize how much you love someone until the thought of them possibly no longer being here happens," Lisa said.

"You sound better than earlier. Is he ok now? I was so worried," Cookie asked.

"Yes, long story short, the doctors think your dad had a mini stroke. They're running some tests now, but based on his heath history they're saying it was probably just over-exertion. Your dad will be 73 this summer. Neither one of us are exactly spring chickens anymore. That man is just like the Energizer bunny though. It's just probably a sign he needs to slow down a bit," Lisa responded.

"Well, I hate to hear that it could possibly be a stroke, but I'm glad he's ok. Ken and I are coming tomorrow. We just have to find a flight that leaves sometime tomorrow morning or in the afternoon. We'll at least be able to help you take care of daddy for a couple days. I'm sure Chelsea will be there too," Cookie added.

"Yeah, I overheard your dad telling you about how she's been acting lately. Truth be told, I think worrying about her has both of us sick. She's been acting weird. Lord knows I love Chelsea with all my heart. I love both of you girls so dearly. Your father and I couldn't have been more happy when both of you were born. But Cookie, I may never have told you this but I really want to thank you for being the rock for your sister. You have made both your father and my life so much easier. It just takes a little extra time with your sister, but she'll come around. I know it. I think she's just probably dealing with a lot right now that she's not ready to share with us," Lisa said.

Meanwhile Chelsea was outside of her father's hospital room seething with anger. The door was left slightly ajar and she could hear everything her mother just told Cookie about her. She always felt like she could never measure up to her sister, but this was yet another example that confirmed her thoughts. She was standing outside the door for so long that one of the nurses came by and asked her if she was lost. "No, thank you. I just was having a little moment. I'm ok, just was nervous about my dad. He's in here. I'm about to walk in," Chelsea said with a smile. She knocked softly on the door and then stuck her head inside.

Before Cookie could even respond to her mother's comment, she could tell by her reaction that Chelsea must have just arrived. "There's my baby! Hey Chelsea. You got here quicker than I thought. Come on in. I made a seat for you right here. I'll move over so you can sit closer to your father. They're about to come bring some food in to him shortly. Cookie, let me call you back baby. Chelsea just got here. I love you. Kiss Ken for me and I'll see you both tomorrow," Lisa said.

"I love you too mom. See you tomorrow and please tell Chelsea I said hello for me," Cookie requested.

"Baby, your sister said hello," Lisa said.

"Oh, hey Ms. Cookie," Chelsea responded, holding her father's hand and waving at the phone with her back turned. She could tell he was waking up. He let out a low groan and opened his eyes.

"Is that my baby girl here to see me? Thanks so much for coming baby," Bill said, mustering up the energy to smile at his youngest daughter.

"Hey daddy, so glad you're ok. I love you," she smiled back at him.

"It's so good to see you baby. You got here faster than I expected," Lisa said.

"Oh yeah it didn't take me long at all. I was getting ready on the phone on my way here. How is Cookie? I talked to her earlier today too and she told me she and Ken were going to try and make it out here tomorrow," Chelsea replied.

"She's fine now after I told her Bill was doing better now. Baby, you all had us worried there for a second," Lisa said, smiling at Bill.

"Well that's great. I'm sure you both will be so happy to see her when she gets in tomorrow. I'll just do what I can in the meantime and let her take it from there. How about that?" Chelsea said.

"Ok, well baby I don't think anyone is insinuating there's a competition. Your father and I are happy and appreciative to see both of you. Maybe you can help me in the kitchen cooking tomorrow. Hopefully they'll release your dad by then and we can have a nice family dinner," Lisa responded in a stern tone. She read the irritated expression on her daughter's face and wondered what could be troubling her so much.

CHAPTER SIX

For as far back as Chelsea could remember, she always felt inadequate compared to Cookie. Even when they were of elementary school age, people raved on and on about how beautiful Cookie was. She had the brightest eyes, the most amazing smile, and the longest hair. People would probably think she was crazy if she ever outwardly acted upon her thoughts. However, they were more than validated based on several occasions; the latest being her overhearing her mother telling Cookie how "difficult" it's been for her parents dealing with her and all her problems.

One of the most vivid memories when Chelsea felt inferior to Cookie was the year Cookie entered high school as a freshman and Chelsea was just entering middle school. It was an interesting age for both girls and Cookie was always her own worst enemy. She felt pressure to outdo herself from the last big accomplishment she made. It was part of what made her so successful. As for Chelsea, she always felt like a hamster in a wheel, Cookie's world; just trying to keep up the momentum.

Cookie was a prissy tomboy, who could easily turn her athletic and girly switches off and on. During her freshman year in high school, she tried out for the volleyball team and earned a spot with the varsity team. During that same time, Chelsea tried out for the cheerleading squad and failed to make any of the teams. The coach even had the audacity to tell her that she was surprised at Chelsea's inability to get the routines down as quickly as her sister, Candice did. Yes, Candice was a star on the cheerleading squad as well.

While Chelsea was talented in her own right (a gifted saxophonist and an excellent debater in high school), she felt like her victories were always one step behind Cookie's. Then there was the time of both of their high school proms. She could never forget it. Cookie won the coveted title of prom queen and her date barely missed being prom king, although he was on the homecoming court as well. However, people were so smitten with Cookie that everyone said he was the real king to have had Cookie on his arm for the night.

Chelsea, unfortunately did not follow in her sister's glorious footsteps. She did make it to the homecoming court as well, but didn't win. The knife was driven deeper when people kept her comparing her to her older sister who won a few years before. Cookie probably didn't even remember many of those things. All the water under the bridge that Chelsea had to create still didn't mean that her hurt behind it was gone. It was there lurking and waiting to be resurfaced.

One of the most embarrassing moments of Chelsea's life was one that she kept to herself, even to this day. It was no secret that Cookie's ex-husband Brandon was one of the most sought after men on campus when they were in college. Chelsea was a beautiful woman in her own right. At that time, she didn't know Brandon or his twin brother, Brian, that well. Although both brothers were attractive, Brandon had that extra swagger that really made people gravitate towards him. Chelsea was no exception.

In a bit of a drunken act of courage, Chelsea danced with Brandon at one of the biggest parties that happened that year. Brandon was a fraternity man, plus he was popular and could basically have any woman he wanted. After dancing with Brandon, she mustered up the nerve to ask him if he would like to go out to dinner with her sometime. Honestly, she thought she had it in the bag. She looked amazing that night and many men at the party were trying to get close to her, but she only had her eyes set on Brandon. He politely turned her down by saying, "Chelsea, I feel a little weird saying this to you. You are a beautiful girl, you know. Very beautiful." He emphasized the word beautiful, with a look that said he could have eaten her alive right there on the dance floor. "But I'm into your sister, Cookie. I just can't break her. She keeps playing so hard to get. You have any ideas on how I could get to know her better?" he asked.

Chelsea wanted to drill a hole into the floor and sink into it, never to return. She was never one to let people see her sweat though, so she played off her crushed feelings smoothly. "Ah Cookie. Yep, that's my sister. Well, I'm sure if you keep plugging away at it, she'll give in. She's stubborn and just takes some time to crack. Keep trying and you'll get her one day," Chelsea responded.

Brandon gave her a hug, thanked her and walked away as one of his frat brothers summoned him to a circle of some other guys in the corner. Cookie did eventually end up marrying Brandon and Chelsea soon found out that he wasn't nearly the prize possession she thought he was while she was in school. Hindsight was truly 20/20.

****

Cookie and Ken arrived in Chicago around 5:00 pm the next day and went immediately to the hospital, after checking in to their hotel. Had it been just Cookie by herself, she probably would have just stayed with Chelsea. However, since Ken was there too, she thought it would be more appropriate to just get a hotel room. Either way, Chelsea really didn't offer for them to stay at her home.

When they got to the hospital, Bill and Lisa were in the room talking to his doctor. Cookie was glad to get there when they did so she could hear firsthand what was going on with her dad. Bill smiled brightly as they entered the room and Lisa walked over quietly to give them both a hug.

"This must be your beautiful daughter, Candice, and handsome son, Ken, you were telling me about," the doctor said. He extended his hand to greet Cookie and Ken.

"Thank you. Hello doctor. Nice to meet you," Ken responded, with a serious look of concern on his face. He developed a genuine bond with Bill and couldn't really fathom him lying on a hospital bed.

"Hello doctor? Yes, it's very nice to meet you. You can call me Cookie," she answered.

"Forgive me for my bad manners. I'm Dr. Calloway. Cookie? Okay, well Cookie and Ken. That has a nice ring to it. You'll be happy to know that your father is doing much better than when he first came in. He did suffer a mild stroke. Bill has been directed to give up red meat, stay away from high stress situations and avoid any extra strenuous activity," Dr. Calloway responded.

"Well, I'm just glad you're doing better. You gave me quite a scare, dad," Cookie admitted, smiling at the doctor while looking over at Bill. "Where's Chelsea?"

Bill and Lisa looked at each other before Lisa responded. They looked as if they were trying to get their story together before responding to Cookie. "Well baby, she left here a little while ago. Probably about an hour before you and Ken got here. She said there was something urgent that she forgot to do and for me to call her when we were leaving the hospital. I told her you were on the way. I assume you probably talked to her too," Lisa responded.

"I did, but that was before we caught our flight today. I told her what time we would arrive and I texted her when we got to the hotel. Maybe she was just busy," Cookie concluded. She didn't believe the words she was saying herself, but she didn't want to deflect from the more important issue at hand – her dad's health. Something was definitely going on with Chelsea and now Cookie wondered if it had something to do with her.

As Cookie and Ken got in their rental car to follow Bill and Lisa back to the house, Cookie's phone rang. She looked down and saw it was Sheila calling her. Cookie realized she didn't get a chance to tell Sheila about her father. Everything happened so quickly. She didn't have time to go into it now so she decided to just give her a call back later.

Cookie's phone rang again once they got inside the house. It was Chelsea this time. Lisa immediately went into the kitchen to start preparing a meal for the family. Bill sat on the couch and asked Ken to turn on the TV for him, but not before he showed off his new cabinet that he made for Lisa. His face gleamed with joy, proud of his accomplishment.

"Hello? Chelsea? Hey girl, we just got over to mom and dad's. What are you up to? Not sure if you got my message earlier when we got here. Dad looks pretty good. He's sitting here now watching TV," Cookie said.

"I'm just fine. Glad you and Ken made it safely. I'm just wrapping up a couple things here at home and I'll be on my way over there. It's been a long time since I've seen you. I love you sis," Chelsea replied.

"I love you too. Hey Chelsea, are you sure everything is alright?" Cookie asked in a fretful tone.

 "Oh yeah, I'm good; just concerned about dad. That was quite a scare he gave us, wasn't it? What makes you ask that?" Chelsea rebutted.

"I guess you could say it's just big sister's intuition. But if you say you're good, then I'm good," Cookie responded.

"Cool, well, I will see you all in about 30 minutes. How about that? I'm getting ready to walk out the door now," Chelsea said.

"Ok girl, bye. See you when you get here," Cookie smiled and hung up the phone.

Before Chelsea left home, she felt a pang of nausea hit her in the stomach. She couldn't believe this was happening again. After vomiting for the second time that day, she looked over on the bathroom counter to read the pregnancy test. Positive. This couldn't be. She was on birth control. Although she wanted to have kids, this couldn't be the way it was supposed to happen. Frustrated and angry about her new fate, she threw the pregnancy test at the mirror and yelled as she slumped on the bathroom floor. She couldn't hold back her tears, but she had to pull it together to go meet her family.

Chelsea grabbed a light jacket, along with her keys and walked out her front door. Her car was still parked in the driveway and she noticed a peach colored piece of paper sticking up from her driver's side window. As she got closer she saw there was a handwritten message on the paper that read:

"You think you can hide, but I KNOW what you've done".

Chelsea wasn't sure if this could have been the same man who walked up to her door in the rain a few nights prior. This was just too much to deal with in one week. She crumbled up the paper and threw it in her passenger seat. Chelsea drove in complete silence on the way to her parents' house, in an attempt to sort out all her thoughts.

Chelsea exhaled deeply before getting out of her car. She parked parallel to Cookie and Ken's rental car. Lisa opened the door before Chelsea got a chance to ring the doorbell. "Hey baby, you look like you've just seen a ghost. Is everything alright?" Lisa asked.

"Oh yeah, I'm fine mom. Just a little light headed but other than that I'm ok," Chelsea responded.

"Well, come on in. You're just in time for dinner. I made some grilled salmon, baked potatoes and fresh green beans. I'm going to make sure your father and I start eating healthier. I think it will do us both some good," Lisa said, smiling at Bill.

"Hey Daddy, don't you get up. You just relax. I'll come to you," Chelsea told her father, who was already attempting to get off the couch to come greet her.

"Thanks for coming to check on an old man baby. I love you," Bill said, giving his daughter a tight hug. At that same moment, Cookie and Ken were coming out of the bathroom from washing their hands.

"There's my baby sister. Hey girl, come over here and show me some love," Cookie said, with her arms outstretched towards Chelsea. "I love you. I've really been missing seeing you. I hate that it's under these conditions that we're seeing each other but I am extremely glad to see you".

"It's so good to see you too, Cookie. And is that the most handsome brother in law I see?" Chelsea asked.

"Well, only if it's the most beautiful sister in law ever. It's really good to see you Chelsea," Ken said after giving her a hug.

"Alright, now that we're all here together, let's eat. Girls, do you mind helping me set the table please? Ken, please make sure Bill doesn't over exert himself over there in the meantime. I have this lovely new red wine that your father and I got last week. I have a brand new bottle and would love for you all to try it. I think this occasion is special enough to pop the cork," Lisa smiled.

"Oh mom, I don't think I want any wine. I'll try some later. Just probably not today. You know, I'm kind of hit or miss with red wines anyway," Chelsea responded.

"Ok, well suit yourself then. You're missing out. It may help that headache too. It's not like you're pregnant. Come on everyone, let's eat!" Lisa said cheerfully.

Chelsea was frozen for that moment in time. There was no way her mom could have known she was pregnant. She felt like the room was spinning and she just wanted to hide under a rock. This was just another reality check that she had to figure out what she was going to do quickly. She also had to let Mel know he was going to be a father.

CHAPTER SEVEN

Several hours later, everyone was in the living room watching TV and telling family stories. Cookie looked at her watch and didn't realize it had gotten so late. It was just after 10:00 pm. Cookie and Ken said their goodbyes. Chelsea decided to leave shortly after they did.

"I'll call you tomorrow and we'll be back over in the morning as well," Cookie told her parents. "Dad, please make sure you get some rest, ok? No late-night carpentry. I love you," she smiled and rubbed his shoulder.

"I sure will baby. I love you too. I'm going to just relax right here. Thanks so much for you and Ken coming all the way here to see me. I'll see you tomorrow then," Bill responded.

"Sounds like a plan. Mom, the food was delicious. Love you," Cookie told her mother.

"I love you both. Now I know you must get on the road and get back to that hotel. You know you were more than welcome to stay here," she said.

"Thanks Mom. I guess I honestly didn't think about it. We were just trying to get here as quickly as we could. Next time we come up, it will be just for a visit and we can do just that," Cookie said, glancing back at Ken. He smiled back approvingly.

"Bye baby sis. I love you. Maybe you and I could have lunch tomorrow. Just the two of us. How about that?" Cookie asked.

"That sounds perfect. It's been forever since we've had some good sisterly bonding alone. I'm looking forward to it," Chelsea smiled and hugged Cookie.

As she and Ken got in the car, Cookie let out a long exhaling breath. "Hey, you think he's going to be ok?" Cookie asked Ken, hoping he wouldn't have anything unfavorable to say.

"Absolutely. He'll be ok. Your father is such a strong man. I must admit, it was quite a scare to me too when you told me what happened. After hearing the doctor break everything down to us though, I don't think there's anything to worry about. He probably just needs to slow down a bit like you said. He's always been very active as long as I've known him," Ken reassured Cookie.

"Thank you baby. I was thinking the same thing, but just wanted to hear it from you, just to make sure I wasn't being too unrealistic," she said.

Ken had just entered the highway to head towards their hotel, when their rental car began to wobble on the passenger side. "Do you feel that?" Ken said, in a concerned tone. He immediately turned on his hazard signals and stayed in the far right lane.

"Uh yeah, that's weird. Kind of makes me a little nervous. I don't know what's wrong. We checked everything with the car before we left. Maybe it's just something on the road," Cookie replied.

"No, I don't think so. I'm going to get back off at the next exit. Something isn't right," Ken said. At that same moment, the passenger side front tire began to shake violently. Ken tried to slow down even more, but there was a car speeding behind him. The car looked strikingly similar to Chelsea's, but that couldn't have been her. She wouldn't have whizzed past them like that.

The next thing they knew, the passenger tire started coming off the car. Ken tried to slam on the breaks, while watching the oncoming traffic behind him. The car swerved as the tire rolled across the freeway. When the car finally came to a stop, they were facing traffic and the front of the car had slammed into the ground on Cookie's side.

"Get out! Let's get out now baby!" Ken unbuckled Cookie from her seatbelt and then took her in his arm across the console. They both got out of the car and stood on the side of the freeway as traffic came to a sudden halt. An SUV stopped just a foot or so from the car.

"Thank you. I was so scared. I...I don't know how that happened," Cookie said, as tears began to stream down her face. She couldn't stop staring at the car, picturing just how close of a brush with death that she and Ken had escaped.

"It's ok now. I'm just glad we made it out of there without getting hurt. I'm going to call AAA so they can come tow this car," Ken said.

Cookie decided not to call her parents or Chelsea to tell them the news. She didn't want to risk worrying them, especially her dad. She and Ken waited about 20 minutes until a tow truck arrived to pick up the vehicle. A man with long silver hair pulled back in a ponytail jumped out of the truck and greeted them. He was tall, about 6'2, with a slim, but muscular build. He looked like the type of guy that would be the President of a motor cycle club. He had a calm demeanor, but a stern face.

"Hi, I'm Ted. Looks like you two are some very blessed people. This could have been so much worse than it is. Are you ok?" Ted asked.

"Yes, we're fine. You're right though. Thank God we made it out ok," Ken responded.

"Um, I hate to ask this, but do either of you have any known enemies that would want to cause you any harm?" Ted said.

"Not that we're aware of. Why do you say that?" Cookie asked. She and Ken now had a very perplexed look on their faces. Ted motioned for them to come around to the front of the car, when it was safe to do so.

"See that? Those lug nuts on the tired had to have already been loose. The studs are completely stripped from the tire. This wasn't a regular blowout. Someone loosened these lug nuts. That's how your tire came off. Wow, I haven't seen anything like this since 2011. My ex-wife did the same thing to me right after we got a divorce. Never had any concrete proof, but I knew it was her," he said.

"Well, can you just take us back to our hotel? I know the rental place is closed and out best bet may be to wait until in the morning," Ken said. He was getting frustrated with Ted's anecdote and was more interested in what their next plan of action should be.

"That is a good point. We just really want to get back to the hotel. It's getting late. But thanks so much for coming out here. Could we take the car to a vehicle repair shop on the way and leave it there overnight?" Cookie added.

"Sure, we can do that. Go ahead and get in the truck and let me know where to go. I'll get you there," Ted said.

"Thank you. We're just a couple exits up the road. Take the Canal Street exit and then make a right. Take that down about four lights I think and the hotel is on your right," Ken said, climbing into the backseat with Cookie.

"Alright, I'll get you there. We'll just drop off this rental car first at the shop. There's one on the way there, so that should work out perfectly. I don't mean to pry, but how long have you been married?" Ted asked.

"Three years now," Cookie answered. She wanted to give just enough information for what he asked for. After all, they didn't know this guy from a can of paint. However, he did seem to be really nice.

"Well that sounds good. I just really like seeing young love. I see things. I know it may sound strange, but I can read people very well. Please don't be alarmed when I tell you this. Someone close to one or both of you is not happy about this union. There's some deep rooted pain going on that you don't see; at least not yet. It's coming though. Just around the corner. Yes, just as sure as that tire came off your car tonight, that's not the end of it. This is just the beginning. You must...." Ted ranted, until he was cut off by Ken.

"Sir, I'm sure you mean no harm. My wife and I have had a long day and we're just trying to get back to our hotel please. We don't really have the energy to process all this negativity right now," Ken said sternly.

"Ah ok, well here we are. Let me just unhook the car and leave it parked here at the shop. I just have to enter some notes in the computer and I'll be right back. You both just sit tight for a minute if you don't mind," Ted said.

When he got out of the truck, Cookie gave Ken a very confused look. She turned around to make sure Ted wasn't in earshot for what she was about to say. "I don't know baby. What if he's right? What if there really is someone that's doing these things to us? Like a force or something. I don't know. It just all seems so strange and too big to be a coincidence. Don't you think?" Cookie asked.

"I do agree that this is very strange what happened tonight. But we're in Chicago. The only people here are your parents and your sister. I mean, really. Who else could be doing this besides some bad kids? Someone probably had a crazy dare to loosen up the lugs on the tires. Hold on, he's coming back now," Ken said.

"Ok kids. We're all set now. I hope you don't mind me calling you kids. I'm sure I'm old enough to be both of your parents. I'll be 60 in just a couple of weeks," Ted said.

"Oh, well, I wouldn't have guessed that. You don't look like it at all," Cookie said. Ken remained silent and Cookie tapped his leg.

"Yeah I'm shocked man. You're keeping yourself up really well," Ken added in, with a slightly sarcastic tone.

"It's the coconut oil. That stuff works wonders," he laughed.

The three rode in a bit of an uncomfortable silence the rest of the way to the hotel. All in all, Ted seemed like a nice guy, a bit cynical, but nice nonetheless. As he pulled into the front of the lobby of the hotel, he smiled and waited patiently for them to get out. "Hope everything goes well with getting the new rental. I want to leave you both with this: You will get another chance at introducing a new life in this world. Just make sure you guard it carefully. Have a good night," he said.

CHAPTER EIGHT

Cookie laid awake while Ken was sound asleep. She looked over at the clock and the time was 2:36 am. Every time she fell asleep she kept having this recurring dream of someone, a lady, with long hair whispering in her ear, with a blade across her forehead. The stroke of the blade wasn't deep enough to cut but forceful enough to scratch the surface of her skin. She couldn't keep this up all night. She had to get some rest.

Ken tossed a bit in his sleep and held on to Cookie tightly. She felt secure and safe in his arms. Finally, she went to sleep. About three hours passed and she woke up again. Ken was still holding her but as she opened her eyes, she saw the most frightening thing in the hotel room. Although the room was dark, it was light enough for her to still see without turning on a light.

Standing right in front of the door was a tall person, possibly of a female stature. The only thing that seemed female about this person was their hair. Could it be Ted? He did know where they were staying. He had long hair. There's no way it could have been him though. He wouldn't have been able to get through the door. At that same moment, she heard the sliding of the chain lock at the top of the door. She could feel herself breathing heavier, as her head and heart felt as if they were about to explode.

The person moved closer towards the bed. The moonlight revealed something metallic and shiny in their hand; the blade. She kept trying to shake herself out of this nightmare, but this time she wasn't dreaming. There was clearly someone in their room that wanted to harm them, or at least her. She couldn't hold it in any longer. She wasn't going to take defeat lying down. If this was her last night alive, so be it.

Cookie screamed as she leaped out of the bed and started swinging at the woman standing before her. Her adrenaline was pumping so strong that Ken even had a difficult time holding her back. He turned on the light, panting heavily and looking irritated that he had just been woken up so abruptly. "Baby, do you want to tell me what's going on here?" he asked, with a concerned and slightly angry tone in his voice.

"Huh? I just....Ken, someone was in here. She's gone now, but I saw her. I promise I did. I kept having these dreams about this woman; well at least I thought it was a woman. She was standing over me with a hooded sweatshirt and a sharp knife in her hand. That bitch kept rubbing it across my forehead like she was taunting me. It wasn't a dream. That was too real. She was here, but she's gone now. I know. Just look at the..." Cookie continued, going a mile a minute.

"Babe. Stop! There is no one in here. Look around. It's just you and I. Let's go back to bed and get some more rest before daybreak, when we have to find a way to get over to the car rental place," he said.

"Didn't you lock the door before you got in the bed? I know you did. I know you locked that door Ken. I'm not crazy," Cookie pleaded as she stared at the door.

Ken looked over at the door and couldn't say a word. The door was left slightly ajar and the chain lock was not latched on the back of the door. Now he wasn't so sure if Cookie was being delusional. He didn't see anyone in the room, but he would have bet money that he put both locks on the door before he got in the bed.

"Baby, I'm sorry I didn't believe you. I'm sure I locked that door too. There's definitely something strange going on here. It's almost 6:00 am now. Let's get out of here as soon as the car rental place opens," Ken said. Cookie was convinced that he was now spooked too by who could have possibly been in their room. He was trying his best to remain calm, but she could tell that he was frightened by the whole experience.

"Ok, that sounds like a plan. Looks like they open at 7:30 am. We should start getting ready now. I'm going to hop in the shower if you don't mind," Cookie replied.

"Go ahead baby. I'll be right here. I'll just wait until you get out to take mine. I'm going to be here in case anyone tries to come in. We're going to be ok baby," he assured her. Ken watched the room like a hawk, while Cookie was in the shower. He even looked around for any remnants of an intruder having entered while they were sleep. The only clue that gave an inkling that someone had been inside the room was that the door was left ajar, with the latch hanging down.

When Cookie got out of shower, Ken had already gathered their things together in the suitcase. He was about to put her shoes that she wore from last night inside the bag, when he found a note inside of her left shoe that read *tread lightly*. The handwriting was very neat, but looked like it had been written in lipstick or makeup of some kind. By this time, Cookie was already out of the shower. She walked over to the suitcase before Ken could change his expression.

"Babe. Everything ok? Your face looks really flushed," Cookie asked, with a concerned and fearful look on her face.

"I...I think I'm ok. But I don't know where this came from. It was in the bottom of your shoe," Ken said, handing her the note. Cookie's mouth dropped open as the note fell out of her hand and onto the floor.

"We need to hurry up and get out of here. Right now! Go shower, so we can leave baby. I'm really not comfortable here," Cookie demanded.

"I'll make it quick. Everything is else packed except for the clothes I'm wearing," he said. He went into the bathroom and showered vigorously, as if he was trying to wash away the eerie cloud that was looming over them. But this was a storm that had to run its course. There was nothing he could do about it.

After Ken got out the shower, they both finished getting dressed quickly and did a once over to make sure they weren't leaving anything. As they walked out into the lobby, Cookie had a thought that may give them both some peace of mind about what really happened last night.

"Hello. How was your stay here? I hope everything went well," an enthusiastic young lady by the name of Emily asked as Cookie and Ken approached the front desk.

"Well the stay was nice, considering the circumstance. We had a feeling that someone may have come in our room last night though," Ken answered.

"Yes, is there some way you could play back the surveillance tape to see if anyone passed by the room last night?" Cookie asked. If she saw anything suspicious on the tape, that would at least help give her some closure.

"Ok…wow, I'm so sorry to hear that. Let me go get the manager. I'm sorry, but I don't have access to the tapes here. I'll be right back," Emily said.

Ken and Cookie waited patiently until Emily came back with the manager to review the tapes. "That was a really good idea baby. I didn't think about the surveillance tapes. Hopefully that will give us some kind of answer to all of this," Ken said.

"That's what I'm hoping for too. I didn't even think about it until we were about to get on the elevator," Cookie said. Just then, a tall burly man, with a scruffy beard and bedroom hair came from the back of the office behind the front desk.

"Good morning. I'm Cliff and I heard there was a disturbance in your stay last night. Please, come around to the side door. I'll review the tapes with you to see what may have happened. We'll take a look at your floor and the video from the actual room itself. You were in room 622, right?" Cliff asked.

"Yes, that is correct. Room 622," Ken answered. He and Cookie walked around to enter Cliff's office, hoping there would be something on the tapes to confirm their suspicions. They sat down in the two chairs in front of his desk, as he turned the computer screen towards them.

"About what time would you say you noticed the disturbance in your room?" Cliff asked.

"I would say it first started around 3:00 am or so. I kept falling asleep and waking up. There seemed to be a woman who was standing at the front of our door with a hooded sweatshirt on and she seemed to have something shiny and metallic in her hand. I think it was a knife," Cookie responded.

"I never saw the woman myself, but I woke up around 5:30 and that's when my wife showed me the door. I could clearly see the door was slightly open. The latch had been removed and it was hanging from the door," Ken added.

"Mmmh hmmm. Now, I do not doubt that there could have been some foul play going on. Chicago is after all a dangerous place at times. We do have security patrolling the hotel at night though. I'm just wondering if there was any chance the door could have been left open by mistake," Cliff asked.

"We're positive that the door was closed. Do you mind if we just review the tape now?" Ken responded in an agitated tone.

"Yes, certainly. Let's take a look at it," Cliff said.

They reviewed the tape of the outside hallway for 1:00 am. Nothing suspicious. Then they looked at the tape for 2:00 am. The beginning of the tape showed the same kind of footage. There was nothing questionable until they got towards the last couple of minutes just before the 3:00 am hour began. That's when they noticed a person in sweatpants and a hooded sweatshirt with long hair peeking out of the sides of it. They couldn't really make out the person's features well, but it appeared to be that of a woman.

The unidentified woman showed more activity during the tape of the 3:00 am hour that was reviewed. She paced back and forth in the hallway, stopping several times before she halted in front of one of the rooms. "That's it! Don't you see? She's stopping in front of our door. Can you zoom in any closer?" Cookie demanded.

"I can't believe this. Sure, let me just push this button to zoom in a little closer," Cliff responded. As soon as he clicked the button to advance the film closer, there was a gray haze that started forming over the camera. The footage went black and then skipped. The time jumped about five minutes ahead. Cliff tried to rewind the tape, but there was no way to retract the footage. "I'm terribly sorry. I don't know what is going on with the tape. We've never had this happen before," Cliff said.

"Can we look at the actual room footage? Maybe something will be there," Ken asked.

"It will only show the area immediately by the door. I supposed it's worth a shot though," Cliff responded as he flipped screens to show the view of the inside of the hotel room. They all looked intently to see what activity would transpire in the video. They checked all the same times as the other footage and there was absolutely nothing.

"Wow, that's crazy. There's got to be a glitch in the film somewhere. We should get going though. We have to get an uber to take us to get the rental car. Well, thank you for your time Cliff. We really appreciate it," Cookie responded.

"For all the trouble, please let me have one of my staff members take you to your next destination. It's the least I could do. I really do apologize for the both of you having such an unpleasant experience during your stay here," Cliff said.

"Thank you. We really appreciate that. The place where we're going is just right up the street," Ken stated.

Cookie and Ken finally made it to get a new rental car, thanks to Don, from their hotel, who drove them there. They were able to get a blue Toyota Camry in place of their previous vehicle. Once they were on the road again, Cookie called Chelsea to see where she wanted to meet for lunch. Ken had just decided to stay at Cookie's parents' house while she and Chelsea went out for lunch.

"Hey Cookie. How are you? I'm almost ready for lunch. I'm just trimming my edges a bit. My hair has been growing like a weed lately. I'm looking forward to us catching up. Is Ken going to be ok to be away from his 'snookems' for a little while?" Chelsea joked. She seemed to be in an exceptionally chipper mood, unlike her stoic attitude when she and Ken arrived yesterday.

"You've got jokes today, I see. Yes, he will be quite alright. Plus, I'm sure dad will enjoy his company. That is if he's not up trying to build something again," Cookie smiled.

"If you say so. I can be at mom and dad's in about 45 minutes. I'll come by and pick you up. How about that?" Chelsea asked.

"Sounds perfect. I'll see you when you get there then," Cookie answered.

****

Cookie and Chelsea walked into a new Italian restaurant that Chelsea suggested and were seated in a quaint corner near the entrance. "This place is nice. The food smells amazing too. I can't wait to try it. I'm so glad to be here together with you, although I hate it's under these circumstances. Dad really had me scared," Cookie said.

"Yeah me too. Hopefully, this will make him realize that he needs to relax. But I guess he passed on that trait to his girls too," Chelsea laughed.

The waiter came up to the table and introduced himself as Chad. He rattled off a list of the daily specials and specifically recommended their signature mimosas. Chelsea had totally forgotten about that. As fate would have it, Cookie just had to try the mimosas. Under normal circumstances, Chelsea would have been excited to share mimosas with her sister, but not today.

"I know that was quite a bit to take in. Shall we start off with drinks for you beautiful ladies?" Chad asked.

"Well, let's see. How about two of those delicious mimosas you mentioned earlier? I could really use one of those right now," Cookie responded.

"Could we also get some of the spinach and artichoke dip for an appetizer? Oh and make that one mimosa. I'll just have a blueberry lemonade," Chelsea added.

"Ok, coming right up. I'll be back with your drinks and spinach dip shortly. Then I can take your entrée orders, ladies," Chad said.

"Hmmm...what's really going on Miss Thing? This is your second time passing up alcohol since yesterday. If I didn't know any better I would say someone is pregnant," Cookie laughed.

"Hmmm...Really? Well, what would you say if I told you I was?" Chelsea rebutted. Cookie knew from the way she answered that there must be some truth to her statement. Not only had her sister hid her pregnancy, but Cookie was doing the exact same thing. She didn't let her know about her pregnancy either and then had a miscarriage. If Chelsea was truly pregnant, she would have to face the music and tell her about her miscarriage too.

CHAPTER NINE

"What? Wow, you're not kidding. With whom? Come on, tell me. Somebody is going to be an aunt soon," Cookie smiled. Although she was concerned about her sister having a baby out of wedlock, she was still excited for her.

"I just found out yesterday actually. My mind was in so many places. I haven't told Mel yet. I don't even know if I will. I'm debating even having this baby. Don't get me wrong, having a baby would be nice. It's something I've always wanted. But I didn't want it like this. I may get an abortion," Chelsea replied.

"An abortion? Don't you think you may be moving too fast with all of this? Give yourself some time to think about it," Cookie said. Tears started welling up in her eyes. Hearing her sister say that she was not only pregnant, but also thinking about getting an abortion, made her think about her miscarriage. She was so excited about having a baby with Ken. She was nowhere near over it and now all the feelings she tried to tuck away came rushing back to her at once. The feeling was overwhelming and she couldn't take it.

"Cookie, why are you crying? What's wrong? I'm sorry, I really didn't mean to upset you by telling you this," Chelsea rubbed Cookie's back. As fate would have it, the waiter was just making his way back to their table and witnessed Chelsea trying to console Cookie. He sat the drinks down on the table, along with their spinach and artichoke dip.

"Ladies, is everything ok? Please let me know if you need anything. I can give you a few more minutes and then come back," Chad said.

"That would be great. Thank you so much. We'll just need a few minutes and we'll be ready," Chelsea responded.

"I'm sorry. This isn't the right time for all of this. I'm happy for you. I'm really happy that you're pregnant. But I do support you either way, no matter what. I hope you know that," Cookie said.

"Well thanks, but don't bullshit me sis. I know something else has you upset. Spill it. I've got all day. You're the one that has to catch a plane tonight, not me," Chelsea replied.

"Well I was pregnant too recently. I was about three months pregnant when I had a miscarriage. Ken and I decided not to tell anyone until we had gotten past the first trimester. It was the same day we got back from our trip. I was so devastated. I didn't even mind so much with Brandon. I actually want a family with Ken though. I guess I haven't really allowed myself to deal with it," Cookie said.

"Cookie! Why didn't you tell me? I thought we were better than that," Chelsea exclaimed, raising her voice. By now, some of the other patrons in the restaurant started looking in their direction but, Chelsea was never one to care about causing a scene. If there was something she needed to get off her chest, she did just that – no matter who was around.

"I know. I get it. Well, for the miscarriage, it was the same day you were telling me everything about Mel. It happened right after you dropped us off at home. I figured you already had enough bad news for the day. Honestly, I couldn't even stand to talk about it without breaking down," Cookie said.

Chelsea felt like the worst person in the world at that moment. Here she was complaining about an unwanted pregnancy with Mel and Cookie was still suffering the after effects of her second miscarriage. She had to take a moment to collect her thoughts because she had no idea what to say to make Cookie feel at ease. "Cookie, I'm really sorry. I didn't know. I wouldn't have even talked about me being pregnant so nonchalantly. I'm here. Damn, we've really been through a lot, haven't we?" Chelsea laughed, trying to make some humor out of the situation and lighten up the mood.

Cookie couldn't help but laugh back when all the thoughts of the last 15 years of their lives flashed before her eyes. "You know what? You're right. We're going to be ok. We've been through worse. I really wish you could share this drink with me right now. Damn, this is good," Cookie said, raising her glass to the air for an imaginary toast with Chelsea.

The waiter came back to the table a couple minutes later to take their entrée orders. Cookie ordered a pineapple and chicken personal sized pizza. Chelsea ordered crispy chicken tenders with seasoned fries. The ladies talked and reminisced about the good ole days before wrapping up their lunch nearly two hours later.

"Hey, how is Sheila doing? You haven't left her alone with Ken, have you?" Chelsea asked Cookie with a sinister grin. They had just gotten in Chelsea's car and they were on their way back to their parents' house.

"Chelsea. There you go again. She hasn't tried anything on Ken. Funny you mention her, though. I need to call her back. She called me a couple days ago. I haven't even had a chance to tell her about dad yet," Cookie revealed.

"Mmmm. Ok then. She's got a good heart. We all make mistakes. I was just giving you a hard time. You know I couldn't resist," Chelsea joked.

"You are too funny girl. I had a great time hanging out with you today. Even with my meltdown. I was serious about what I told you too. Whatever you decide, I support it. It's your life and your body. Don't feel pressured either way. I love you," Cookie said.

"Thank you. I love you too. I'll be sure to let you know what I decide. I'm just so unsure about it right now. I still have to talk to Mel. That bastard: I get sick to my stomach just thinking about him. Ugh!" Chelsea laughed, as she pulled into their parents' driveway.

Cookie got out of the car and had to sit back down in the seat for a second. She felt a quick dizzy spell and then tried to get out of the car again. This time, she was unable to catch her balance as she started to fall against the car. She caught herself on the door handle of the back passenger door. "Chelsea, something's wrong. Whoa," Cookie mumbled.

"Cookie! I'm here. Lean on me," Chelsea said, running over to the passenger side to help Cookie stand up. She kept her in one spot, standing straight up after she picked her up from falling. Cookie started to gain her balance back and shook her head in an attempt to regain her composure. She seemed to be back to normal, but Chelsea kept her still to make sure she didn't stumble again.

"Damn. Well, that was pretty scary. That was really weird. I've never felt like that before. But, I think I'm ok now," Cookie said, trying to collect herself together before they walked inside the house. Although she was fully able to keep her balance now, her head still felt hazy. She didn't understand where it was coming from, but she brushed it off and tried to act as normal as possible when she and Chelsea walked inside. When they stepped into the house, Bill and Ken were having a debate about who would win the NBA Championship this year. Cookie was glad to see her two favorite men enjoying each other's company and getting along so well. At that moment, she really enjoyed being in Chicago. She missed the quick accessibility to her parents. Each time she visited, she realized there was something she missed out on from living so far away.

"There are my girls. Cookie, you saved your husband over here. He was going nowhere fast with this argument. I keep trying to tell him that it's the Bulls all the way. He'll learn one day," Bill laughed, patting Ken on the shoulder.

"Hey baby. Hey Chelsea. I need you both to remember this day. Mom, do you mind taking a picture for us? We need to document this," he laughed.

"Oh no, you and Bill are not getting me roped up into this. You know, I could get used to this. It's great having everyone here. We aren't used to having this much company. Ken, doesn't your company have an office in Chicago?" Lisa joked. Although she was making light of it, Cookie knew that her mother was serious.

"Well I guess I don't have a say in at all, huh?" Cookie laughed. She looked over at Chelsea, who was quiet the whole time.

Once she knew Cookie caught her unsavory expression, she quickly joined in on the conversation and said how great it would be if they lived in Chicago too.

Bill was nobody's fool. Cookie could see that he noticed the quick change from the negative expression Chelsea had on her face at that moment too. Being the clever man that he was, he quickly deflected the situation to make it less awkward than it already was.

"Well, it would be nice to have another guy to watch some of the games with. Ken, I'll forgive you for your uninformed opinions. Those can change in time," Bill said, while everyone laughed. Cookie and Chelsea took a seat on the couch with the rest of the family as Lisa surfed through the channels to find something on TV to watch.

They all watched a couple of lighthearted comedies on Netflix before Cookie and Ken started getting ready to head towards the airport. Bill gave Cookie and Ken some snacks for the road and everyone exchanged their goodbyes. Cookie felt another brief wave of dizziness take over her again.

"You take it easy now. I know that's hard for you to do, but we need you to stick around here for a while. I love you dad," Cookie told her father.

"I'll try my best. The best that I can do at least. I'm not going to let one little fall stop me from living. If it's my time to go then it's just my time," Bill said, with a half-smile and a glossed over gaze in his eyes.

CHAPTER TEN

Cookie was nervous about breaking the news regarding Chelsea's pregnancy to Ken. She was primarily concerned not with her sister's business, but with his reaction once he found out that she told Chelsea about their miscarriage. Naturally, he asked how their lunch went. This was her cue to tell the truth.

"Um, it was good. Really interesting. Bet you won't guess what I found out about Chelsea," Cookie said.

"Don't tell me she's back with Mel. Hopefully she leaves him alone. That just seems like a toxic situation all the way around," Ken responded.

"Well, not exactly but you're really close. She's not back with Mel, but she may be tied to him forever now. She's pregnant," Cookie said.

"Pregnant? How far along is she? I must admit, I didn't expect that," he said.

"Tell me about it. Me neither. She literally just found out yesterday, apparently right before she came to the hospital to come see dad," she said.

"Hmm…maybe that explains how strange she was acting then," Ken replied, in a matter of fact tone.

"Wow, so you thought so too? I'm with you on that. She seemed a little cold towards me at times. I guess to you too. I do have a confession to make though. I did tell her about the miscarriage. I didn't mean to, but she mentioned she may get an abortion. I think hearing that just broke me down. We're trying to have a baby and she's contemplating getting rid of hers. I couldn't take it and I kind of had a meltdown at the restaurant. I'm so sorry. I didn't want to tell anyone until we both talked about it first," Cookie said. As nervous as she was, she felt a weight lifted, after she got that off of her chest.

"You don't have to apologize. At least you're talking about it to someone. We haven't really talked about it together since it happened. I'm honestly glad you got to talk it out with her. I haven't told anyone yet, but I can definitely see how you would have felt led to tell her then.

"I know. We should talk about it. Maybe we should go see someone; a counselor, maybe? I honestly don't even know where to start. Would that even be something that you would be open to doing? I know that's not a typical guy thing to talk to a therapist," Cookie said.

"Um, well it's not something I've thought of doing. I thought we could talk it out amongst ourselves. But considering we haven't done that yet, a therapist may be a good idea. So, yes, I'm open to it," Ken replied.

"What did I do to deserve you? You are so perfect for me. You never cease to amaze me, even after all this time," Cookie smiled.

"Well I'm far from perfect. I love you Cookie," Ken said to Cookie.

"You're about as close to perfect as it gets. I love you too," Cookie said, resting her head on his shoulder.

"Now boarding for flight 704, from Chicago to Dallas," the flight announcer said. It was time for them to get in line to board the plane. Cookie stood up and had to grab Ken's arm to keep her from falling. He was caught off guard but quickly caught her and helped guide her to their seats.

"Baby, what's wrong? Are you ok?" Ken asked as they walked towards the middle of the plane to find their seats.

"I'm ok. I'm good. I think so at least. The same thing happened to me when Chelsea and I got back from the lunch, in the driveway. Right before….right before….we….um got inside. Yeah that was it," Cookie said. She was able to stand up on her own now, but now Ken was concerned about her speech now. Her sentences didn't make sense. He asked the stewardess for a bottle of water for her.

"Here, drink this babe. Let's go ahead and get you seated. Maybe the stress of the weekend has gotten to you," Ken told Cookie. He didn't really know what to do or say at that point, but he knew he was definitely going to keep a close eye on Cookie. Although he was still tired from last night, he couldn't rest now.

Just as he was about to put his phone on silent, it rang. He started not to answer, but it looked like the phone number from their hotel. Considering everything that happened last night, he decided to answer it.

"Hello?" Ken said.

"Um, yes this is Christine from The Royal Plaza. Please don't tell my boss that I called, but I have something to tell you about the video footage from your room last night," she said.

"Ok, you have to make it quick though. I'm on a plane and will have to turn my phone off soon," he said. By this time, Cookie was fully coherent and eavesdropping Ken's phone call. She listened hard to hear who was on the other line.

"Yes sir. Long story short, you and your wife were right. We have a guy here that's really tech savvy. He was able to get the footage of the inside of the room to show up somehow. There was definitely a person in your room last night. It appeared to be a woman, just as you and your wife described," Christine said.

Ken fell silent on the other end of the phone, just as the announcement came over the speakers for everyone to turn off all electronic devices.

****

Meanwhile, Chelsea was at home getting running a hot bath. She was about to pour herself a glass of wine to accompany her soft music and candles. Just that quickly she forgot about being pregnant. She did another test when she got home just to be sure and the results were still the same. Although she was leaning more towards the side of having an abortion anyway, she didn't want to start drinking knowing she was pregnant. Somehow that seemed more wrong in her mind than going through with getting an abortion.

Just as she put the wine back in the refrigerator, she heard a knock at her door. She wasn't expecting any company tonight. She waited a few moments before walking towards the door. She thought the knocking would stop, but it picked up again about a minute later. She walked slowly towards the door and looked through the stained glass. There was definitely a person standing at the door, but it was too dark outside for her to tell who they were. For some reason her light motion detectors were not working properly lately, making it even harder for her to see anyone coming up to her front door. The only she could see was that the person had on a dark colored sweatshirt with the hood pulled over their head.

Her water was still running and she decided to ignore whoever was at her door and go cut her water off. She walked upstairs to her bathroom quietly, still looking back at the front door. She loved her house, but it did make her feel uncomfortable at times that if anyone was ever to break in her house through the front door, they could run directly up the stairs into her bedroom. Chelsea exhaled deeply as she waited a couple of minutes before finally getting in the bathtub. She turned off her music so that she could easily hear any foreign sounds coming from downstairs.

The steam from the water rolled off of the surface, just as Chelsea eased into her chamomile and lavender scented bubble bath. She could really use that glass of wine right about now to take the edge off. She tucked a rolled up towel behind her head and deeply inhaled the relaxing fragrance. She closed her eyes, propped her feet up on the edge of her spacious garden tub and that's when it happened. Smash!

Chelsea could tell from the direction of the sound that the broken glass came from the window near her front door, downstairs. She sat up in the water, preparing to ease out of the tub. Thankfully the room was only lit by candlelight, which would allow her to cast less shadows as she eased to grab her robe as she stepped out of the tub. She heard someone fidgeting with her door knob downstairs and stopped dead in her tracks. Whoever this was must have been trying to come after her. For the first time in a long time, she was extremely fearful for her life. She crept towards the bedroom door and slipped her cell phone inside her robe. Then she lifted her mattress for her gun and pointed it straight out in front of her. She leaned her head forward just enough to see outside the bedroom. Surprisingly, no one was in plain sight that she could see. However, Chelsea wasn't going down without a fight.

The house was quiet yet again and she thought now may be a good time to walk down the stairs. As she made her way down, she noticed there was something wrapped up in a towel on the floor. There was shattered glass through her side window but the front door remained intact. Chelsea looked around downstairs and turned on all of the lights. The gun stayed pointed in front of her wherever she turned.

With all of the excitement going on, she forgot she didn't call the police. As soon as the operator answered, she spilled out the whole story of what just happened and waited for the police to arrive. Now she felt fearful again. What if the person was still lurking around when they showed up? They would know she was a snitch and possibly try something more drastic the next time. That's when she got a good look at what must have been used to break her window. Although she was curios to find out what it was, she decided not to touch anything until the police arrived.

A couple of minutes later, she saw the red and blue lights flashing outside of her window. Two men got out of the car and walked up to her front door and greeted her. She noticed there was a third officer who trailed behind the other two men. He primarily kept an eye on the outside perimeter of the house.

"Good evening mam. I'm Officer Mallory. Are you ok?" the first police officer said. He stepped over the wrapped object that was thrown through the door and landed at the front of her the hallway.

"Yes, thankfully I'm fine. I was upstairs about to take a bath and that's when I heard the noise of the glass from the front door being shattered. I actually heard a knock at first, but I had a strange feeling so I decided not to answer the door," she stated, recounting the series of events.

"Well, you are really blessed. That's for sure. I'm Officer Jones. Can you recall how much time passed between when you heard the knock at the door and then the shattering of the glass here through your front door?" Officer Jones said.

"I would say it couldn't have been past five minutes. There wasn't a long span of time in between at all," Chelsea answered.

"Ok, well we'll assign extra security in the neighborhood for the next couple of weeks. We definitely don't want you feeling unsafe in your own home," Officer Mallory said, while looking back outside at his counterpart who was surveying the driveway and front yard with a flashlight.

"That would be really nice. I've never felt unsafe in this neighborhood before, until now," Chelsea said. She intentionally left out the odd occurrence of the man who came to her house before and knocked on the garage door, leaving an eerie note on her car.

"I am concerned about this mass that broke your window here on the floor. There's got to be a reason why they wrapped up whatever this object is before they threw it at your door," Officer Jones said. "Do you mind stepping back a bit while we take this outside?"

"Um, sure. I don't mind at all," Chelsea responded obediently. She also thought it was weird that what appeared to be a single brick was wrapped in such tattered fabric.

The police officers weren't even gone two minutes before they came back in the house. They showed her the contents of the sheet, which was a brick as she expected. "I know this may seem like an odd question to ask, but do you have any idea why someone would send you a note like this?" Officer Mallory said.

He turned the brick over so she could read the message that was taped on it. The letters were clipped with different fonts on a piece of pastel yellow paper. Chelsea's eyes widened and she gasped as she read what the note said, "You can't run forever. You WILL pay."

CHAPTER ELEVEN

Chelsea didn't sleep well at all for the next couple of days. She was unnerved partly because of her newfound gift of morning sickness. The incident that happened at her house the other night didn't help either. She didn't tell her parents about the break in and at this point, she had still only revealed her pregnancy to Cookie. She tossed and turned all night, unable to fall into a sound sleep. Her stomach was tied up in knots. She looked over at the clock. It was already 8:15 am on a Saturday morning. She rushed to the toilet quickly to vomit. It was her second time heaving over the toilet that day. The first time was about three hours prior.

That was it. She finally had enough. Although she still hadn't made up her mind about whether she was going to keep the baby, she had to let Mel know. She took a long, hot shower, cooked breakfast and called him shortly after 11:00 am. She almost didn't even expect him to answer. Ironically, ever since she found out she was pregnant, she stopped hearing from Mel. Before then, he was reaching out constantly, several times a day, attempting to get any kind of response from her.

Surprisingly, he answered. "Hello? Chelsea? Hey, um this is a nice surprise. How are you?"

"I'm ok, I guess. Hey, I know this is probably a little awkward for me to call you like this. But I guess there's no better way than for me to tell you than to get straight to it. I'm pregnant. I just found out a few days ago," Chelsea responded.

"Really? Oh wow," Mel responded.

"Oh wow? What the hell do you mean "oh wow"? I was expecting something a little better than that," she said.

"I just...I know there were only a couple of times that we didn't use a condom. I guess it would have been then. Are you sure?" Mel asked cautiously.

"I know you're not trying to say that I could be pregnant by someone else. You've got more balls than I gave you credit for. How dare you even insinuate some bullshit like that when you were the one running around with cheap sluts?" Chelsea screamed.

"Wait. I'm not saying that. I just don't see how it happened. That's all. Well, I'm here. I'm ready to do whatever I have to do to support the baby. I'm going to take care of my responsibilities," Mel replied. Chelsea was trying to keep her cool, but she was boiling inside. Sure, she was pissed that Mel even questioned if the baby was his. But the real issue was that he said he would be a father to his unborn child without trying to get back with her. She was shocked, even offended.

"Well, at the end of the day, Mel, it really doesn't matter what you think. Since you don't even think this baby is yours, I'm not really expecting much support from you on this. To be honest, I'm not even sure I'm keeping it," Chelsea responded.

"What do you mean you're not sure if you're keeping it? How could you just get rid of our baby like that?" Mel rebutted. Chelsea could tell he was starting to get heated now.

"Look, we're not getting back together. That's a done deal. I refuse to start a family off like this. This isn't the right way to do it. Whatever I decide to do, I'll let you know," Chelsea said coldly.

"Umph, just like that, huh? Ok, well you just let me know what you decide. I'll support you either way," Mel said.

"Thanks. Well, I have some business I need to take care of, so I should go ahead and let you go now. But you have a good day Mel," Chelsea replied.

"Yeah, you too Chelsea. Take care," Mel responded abruptly, before hanging up the phone. Chelsea threw her phone on the counter and put her head in her hands. Talking to Mel didn't make the situation any better. She couldn't believe that bastard could be so insensitive. There was one good thing that happened from their conversation though. She was one step closer to her decision about the baby.

****

"What? She speaks! The world must stop because the queen has called," Sheila joked as she answered the phone. She really wasn't upset but was just giving Cookie a hard time for taking so long to return her call.

"Ok, alright I guess I do deserve that. There is so much I have to fill you in on. It's been crazy, but first I want to hear about you. How is Sean? If I know you like I think I do, you are already making wedding plans," Cookie laughed.

"I'm wonderful, just busy as ever, balancing the business and day to day to life. Sean is fine. I'm still on cloud nine. You know what? I'm actually just trying to take it slow. It won't be a long engagement at all. We're doing some basic planning but it won't be anything really extravagant. We're too old for all of that. I just want to walk down the aisle, become Mrs. Tipton, sweat from dancing in my dress and then sweat with him later that night. It's just that simple," Sheila said, in a matter of fact, but lighthearted tone.

"I know what you mean. I am so excited for you. I cannot wait for your big day! I'm here if you need help with anything. Just let me know. I promise I won't take this long to call you back either," Cookie laughed. She wanted to fill Sheila on what was going on in her life, but didn't think this was the best time to tell her about the miscarriage during their discussion of upcoming marital bliss.

"Thank you so much. You know you will be there for me right? I want you to be my matron of honor in the wedding. Monica will hopefully be my maid of honor, but I wanted to ask you first. We don't want to have a large wedding party. We're just keeping it intimate and simple, with our closest family and friends," Sheila responded.

"Of course! Yeah! You know I'm so ready. I would be honored to be your matron of honor," Cookie said. She and Sheila endured their share of trials throughout their friendship, but she was a tried and true friend. She considered Sheila more of her sister than a mere friend.

"Oh and there's one more thing that I want to run by you. You must say yes. Well I'm hoping you say yes, at least. I have an extra ticket to the New Orleans Jazz Fest and Sean isn't going to be able to make it. He has a business trip that falls during that same weekend. It worked out well in a sense. It will give us some time to really catch up and just have some one on one girl time. We'll leave next Friday morning and come back Sunday. Check with Ken, but he's cool so I know he'll say yes," Sheila ranted.

"You just have it all planned out, don't you? I would love to go with you. I'm sure Ken will be alright with it, but I'll ask him just to be sure. I haven't been to the Jazz Fest in forever. That will be so much fun. I've got to hit the gym extra hard this week so I can be ready," Cookie and Sheila laughed. This would be the perfect opportunity for her to really fill Sheila in on everything that had transpired in the last couple of weeks. She was glad to finally get that opportunity.

"Ok, well just keep me posted. I'm looking forward to us getting a chance to hang out. Cookie, I have to ask you a question. I've known you long enough to know when you're hiding something from me. I can't get off this phone without at least asking you. What's really going on with you? How have you really been doing?" Sheila asked.

Cookie thought she would be able to get through the conversation without discussing anything serious. However, she should have known that wouldn't fly with Sheila. They knew each other like a book, so it was only a matter of time before she would pry to find out what was going on in her head. "Um, I'm ok. I'm doing well. There's been a lot going on. Ugh, I hate this. You always know me so well. Ok, I know I should have told you this already, but my dad got sick and I had to go up to Chicago to see him. That's why I missed your call the last time," Cookie said.

"What? Oh my God! Is he ok now? What happened?" Sheila asked.

"We were on the phone, just talking like normal. He was working on a shelf for my mom. You know, doing some construction work like he always does. His speech started getting slurred all of a sudden and then I heard him fall to the floor. Thankfully, my mother was there too. Basically, when he got to the hospital, they told him he had a mini stroke," Cookie confessed. Although she didn't want to relive the whole situation again, she was relieved in a sense to get it off her chest.

"Thank goodness he's ok! I know that had to have been hard for you. I'll be praying for him too. How does he feel now?" Sheila asked.

"He's much better now. I think he just need to learn how to rest. That man cannot sit still. I'm concerned about him though. I'm going to make another trip home soon," Cookie replied.

"Well look who's talking, Mrs. Busy Body. I guess the apple doesn't fall too far from the tree, does it? You're a lot like your dad, but in a way that's good. Just make sure you take care of yourself too. How are your mom and Chelsea doing?" Sheila questioned.

"Umph. Well, I guess you do make a good point. They're both doing well. They were both pretty freaked out about dad too. The next time I go home, I'm looking forward to getting some more quality time in with them," Cookie said.

"Hmmm....ok, well that's understandable. Cookie, I don't know how to say this. I know that what happened with your dad is a pretty big deal. But, I also know when you're hiding something too. Tell me the truth. What else is going on that has you worried or upset? I can tell there's something else bothering you," Sheila asked.

"Oh no, girl. Really, I'm ok. I'm good, I promise," Cookie replied. She didn't know why she just lied to Sheila. No, she did. She would eventually come clean about the miscarriage and even her uncomfortable feelings towards Chelsea lately; just not today. Up until this point, Cookie had done a superb job of controlling her emotions, considering everything that had been going on in her life recently. But she could feel herself at a breaking point. Honestly, she didn't know how much longer she would be able to hold it together without having a meltdown.

CHAPTER TWELVE

The weekend came quickly and Cookie couldn't be more excited to see it arrive. Although she had to do some work to wrap up some presentations for the quarter's closing, she was excited about getting to spend some uninterrupted time with Ken. Saturday morning he asked if she wanted to go on a run with him. He thought it would be great for both of them to clear their minds. She called her dad before they left to check in on him. He sounded vibrant as ever, which made her heart melt. At least that was one burden lifted from her shoulders.

Ken laced up his tennis shoes while he waited on Cookie to change into her workout gear. "Oh, so fancy. He's matching his shoes with his sweats," Cookie joked. Ken's shoes were gray and white, with specks of orange at the soles. His gray sweatpants had an orange drawstring and the emblem on the side of them was orange as well. It was one of the things Cookie appreciated about Ken. He wasn't stuck on himself, but he did care about his appearance. He was a head turner even in workout gear.

"Well when you have a wife as breathtaking as you, then it makes you step up your game a bit. I don't want to be left behind in the dust," Ken smiled. They walked outside the front door and were greeted by a warm, brightly shining sun. The weather was perfect, with a nice breeze to boot. There was a beautiful trail just about a half a mile from their home and everyone else seemed to have had the same idea to go for a run.

They decided to run the whole 6 mile track, taking in all of the beautiful natural scenery. Every now and then they would cross paths with someone else running on the trail. About halfway in, they passed a young woman that favored Cookie who was bending down to help her daughter tie her shoe. Cookie heard the woman say, "Mommy loves you". The little girl smiled wide and hugged her mother as they continued along the trail.

Cookie felt a lump forming in the back of her throat. Then water began collecting at the corners of her eyes. In her mind she was saying, "Stay strong. It's ok, your time will come. God doesn't make mistakes". But right at that very moment, she didn't feel like being strong. She wanted to crumble inside of herself and hide from the world. She didn't want the world to see her poker face compromised. Judging from her and Sheila's conversation that week, she wondered if the only person she was fooling was herself.

"Ken, is it ok if we stop for just a second? I'm getting a little winded," Cookie asked.

"Oh ok sure baby. What's wrong, you can't keep up?" Ken responded, tapping her shoulder. He loved the friendly competition they had with each other. It was one of the things that always kept their love life spicy. However, as he looked in Cookie's eyes, he could tell something was seriously wrong.

"Haha. You've got jokes mister. Just need a quick second to um, regroup. That's all," Cookie answered, turning her head away so Ken wouldn't see the tears beginning to walk down her cheeks.

Ken grabbed her face gently and turned it towards him. "Baby, talk to me. What's going on? Is something hurting?" he asked. Grief and pain impact people so differently and it just clicked in Ken's mind the reason why Cookie may be so upset. He saw the woman and the little girl on the trail as well. He felt a pang of sadness, but he was hopeful that one day soon he and Cookie would get to experience the joy of being parents. Cookie apparently had a different reaction. He guided them to have a seat on the rest bench a few steps ahead.

"Nothing on the outside is hurting, although I feel like my heart is being ripped to shreds. I'm really trying hard not to be angry at God right now. I can't lie though. I'm so pissed. I just can't take it. I know you're hurting too, so I try to keep quiet about it. I know I'm just preaching to the choir," Cookie revealed. People running past them began to look intently with nosey stares. She didn't care what they thought. She needed to free herself of the bottled up emotions she had been holding back. Right then, she could care less what they thought about her.

"I'm so sorry baby. It's ok, let it out. I should have checked in more with you to see how you were feeling. It does hurt. It hurts like hell. We will get through it together though. You do believe that right, baby?" Ken asked, leaning back so he could see Cookie's eyes.

"Yeah I know. At least I think I do. Sometimes I'm strong and other times, I just... I guess this is just a really weak moment for me. I've been thinking about something. Remember when I mentioned us going to see a counselor? Maybe we can find someone sooner than later," Cookie asked.

"Yeah, sure we can go baby. Let's go for it," Ken replied.

"Ok, maybe we can start looking up some people tonight?" Cookie asked. She was relieved that Ken still agreed to the idea but nervous that it may be something he was just going along with to please her. Then again, Ken was far from a yes man and would have likely spoken up if he didn't feel comfortable going to see a counselor.

Cookie and Ken finished out their run and Cookie felt good running off her pain. Although, when they finally arrived back at home, she still felt a weight of heaviness on her heart. She and Ken walked in the house and soon after, Cookie's phone rang. It was her mother calling. She breathed a deep sigh before answering the phone. She tried to remain positive and remind herself that her mother could be calling just to talk and not to deliver any bad news.

"Hello? Mom. How are you? Everything ok?" Cookie answered, still trying to get her breathing pattern back to normal after the run.

"Hey baby. Oh yeah, everything is ok. I was just calling to chit chat. I didn't want anything major. Sounds like you're out of breath over there. I didn't catch you at a bad time, did I," Lisa asked, with a tinge of sarcasm.

"No! We weren't doing that. Ken and I just finished running mom. You are too funny," Cookie laughed. Though she was slightly embarrassed by her mother's comment, she was ecstatic just to be able to laugh and really feel it.

"Oh ok, I see then. I love that you both workout together to stay healthy. Smart thinking to keep your marriage together too. Look, I don't want to hold you up. I know you both probably have to work tomorrow. Your father went to Home Depot to pick up a couple things for the shelf he's making me. He's insistent on continuing to work on it. But I made him slow down and only do a little bit at a time. You know I can't tell him anything," Lisa said and laughed.

"Yes, he is definitely going to be his own man. I think someone over here has that same syndrome too," Cookie said, playfully nudging Ken. "What was it that you wanted to tell me though?"

"It's your sister. I just can't shake it. I keep having this strange dream about her every night. What's crazy about it is it's the same exact dream over and over again. Last night was my fourth time having it. I haven't mentioned it to your father and I really don't mean to dump this on you either. I just have to tell someone though. It's driving me crazy keeping this to myself," Lisa said.

"Okay, mom, you're not being a burden on me. You know you can tell me anything. What is this dream that you've been having?" Cookie asked, grabbing a bottle of water from the counter as she sat on one of the stools in the kitchen.

"I'll try my best to describe it, but it's weird like I can't make out her face in the dream. I know it's Chelsea though. I can feel it. In my dream she has on these dark sunglasses and a gray hooded sweatshirt. She's walking on this deserted road and I see her coming towards me. She eventually passes me but doesn't say a thing. She acts like she barely knows me. The closer she gets, I can see a red glow permeating around the rims of her shades. I call her name and she never answers. She just keeps walking and that's when I look up in the sky and it's burning. The sky is literally on fire. I just can't figure out what it all means. I know she's been acting strange lately, but I just don't get it," Lisa vented.

"Wow, mom that is a really weird dream. Hopefully, it's not anything major. I can't believe you keep having it over and over again. You haven't been eating anything spicy before bed, have you?" Cookie laughed.

"No, I haven't Missy. I'm serious though. Cookie this dream really has me shook," Lisa responded.

"I know and I promise I'm not trying to negate your feelings. Let's just pray that whatever is causing you to have the dream goes away. That's got to be frightening to keep having it every night," Cookie responded. She couldn't let on to her mother, but she was trying to make light of the fact that hearing about the dream was spooking her out too. The part when she said Chelsea was wearing a gray hooded sweatshirt immediately reminded her of the woman she saw in the hotel room a few nights ago. Something weird was definitely going on, but she couldn't allow it to have power over her or her mother.

"You're right baby. That is the best thing is just to continue praying that it will eventually stop. I hear the garage door coming up, so your father's back. I'll talk to you later sweetie. I love you," Lisa said.

"Ok mom, I love you too. Don't let that dream stuff get you worked up. It's going to be alright," Cookie said, trying to give her mother a calm reassurance. They said their final goodbyes and got off the phone. Cookie could tell her mother was shaken by the incessant dream of Chelsea. She felt powerless and didn't know what to do to help her. She buried her face in her hands and let out a deep sigh as Ken took off his sweaty shirt and placed it inside the empty washing machine.

"Everything ok with your mom? You looked a little worried when you were talking with her" Ken questioned.

"Yeah, in the whole scheme of things she's fine and my dad is doing well. She keeps having this strange dream about Chelsea. Something about her wearing a hoodie, with shades on and red lights glowing from her eyes. It was really spooky. Then she said she was trying to call her name in the dream, but she never answered. She just kept walking down this abandoned road. My mom said there was a lot of fire in the sky too. It's just crazy. I don't get why all of these things are happening," Cookie said.

Ken was very quiet, almost dazed. Cookie was about to ask him if he had even heard anything she said. Right before she could get the words out, he spoke. "I didn't tell you because I was trying to find the right time. I had that same dream last night".

CHAPTER THIRTEEN

Chelsea laid on the operating table inside of the cold hospital room. The room was so silent that she could hear the second hand on the clock ticking. The noise was so loud that she couldn't even hear herself think. Maybe that was the point. She toyed with this idea back and forth. She just couldn't see herself bringing another life into this world with such a scumbag of a man. She didn't even bother to tell him that she was actually getting an abortion. He didn't need to know. The decision was hers to make alone, since it was her body anyway.

She waited for what seemed to be an eternity for the doctor to come back in. Of course, she had kids and she warned her of her decision. She asked her for the umpteenth time if she was sure she wanted to go through with it. "I've made up my mind. Yes, I'm sure," Chelsea responded, with a slightly agitated tone. Right now, she wanted a burning bush answer that she was making the right decision. Her mouth said she was, but her mind spoke otherwise. At the root of her thought process, she couldn't picture herself having her first child with a man who cheated on her. That wasn't exactly in the cards for her thoughts of early stages of motherhood.

"Ok, I understand. We will move forward with the procedure then," the doctor answered curtly, but with a sense of warmth; sympathy even. She had some complicated name that she didn't care to begin to recall. Chelsea still hadn't told a soul outside of Cookie (and Mel, of course) that she was even pregnant. She wondered what her mother would think. What would her father say? All of that didn't matter right now because the decision had been made.

Although she felt sorry for her sister for having yet another miscarriage, she felt a pang of resentment towards her. How could she be so heartbroken when she could just try again? She had the perfect career, perfect husband and the perfect life. So what that her first marriage ended up being hell in a handbasket. Cookie escaped unscathed, largely because of Chelsea's help. Cookie may have missed her opportunity for being a mother for now, but she could at least try again with someone who she loved. Someone who was worthy of her company and she was worthy of his. All Chelsea had was the remnants of a beautiful nightmare from a man she thought loved her solely and genuinely.

When the procedure was over, Chelsea was asked if there was anyone coming to pick her up or if there was someone in the waiting room for her. "No, I came alone. I'll be fine. Thanks for asking," Chelsea responded. Her eyes were now blank and the feisty spunk she possessed was absent. She was more cooperative and calm. Chelsea's ride home seemed like the longest one ever. She rode in silence because her thoughts were loud enough. She didn't need the radio competing with what was going on inside her head. Once she got home, she put on her plush pink robe and curled into the bed. She slept for several hours and felt like she was in another world when she finally did wake up.

****

"Good afternoon Candice and Ken. Please come in and have a seat. May I offer you some water?" the counselor asked. Cookie found a counselor she thought would be great for them to move towards restoration and healing. Ken was surprisingly still on board, although they were both apprehensive about their first session. Neither one of them had ever seen a counselor before. The woman, Melissa Kenton, was strikingly beautiful. She looked even better than the pictures Cookie saw online. Cookie briefly looked her up and down in the slightly judgmental way that women do, as she caught Ms. Kenton (who appeared to be unmarried) subtly doing the same. Even in form fitting, but nonrevealing clothes, Cookie could tell that she had a striking figure. She looked at Ken and smiled, thinking that there was no way he missed her physical appearance as well. But she had to focus. They were there for a specific purpose.

"Oh yes, thank you. We would love some water Ms. Kenton," Ken responded as he and Cookie extended their hands to greet her.

"Please, call me Melissa. I'm not quite that old yet. I won't be 40 until later this month. I'm debating whether or not I should celebrate it as my second 39th birthday," she laughed. She walked over and handed each of them small sized bottles of cold water. Her office was pristine and simple, with no semblance of family or her personal life, except for a few plaques that were hanging on the wall.

"We're not far from it ourselves. You look great. I say embrace it," Cookie responded, starting to loosen up more.

"Well, thank you. You two look like a young, vibrant couple with lots of chemistry. I know there has to be a reason you're here today though. Where would you like to start? I'm all ears," Melissa said.

"We just recently suffered a miscarriage. It's actually my second one. I had a miscarriage from my previous marriage as well. We've been so busy with work and just living life that we really haven't grieved and accepted it. At least, I know I haven't for sure," Cookie said. She figured she would speak first since it was her idea after all.

Melissa looked at both of their expressions before responding. She noticed that Ken's face changed when Cookie mentioned the miscarriage, but especially when she mentioned her ex-husband. She would get back to that later, but for now, she wanted to get his take on how he felt.

"I'm so sorry Candice. Well, let me rephrase that. I'm sorry for both of you. As a woman, I know how you feel Candice, from personal experience. Ken, I want to talk to you for a moment. How does the miscarriage make you feel?" Melissa asked.

"I hate it. I really do. I feel like there's something I could have done. But the reality is, I couldn't do anything. I've always wanted children. I love Candice. I really do. She's going to be an amazing mother one day. It's just not our time yet," he said.

"Is that all?" Melissa asked curtly.

"I'm not exactly sure what you mean. Yes, that's the gist of how I feel," Ken responded with a matched tone.

"We basically are devastated by this. I was so excited to be a mother and especially with Ken. I just want to still have that chance. The doctors haven't said there's anything wrong with either of us that we know of. Oh, and you can call me Cookie. That's what most people call me anyway," Cookie added.

"Ok, well Cookie and Ken, there's a reason why I lead off with asking you both how you really feel about the miscarriage. You have to dig deep into the pain. Rip the band aid. It hurts. I know it does, but that's the only way you're going to get to the other side of healing," Melissa replied.

Cookie began to cry as Ken wrapped his arm around her shoulder. The more he rubbed her shoulder, the more she continued to sob. His eyes were now glossed over at the thought of her being in so much pain. "You know, it wouldn't be so bad if this was the first time. Granted, with my first husband, that was a blessing that we didn't have any children. He was abusive. I didn't know what real love was until I met Ken. I thought everything would be in sync now and we would be blessed with having our own child," she said.

"Do you feel as if this is somehow your fault, Cookie? I'm going to eventually have separate sessions with you both as well. Although you both appear to be happily in love, I may be able to go deeper beneath the surface one on one and then we'll of course, continue with our joint meetings. I also want to go back to something you just said. Did you not think your ex-husband was fit to be a father?" Melissa said.

"In some strange way, I do. I think that maybe there's something I'm doing wrong for this to have happened two times in a row. To answer your question, my ex was in no way, shape or form prepared to be a father," Cookie sobbed, less urgently now.

"Baby, there is absolutely nothing wrong with you. You are perfect and we're going to talk through this so we can just move forward with our lives," Ken said, trying his best to comfort his wife.

Melissa crossed her legs and rubbed the bottom of her neck before answering. "Ken is right. You can't blame yourself for what happened. I do want to know more about your ex-husband though. I think that may help me understand why you feel you should carry this weight of blame on your shoulders. Can you briefly tell me what happened during your courtship and marriage with him?" Melissa asked.

"Briefly? Ha, there's no way I could tell that story briefly," Cookie smiled sarcastically. This would be her first time in a few years that she had to relive her experiences with Brandon. She was scratching an old wound that hopefully make the new one heal quicker. She looked nervously at Ken as she began to sift through her thoughts about Brandon's difficult upbringing, their tumultuous marriage together and most uncomfortably, his death.

CHAPTER FOURTEEN

Brandon's mother, Maureen, was a beautiful woman; striking even. She had slanted, bedroom eyes, full lips, high cheek bones, wavy auburn hair and a figure to die for. People around the neighborhood called her Mean Green, not only for her mesmerizing hazel eyes, but also for her rude attitude. Their father, Myles, was always smitten by her, regardless of how much trouble she caused him. He was always getting into brawls with some man who wanted to test him, because of Maureen's good looks and smart mouth.

Myles was a quiet man, who looked meek and docile. When people talked about him though, they often said, "Don't let the smooth taste fool you". When it came to Maureen, he would literally go to any length to save her. As bad as Myles knew that Maureen was for him, he never left her. Despite Maureen's beauty, she battled many demons. Before she got pregnant with the twins (Brian and Brandon), she started experimenting with drugs. First, there was marijuana and then she graduated to cocaine.

Myles tried drugs with her too in the beginning, but stopped once he realized how hooked Maureen had become. Miraculously, she stopped when she got pregnant with the twins, but things went downhill as soon as they were born. She suffered severe post-partum depression and picked up her drug habit again. This time she skipped marijuana altogether and went straight for the cocaine. Heroine was even brought into the mix on some occasions. She lost her job because of her increasing erratic outbursts. Myles soon found himself serving the role of mother and father for the boys.

One night she came home late at 1:00 am in the morning. It was the day before the twins' second birthday and there was a big party planned for them that weekend. Maureen finally stumbled in, while Myles was in the front room watching TV. He was drinking directly from a bottle of Bulleit Bourbon. His nerves were eating him alive and he was going crazy with his own thoughts. Maureen crept in and could see the TV was on in the front room. Myles flicked on the light, just as she thought she was about to get by.

"Where the hell have you been, Maureen? I've been trying to get in touch with you all day. I went up to your job and Connie told me that you haven't worked there in a week. Said you got fired. I pray to God that's not true. Look at your face. You've got to stop this!" he said, fuming with anger as he spoke to Maureen.

"Myles, cut the lecture ok. I'm just fine. Come on, let's go to bed. It's been a long day," she said, acting totally oblivious as to why he was so upset with her.

"Are you freaking crazy? These boys can't grow up in a house like this. You are ruining your life and frankly ruining ours. I'm leaving you if you don't get your act together. I love you with all my heart, Maureen. I really do. You know that and that's why you try to use it against me. But I swear to you, I love those boys in there too and they deserve a chance at a good life. So you decide today, either you make the right decision or you pack your bags and go back to wherever the hell you just came from," he said.

"Oh, now you want to play the family man, huh? So says the man that's drinking a fifth of bourbon straight. Give me this.

That's not good for the babies to see," she said, in a mocking tone, while she took a big swig and slammed the bottle on the table.

She walked towards the boys' room and opened the door. Myles followed quickly behind her and grabbed her arm. "What are you doing? You just go in there and get yourself cleaned up. You smell like smoke and alcohol. Don't go in there disturbing those boys," he said.

"I'll do whatever the hell I want. These are my kids. I carried them for 9 months and you didn't do shit! Let me go!" she said as Brandon and Brian both woke up and started crying almost simultaneously. She reached for Brandon and rocked him in her arms. His cries quickly turned to screams as he kicked and squirmed to get out of her grasp.

"Maureen, put him down. Give him to me, please," Myles said. At this point he could tell her stance was shaky and he didn't want to risk her falling with Brandon in her arms. She reluctantly handed Brandon over to him and then reached in the crib for Brian.

"Come on baby. It's your Mommy. Your brother's being a little fussy, but I know you're going to show your mother some love, right?" she pleaded to her son, with an inflection of desperate hope in her voice. Brian was quiet at first, but that moment was short lived. He too began to cry and scream even harder than Brandon did. She turned to see Brandon in Myles's arms, now calm, while he rocked him back to silence. She swallowed the massive lump of embarrassment that formed at the back of her throat.

"Come on Maureen. It's been a long night. Leave the boys alone and let's get some sleep. I have to get up early tomorrow for work," he replied.

"Oh I get it. You and these little crumb snatchers here just want to disregard me. You two and your father here want to just act like I wasn't the one who gave birth to you. I was the one who carried you for nine months! Fed you! Clothed you! Gave you a comfortable roof to live under. Is this the thanks I get? Is it? Answer me!" she screamed in their faces.

"Stop this drunken, crazy talk, right now! Get the hell out of this room. You're scaring the boys," Myles ordered her.

"I'll do you one better. I'm leaving for good! I've got another man across town that I've been seeing anyway. Bet you didn't know that, did you? Get the hell outta my way," Maureen said pushing her way past Myles. He wouldn't budge. She knew she couldn't get around his tall, muscular frame even on her best day. She slapped him hard across his face. Stunned from the reaction, she was able to run past him into their bedroom.

"Maureen, I don't know what kind of shit you've gotten hold to, but you are acting like a damn lunatic. You should be ashamed of yourself," he said. Maureen just kept packing her suitcase like she didn't even hear him speaking to her.

"Myles, you're a good man. You really are. But there comes a point in a woman's life where good just isn't enough anymore. I've reached that point and I have to do what's best for me. You may not see it now, but you'll thank me later," she said, matter of factly, with no hint of remorse in her voice.

"Reen (that's what he called her when he was really upset at her), I'm going to tell you this one time only. So, I hope you get this way up there in the clouds where your head is at right now because I'm never repeating it again. If you walk out of that door right now, I'll live without you as my wife. It'll hurt, but I'll get through it. Honestly, our relationship has been dead for the last couple years anyway. But if you leave, you leave Brandon and Brian behind for good. Don't look back. I'll take care of them on my own. They don't deserve this shit from you," he said.

Maureen knew Myles had reached his wit's end with her. Not only did he address her as "Reen", but he rarely ever cursed at her (except for a handful of times when she made him boiling mad). She still didn't care though. She had reached a selfish point of no return. She grabbed her suitcase and wheeled it right past him, barely missing his foot.

"I probably shouldn't wake the boys; sounds like they're back asleep now. Give them my love. Bye baby," she turned around and leaned forward towards Myles to give him a kiss. He back away quickly to dodge her lips.

"Just get out," he said coldly.

"Alright, suit yourself. You take care now," she said as she closed the door behind her.

It would be 15 years before Myles would ever see Maureen again. Myles did as well as he could have for any abruptly single father, considering the cards he was dealt. He made a great father figure for the boys, despite battling his own addictive demon to alcohol. He wasn't an abusive drunk by any means. But every night he had a Jack and Coke before he went to bed.

After a few years, it escalated to two glasses before bed (with more Jack than Coke). He tried to reach out to Maureen, but she constantly dodged him. A few times, he even spotted her out with different men at dinner or at the local store. The alcohol numbed his pain, although he never let it show on the surface. Whenever he ran out of alcohol, Brandon and Brian were sure to hear about it, because he always made a big fuss.

The day of their high school graduation, Myles was sitting in the bleachers, waiting for his sons to walk across the stage. He couldn't have been more proud. His sister, Nina came with him for moral support. In many ways, she acted as the twins' second mother when she walked out.

Nina stepped inside of the women's restroom while she still had time before the boys' names were called. She hurried, although she had plenty of time before their names were called. Still, she didn't want to miss their big moment. On her way out, she ran into Maureen. At first, she almost didn't recognize her face. However, based on Maureen's reaction, she knew she must have been right in her assumption that it was her.

"Maureen, Is that you?!" Nina asked, trying to not make the moment anymore awkward than it already was. Maureen was dressed nice, but she looked frail underneath her dress. She was always a slightly petite woman, but with curves. Now all of that seemed to have withered away. Her skin was not as clear and her once thick head of hair was much thinner than she remembered.

"Nina. Yes, long time no see. I wasn't expecting us to meet like this. I came here to see the boys," she said in a slightly dismissive tone. She didn't feel like being judged. She had beat herself up enough over the years and really decided to make a change. The pain of her revelation always stung though as she realized her relationship with her sons may never be the same; let alone ever rekindling the love she had with the one man who truly cared for her – Myles.

"I see, well would you like to come sit with Myles and me? I can lead you to where we are. I'll wait outside," Nina replied. She was a bigger woman than most, considering how nonchalant Maureen was towards her. Nina just excused her curtness and chalked it up to life. Truth be told, Maureen wasn't so thrilled to see the woman who helped raised her sons because she walked out on them.

Nina led Maureen back to her seat with Myles. He didn't see them coming and only saw Maureen when she was standing right above them. "Hello Myles. I know this is probably not the best reintroduction after all these years, but I just wanted to be here for the boys on their big day. I'm so proud of them. I've missed you and them. You look nice," she said, as she reached out awkwardly to hug him. He gave her a quick, distant hug and sat back down, looking forward.

"Reen, you know you have some mighty damn good timing, showing up like this," he said. Nina could tell he was getting upset and rightfully so. She shot him a look to remind him to not lose his cool. He rolled his eyes at her and kept looking forward. "Well, it's a good thing you're here. Mighty noble of you," he said.

There were so many people sitting in the bleachers, Brian and Brandon couldn't see their father and aunt sitting up there. They tried to turn their heads to look, but couldn't see them amidst the big sea of people. After the ceremony, they made their way towards the double exit doors that lead to the outside. Brian saw his mother first. He second guessed himself before saying anything to Brandon. His brother took the words right of his mouth as he asked if that was their mother walking with Myles and Nina. They couldn't actually remember how she looked and could only make her out now from the old pictures their father had shown them long ago. Brandon scowled at her with a force strong enough to pierce her as she stopped right in front of him.

"Congratulations! You boys make me so proud. Well, as you can see here, I have someone I'd like you to meet," Myles said. Although Myles was fuming on the inside, Maureen was their mother, after all. He didn't want his anger and resentment towards her to rub off on them. He wanted them to have their own opinions when it came to their mother. Even when he told the story of how she left years ago, he just purely stated the facts. He never tried to bad mouth her.

"Shit, frankly I don't see anybody here worth speaking too. Hey Aunt Nina. Thank you so much for coming," Brian said, stretching his arms to give Nina a hug, reaching around his mother in the process.

"Wait a minute Brian. She deserves to explain herself. Go ahead. Tell us. Why are you here now, 15 years later? You never came to any of our football games, karate tournaments, band performances. Hell, we didn't even get as much as a fucking 'happy birthday' from you. Get the hell out of here. Let's go," Brandon said to Brian. They both walked through the double doors and waited outside for their father and Nina.

"Can you believe she has the damn nerve to show up here after all these years?" Brian asked.

"Nope. And today of all days. I don't want her here. I wish we had driven up here so we could just leave right now. It's like we're living in a dream man. This can't be real," Brandon replied.

When Maureen walked out, the boys could see her crying hard. They felt a little remorse for the way they spoke to her. This didn't change the fact that they still felt she was the definition of an unfit mother. "Hey, I'm going to go ahead and go now, but I just wanted to see my beautiful sons on their big day, that's all. I know I really have no business being here and I've been absent for most of your lives. I do love you, though. I don't know if that means anything to you, but I really do," she said, wiping away the tears from her eyes.

"We love you too," Brandon replied. Brian looked on as his brother spoke, as if to say, "Do we really love her?"

Maureen tagged along for their celebratory lunch and paid for everyone's meal. Myles wondered where she got the money from to pay for it, but didn't question it and just said thank you. He had a feeling she may not have gotten the money honestly and would rather stay in ignorance about it than to know the truth.

From that day forward, Maureen tried to keep a close relationship with Brian and Brandon, but it was honestly too late. She missed too much of their lives to really be able to get in good with them now. They kept in touch with her occasionally and saw her maybe once every couple years after that point. The last time Brian and Brandon would see her together in the same room would be at her funeral. There weren't many people there. Brian and Brandon only shed tears for the pain they knew their father felt. As for themselves, they had no feelings for her and they were completely numb.

CHAPTER FIFTEEN

"Cheers to love, life and a damn good time," Sheila said, raising her glass to meet Cookie's. The savory aroma of classic Cajun dishes like shrimp po boys, crawfish etoufee and seafood gumbo filled the air. The sounds of trumpets, drums and tubas served as the background to their conversation as they could feel the thumping bassline of the zydeco music at the bottom of their seats.

"Yes, this place smells so good. I can't wait until they bring out our food. How did you hear about this one again?" Cookie asked, taking another sip of her potent Swamp Thing drink. She was excited to get some girl time in with her friend alone and get a break from regular life for a bit. She and Ken had just completed their second session with the counselor earlier that week too. Needless to say, she couldn't thank Sheila enough for mentioning the trip to her. She loved the jazz fest anyway and she didn't realize at the time just how bad she would need the escape from reality.

"Hmmm. Well, you remember Marcus don't you?" Sheila asked playfully.

"Sheila. How could I forget? That man had you more sprung than I've ever seen. Don't tell me you're still messing around with that fool. Don't mess up the good thing you have with Sean," Cookie pleaded.

"Thanks for the lecture mom, but you can save it. I'm head over heels for Sean. I'm ready to be with him for life. But Marcus took me here once for a weekend getaway. Those were some good times though. We made some magic," she smiled.

"Oh goodness, here you go. I'm seriously so happy for you though. I've never seen you have such a glow. Whew, can you believe we are about to be 40 years old?" Cookie said.

"Hush! Don't speak such a foul thing. We'll cross that bridge when we get there. It is around the corner though, isn't it? But that's alright, because we look better than most women in their twenties," Sheila responded, taking a big gulp of her drink. To be such a pretty woman, she could drink hard and fast like the guys.

"Girl, you better slow down. You won't even get through the weekend drinking like that," Cookie laughed as the waiter arrived at the table with their meals. She ordered some shrimp etoufee, with garlic bread and southern green beans. Sheila ordered blackened tilapia, topped with crab meat in a garlic butter sauce, a side of mac n cheese and mustard greens.

"Please be careful with the plates, ladies. These are popping hot, straight from the kitchen. These dishes are made with secret bayou sauces that we'd have to kill you to reveal," their waiter said, as he gave a sinister grin while picking up their drink glasses. "Shall I put in another drink order for you lovely beauties?" he asked.

"Oh yes, but we'll take two hurricanes this time. Thank you so much. Matt, right?" Sheila asked, flashing a charming smile back at him. While he was away earlier, her and Cookie chatted about how cute they thought he was.

"Yes, that is correct. I'll be back with two hurricanes. The top shots will be on me," Matt grinned.

"You are amazing. That would be wonderful," Sheila responded.

"Geesh, you are determined to have me wasted in these streets, aren't you?" Cookie laughed.

"Who knows when we'll be back here again? Let's live it up. Have fun. Besides, I have a wedding dress to get into. This is my last hoorah before I start my diet next week. I'm so not ready for that. But for now, let's eat!" Sheila said.

"Well I may not have a wedding dress to get into, but I'm not going to be the chunky friend in your wedding. I can stand to lose a few pounds myself," Cookie replied.

"Please. You look amazing. Speaking of the wedding, we are keeping it simple. It will just be you as the matron of honor, Monica as the maid of honor and Sean's two best friends for his best man. No bridesmaids. No groomsmen. We're too old for all that. I need to get your sister's address from you and I still have your parents' address. I'll mark it down for the invitations," Sheila said, taking bites of the food in between talking.

"I totally understand that. You have to do what makes you happy. I'm so excited for you. I'm honored to be in your wedding. Oh, and I just texted Chelsea's new address to you," Cookie replied.

"What do you mean? You are my ride-or-die, girl. Of course, you were going to be in the wedding. Thanks for sending me Chelsea's address too," Sheila responded.

"You're welcome. Mmmmm, I tell you what. If you ever run into Marcus again, tell him cheers to the mystical magic and all that. This food is amazing," Cookie laughed.

"I don't foresee bumping into him anytime soon, but if I do, I'll let him know. You are too funny. You ok? Your face looks funny. I know you're not drunk yet. What's wrong?" Sheila asked.

"Oh nothing. Nothing major at least. I just, um…With all of the talk about your wedding, I remembered something you told me on the day of my wedding. When you hugged me after everything went down, you told me that it wasn't over. What did you mean by that?" Cookie asked. There was no right time to bring that up, but she had to at least ask while they were alone together.

Sheila's face suddenly became flushed and it wasn't from the alcohol. "There was so much going on that day. I really don't remember exactly what I meant by that. It probably was nothing major. I'm sorry you've been holding that in after all this time. Why didn't you bring it up sooner?" Sheila asked.

"I guess it was just never the right time. But I'm glad to get some closure to it now. If you say it's nothing, then everything is ok. I don't know why I even made such a big deal of it in my head after all this time," Cookie replied.

"Hey, you see that over there?" Sheila asked. "Looks like it's some kind of voo-doo shop or something. I always wanted to go in one of those. We should go get our palms read!"

"What? You are really out of your mind. I don't need a palm reader to tell me that. I'm not going over there. You know I'm not into all of that stuff," Cookie said nervously.

"Well put your fear where your mouth is. They say it's only true if you believe it," Sheila challenged her.

"Ok, I guess it couldn't be that much harm in going," Cookie said. She turned and looked at the small shop behind her. The neon yellow banner on the outside read "Black Magic Fortunes". She felt uneasy about going into a place like that, but Sheila always had a way of getting her to do crazy things. She loved the adventurous side about her friend, although she sometimes wanted to admire it from afar. This was definitely one of those times.

"Look at you. Taking a walk on the wild side. I love it. But we have to try their bread pudding before we leave. I'm telling you, it is to die for. I know you will love it," Sheila responded.

"That sounds good, but where would I put it? These hurricanes are kicking in. I'm feeling a strong buzz now. Can we get it to go and eat in the room tonight?" Cookie asked.

"You do have a good point. That top shot on the last drink is creeping in on me too. Although, it was so good. Ok, when he comes back we'll just order the bread pudding to go. It heats up well too, so it will be just as good later," Sheila said, her face beaming with excitement. Matt had perfect timing. Sheila could see him making his way to their table in the distance.

"Ladies, how were your entrees? I hope you enjoyed the food this evening. May I help satisfy your sweet tooth by offering you one of our dessert menus?" Matt asked.

"Well, we won't need a menu, but we would like a dessert. Do you all still have the bread pudding with the rum sauce? If so, we'd like to get one of those to go and we're ready for the check too, whenever you get a chance." Sheila inquired with a hopeful tone.

"Yes, of course. That's actually our second most popular dessert offered here, behind our praline pecan cheesecake. I'll bring that right out for you ladies, along with your check," he said.

"Thank you so much. You can put it all on one check too," Cookie chimed in. Matt promised a prompt return and walked away briskly to place their order and get their ticket.

"You didn't have to do that. Thank you girl," Sheila told Cookie.

"It's just a pre celebratory token to a major milestone in your life. These are exciting times for you and I'm glad to be experiencing a piece of it with you," Cookie replied.

The ladies received their dessert, paid for the meal and walked outside towards the Black Magic Fortunes shop. "I still can't believe you have me going in here. I'm not into all of that voo-doo foolishness. A part of me has always been intrigued by it though, but just on TV," Cookie laughed.

"They don't pressure you to read your palm and all that. At least most of them don't. I had someone at another shop here read my palm a few years ago. It was a joke. That woman didn't know what she was talking about. I just did it for fun. Relax. We don't have to stay long either," Sheila reassured her.

They walked into the store slowly, as the creaking sound of the wooden door preceded their footsteps. The shop was dimly light with assorted colors of feathers, metal rings and bones hanging from the ceiling. "What the hell is all of this, Sheila? Damn I guess the stuff they show in the movies is real. This is creepy," Cookie said. She glanced at all the dusty books she saw sitting on the shelves. There were all sorts of foreign oils and trinkets on the counters near the middle of the store too.

A long, stringy black and gray-haired woman emerged from the back of the store, through a mass covering of beads that were hanging from the top of what should have been the opening of a door. "Creepy, huh? I've been living here for 56 years and let me tell you, this is nothing you're seeing here. What brings you ladies in tonight? Do you have an enemy you're trying to get rid of? Warding off evil spirits? Trying to catch a husband? Oh, never mind that. I see both of you ladies are married. But we have some things that will punish the hell out of your husband too, if you need it," she laughed.

"Oh, thanks. We don't need any of that. We just came in to explore. Look around a bit. That's all," Cookie responded.

"I see. Be careful of what you go exploring for. You just might find yourself sinking in quicksand. I'll leave you ladies be then, for now," the woman said quietly and walked away.

"Goodness, thanks grandma," Sheila whispered in Cookie's ear. "I thought she would never stop talking. She seems nice though. You should get your palm read before we leave," she added.

"I already told you I'm stretching myself by even coming in here. But you know what? What the hell. We're here to have a good time and like you said, it should be harmless. I'll do it only if you go first," Cookie said.

"Oh so you're just gonna stick me out to take the bullet, huh? Ok I'm not scared. I'll go first then. Hopefully she doesn't try to talk us to death," Sheila laughed as they walked towards the front of the store where the old woman was sitting.

"Did you have a change of heart about anything?" the woman asked, without ever looking up from the table. There were a couple of small, dry bones on her table, along with some red dust in a mini mason jar.

"We want to get our palms read," Sheila answered, glancing over at Cookie to make sure she was still okay with it. There was a cool breeze that she felt run down her back. She looked towards the door and it was still closed. There was also no air vent present above her head. Cookie shot her a look that let her know that she felt a strange aura too.

"Have a seat chile. I'll give you a general reading, but I'll tell you what you really want to know for a small fee too. Now you mam will have to find a seat until your turn. I don't like nobody standing over me while I'm doing my readings. This takes a spiritual connection, with no interference from outside forces. Please, sit down," she said.

"Oh, well excuse me. I'll have a seat right here," Cookie responded as she sat down on a wide wooden stump that looked older than the store it was sitting in. She sat in silence as the old woman began to spread her bag of bones across the table. She placed a small circle of the red dust in the middle of the table.

"Now, before we get started, I'll need your name," the woman said. She shot Sheila a blank, unemotional stare as she waited for her response.

"Oh ok, well I don't have a problem giving it to you. I don't think we got your name though," Sheila answered. She was never one to follow orders well and Cookie was quietly cheering her on from the wooden stump. Her response would have been pretty much the same verbatim.

"Chile, if you want the reading I need the name. My name does not matter. I don't have to give you my name and it's actually none of your business," she said.

"Uh oh, watch out Cookie. She's a feisty one. Well, let's get started, shall we? The name is Sheila," she said.

"Ah Sheila. Ha. Funny. I had an ex-husband who cheated on me with a woman named Sheila. Never liked the name since. But I'm sure you're a fine, upstanding young woman. Give up your left hand dear," the old woman said. Cookie couldn't help but look down at the floor when she heard the woman's comment about Sheila and her ex-husband cheating on her. It all seemed funny to her now. She fought the rising smile that was forming at the corners of her mouth.

"Hmmm, I'm seeing love. It's blinding. A new love. You're about to get married or either you've just gotten married within the last couple of months," she said.

"Well I did just get engaged, but not married just yet. I am in love though. My fiancé is truly amazing," Sheila beamed.

"He loves you totally as you do him. There will be a deep misunderstanding within the first year of your marriage though. You will get past it only if you have the tenacity," she replied.

"What do you mean a deep misunderstanding? Can you tell me more? Maybe I really don't need to know," Sheila responded in a concerned tone.

"You don't, my dear. I just have one more thing for you. Don't let your jealousy consume you. It's an acidic and deadly disease," the old woman told her.

"Thank you, I guess," Sheila said, getting up from the chair abruptly as the old woman picked up the bag of bones again and placed them in the bag. She shook them up as Cookie got up from the wooden stump and took her seat at the table.

"My name is Candice," Cookie said. The woman remained silent as she moved the bones across the table. She added a little more of the red dust as well. Sheila looked on intently, anxious to hear what the woman had to say about her.

The old woman jerked back in her seat as she traced her fingers inside of Cookie's palm. "You have a tremendous amount of pain. You're trying your best to hide it from those you love. Right now, it's working. But you can't keep it up for long. I don't know if you're quite ready for what I have to say next," she said, looking deeply into Cookie's eyes.

"What do you mean? Whatever it is, I can handle it," she said, with a very concerned look on her face.

"Your sister. She cannot be trusted. Get away from her. She's evil!" the old woman screamed.

"What? Come on, nothing is wrong with my sister. You've got to be kidding me," Cookie said, clutching her purse.

"You don't have to believe. Time will show you on its own," the old woman replied with a sinister smile.

"Sheila, come on let's go. This woman is crazy," Cookie said.

"Ha! You haven't seen crazy yet. If you were smart, you would heed my warning. Consider yourself lucky, you foolish girl," the old woman quietly uttered back to her.

Sheila was stunned as she and Cookie walked out the store. The door sounded like it was about to pop off the hinges as Cookie violently flung it open. "Cookie, um, are you ok? That was a pretty heavy statement she just laid on you about Chelsea. I'm sorry I even suggested that we go in there," she said.

"It's not your fault. You didn't make me do it. I just can't believe her. How could she say something like that? She probably doesn't even know that I have a sister. She just pulled something out of her ass. What do those damn bones and dust mean away?" Cookie ranted. She noticed Sheila looked very uneasy and flushed while they were talking.

"Cookie, there's something I need to tell you. Please don't be upset at me when I tell you this. There just may be some truth to what that old woman said," Sheila responded.

CHAPTER SIXTEEN

"Ken, it's your mother. I haven't seen you in a very long time. That wife of yours sure is beautiful. Between you and I, I still don't understand how in the world she got that nickname "Cookie". I'm going to call her Candice. That's much more sophisticated and lady like. I'm not getting any younger. I need some grandkids soon. Have you been trying to make some for me?" Ken's mother said, as she brushed her hand across his face.

Ken woke up panting in a cold sweat. He looked over on Cookie's side of the bed and for a moment, forgot that she was gone on the trip with Sheila. He always felt a little strange sleeping in the house alone whenever she was gone. Ironically, the dream about his mother came as a shock, considering that he hadn't dreamed of her in quite a long time. Time is supposed to heal all wounds, but he still missed his mother dearly.

Darlene was always a very vibrant and warm spirited woman. Ken wasn't close to his father Christopher. His dad used to beat his mother so bad that makeup couldn't hide all the scars he gave her. Shortly after his 16th birthday, he learned that his mother had cancer. She survived it initially, until it came back four years later. By this time, his father had stopped being physically abusive, but kept the mental abuse going. One night, he overheard them arguing and his mother yelled and said, "Nearly all my days with you have been a living hell. If this cancer gets the best of me, at least it will be an eternal break from you. I hate you and I should have left you just as soon as I met you".

Christopher (as Ken always called him, never Dad) was a strong willed man and not one to show any emotions. He came from the old school upbringing where men barely even hugged their children. He, like many of the other men during that time, didn't want to seem soft in any way. He never admitted it, but those words his mother spoke crushed his soul. Ken's father also grew up in a home where his father was abusive towards his mother. In a way, it was all he knew. Ken didn't feel any sympathy for him though and vowed to never follow the same path in his marriage.

Ken was 23 years old when his mother passed. By that time she had gone to live with her sister, Ashley. Christopher repeatedly tried to get her to come back home, but she had finally made up her mind that she was done with him for good. At the funeral, Christopher was so grief-stricken, he could barely stand. Although he never mentioned it to Ken (who was his and Darlene's only child), he suffered greatly because of the way he knew he treated her.

Ken and his father's relationship grew closer after his mother's death, strangely enough. A piece of him hated his father for the pain he brought his mother, but another side of him was sympathetic. He knew his father had done a lot of wrong in his life and now he was faced to pay for it alone. Too much time alone can sometimes be the most crippling thing for the mind. Unfortunately, that's exactly what happened to Christopher.

Ken had decided to pay his father a random visit. He did call him first, but he didn't get a call back from him. He pulled into the driveway and saw his father's car there so he assumed he must have been home. He knocked on the door first and then waited a couple of minutes before he unlocked the door. His dad was a very private man, but he allowed Ken to make a duplicate key since he lived alone. He walked towards the front room, where he heard the TV on in the living room. He surveyed the kitchen and the front room, but his father was nowhere to be found. He walked slowly towards the hallway and began calling for him.

"Dad? It's Ken. Are you there?" he said, as he walked down the hallway. The house was rather large and had four bedrooms with two and a half bathrooms. Ken checked the first guest room. Nothing. His dad wasn't in there. After checking all of the other rooms, he saved the master bedroom for last. He felt a huge lump form in his throat before he even walked through the door. He saw what appeared to be blood splattered at the lower half of the door and on some of the carpet beneath it. He screamed in agony as he walked in to see his father laying in a pool of blood, with a gun at the side of his right hand. There was an old faded picture of Darlene holding Ken when he was a baby, on top of his chest.

Ken rolled over and looked at his phone. It was 5:30 am in the morning. Since he was a natural early riser, he rarely slept in even on the weekends. He didn't quite feel like working out yet, so he decided to cook himself an omelet, toast and grits, with some cranberry juice to cleanse his pallet for his breakfast. He was quite pleased with his meal and sat down on the couch to eat in peace. Although it felt strange not waking up next to Cookie, he did enjoy the leisure and quiet time. He usually had to tip toe around the house when he woke up this early. Cookie would often make fun of him and say that he even beat the dew falling on the grass in the morning.

He turned on the TV to CNN to catch up on the news. Ken was much more politically driven than Cookie and he enjoyed watching the happenings of what was going on in other parts of the world. He had only taken a few bites of his meal, when he heard a rustling in the bushes on their deck behind the kitchen. He kept eating, thinking it was some kind of animal back there. He turned the volume up on the TV and kept eating his breakfast. Just as he was getting up to take his plate to the kitchen, a loud gunshot fired and he heard glass shatter in the house. He looked around quickly and stooped down to the floor. Ken crawled in the bedroom to get his gun out of the closet. There was complete silence now. He didn't hear any more shots, but he quickly ran to get his gun and slowly crept back out of the bedroom. Just then, a blast of shots fired through the front door and he heard someone kick it open.

He stayed securely hidden behind the wall of the bedroom door, as he heard footsteps coming closer towards him. Ken heard the intruder loading another clip into the gun. If he jumped out right now, he could potentially shoot this person before he was able to gather his wits about him. He decided against it and waited. The footsteps picked up again getting closer. The person was walking in Ken's direction so assuredly, almost if he knew the layout of the house.

"Where is she?" he heard the person utter. It was clearly a man's voice. Ken felt his blood boiling and the pang of fear he felt earlier turned to rage. She? Was this guy looking for Cookie? This couldn't be real. Brandon was dead and so was his brother. Ken's phone sounded aloud with a social media notification and lit up the front room. It was still dark outside and Ken had only the kitchen light on, so the house was relatively dim inside. The man made his way towards the coffee table, where Ken's phone was laying.

Ken now had a clear line of sight to the man who had just broken into his home. He was dressed in dark colors, probably black, with gloves, a ski mask and steel toe boots. Ken opened fire at the man and shot him in the leg. Since he mentioned trying to find Cookie specifically, he had a vested interest in making this man suffer and finding out why he was looking for her. The man's right leg buckled as he fell on top of the coffee table. "Who the hell are you?" he yelled running into the front room, with the gun now pointing directly over the man's head as he laid on his back. Ken knew he had the advantage over him.

As Ken glanced down at the man, waiting for an answer, he noticed the gun was still in his hand. He heard him panting heavily as he sat straight up and shot at Ken. He just barely missed his head and Ken immediately shot his right arm and then his left leg. The gun now fell out of his hand and onto the floor. "I'm only going to ask you this one more damn time. Who are you and who are you looking for?" Ken asked. By this time, he was just a few inches away from the man's face.

The unidentified man laughed and spit in Ken's face. In Ken's eyes that was the ultimate form of disrespect. He would rather be punched in the face than to have someone deliberately spit on him. "It's none of your business who I am. She's not here! Where is she? You don't have the balls to kill me, "he laughed, with blood dripping from his ear, around the side of his neck.

"Oh really? Watch me. Say goodnight bitch," Ken said, shooting the man directly in the forehead. He immediately reached over and grabbed his phone to call the police.

"911. How may I help you?" the woman answered on the other end.

"Yes, I just had an intruder break into my home. He fired several shots and I shot back at him in self-defense. He's dead. I need someone to get here quickly, please," Ken said.

CHAPTER SEVENTEEN

At almost the exact same time, Cookie and Sheila were sound asleep in their hotel room. Sunday seemed to have come too quickly for Cookie, but not soon enough. After Sheila cleverly dodged what she said she had to tell Cookie, she finally let her know. It was a door that Cookie was relieved to have opened, but wanted welded shut at the same time. It wasn't until late last night that Sheila finally broke down and told her the truth.

"Sheila, ok seriously. This has been a really great time, even with the crazy old woman and her weird prophecy about my sister. I'm truly grateful to get away with my sister-from-another-mother too. I really need to know the truth, though. Tell me what you were going to say when we left the voodoo shop the other night," she said.

"Okay. Cookie, this is really hard. I must admit, I had my own selfish reasons for not wanting to tell you this sooner. I couldn't risk losing you as a friend again. But there just may be some truth to what the old woman at the voodoo shop told you the other night about Chelsea," she said.

"Huh? Come on now. Is that what you have to tell me? I can't believe she's got you falling for that foolishness. I thought you had something really meaningful to tell me," Cookie laughed, brushing off Sheila's statement.

"Cookie, I need you to listen right now please. I am not playing with you and this is extremely serious. Remember when you asked me a while ago about why I pulled you close at your wedding and told you that it wasn't over?" Sheila asked.

"Yes, of course. You told me that you didn't even remember what it was you wanted to say," Cookie responded cautiously.

"I lied. I'm sorry. I really am, but that was definitely not the truth," Sheila said.

"Sheila, I can't take anymore lies and bad news right now," Cookie replied.

"Well, I think it's high time you hear this from me because it just might save your life one day. I couldn't bear to live with myself if anything ever happened to you without you knowing. Cookie, I think Chelsea tried to kill you on your wedding day. Shit, I've been holding that in for so long," she said, looking like an enormous weight had just been lifted off her shoulders, but also afraid of how Cookie might react.

"Oh my God. Sheila. How? Wait. How in the world could you even think of something so absurd?" Cookie said.

"It's not what I think. It's what I saw. Chelsea never told me this, but I know she had a gun on her at the wedding. I'm also almost positive that she was communicating with Brandon even before your wedding day," Sheila revealed.

"What is it that you saw?" Cookie asked.

"Ok, so while you were getting your makeup done, Chelsea left her phone on the counter by accident. The reason I know it was an accident is because she kept her phone so closely guarded that whole time leading up to your wedding. I guess she just got busy with everything going on and left her phone in the room that we were getting dressed in. She stepped out for a moment and her phone lit up. It was a text message from Brandon. I knew he was still alive. I took a picture of it with my phone. Still have it to this day," she said.

"Wait a minute. This cannot be real. Are you telling me that my sister was in on it the whole time and with Brandon at that?" Cookie asked, with a puzzled and furious look on her face.

"That's what I'm sketchy on. When we thought he was dead the first time, I don't think she was in on that. But this time, there were clearly some things said in those text messages that didn't add up. Basically, there was some sort of package that she brought with her that had a poisonous drug. She was planning to put in your drink. He just happened to have a gun on him at the wedding in case something went wrong. As we both know, she had a gun on her too. She said it was to help protect you," Sheila added.

"I just remembered something. On the day of my wedding, I dropped my wine glass, shortly before we did the toast. Chelsea had the strangest look on her face when I dropped that glass. It was almost as if she was upset at me about it. That makes sense now," Cookie said.

"Wow, you're right. You sure did. I remember that. I wasn't close enough to see Chelsea's expression, but I do remember you dropping the glass," Sheila chimed in.

"Although, I don't know why. First of all, why would she try to kill me? Secondly, why in the hell would she team up with Brandon to do it?" Cookie asked, confusingly.

"That I can't answer. I wasn't sure how you were going to take this, so I wanted to show you myself. I took a picture of it with my phone and I saved it to this hard drive," Sheila said, pulling her laptop out of her bag and hooking up the flash drive to show Cookie.

Cookie's heart felt like it was beating outside of her chest. It felt like an eternity waiting for Sheila to pull up her evidence of Chelsea's devious plan. She turned the laptop towards her and read the capture of their conversation:

Chelsea: Don't you worry about that. Once I put this drug in the drink it will be lights out for her. Trust me.

Brandon: Hmmm, I guess. If you say so. I'll still have my gun just in case. You'll still have yours too, right?

Chelsea: Yep. Well, I gotta go. Don't want anyone around me getting suspicious.

Brandon: Ok, I'll see you later.

Tears began to stream down Cookie's face. "Sheila, I'm so sorry you felt like you couldn't tell me this. You're right. Probably back then, because of everything that happened at the time, there's no way I would have believed you, but I do now," Cookie spoke solemnly.

"Wait, you actually believe me? I was so nervous about telling you. I didn't think we would be friends after this. But, I was willing to take that risk if it meant saving your life," Sheila said.

"Yes, I do believe you. I haven't really told anyone outside of Ken, but my sister has been acting really strange lately. I didn't think she was necessarily out to kill me, but she's made me feel very uneasy around her. You never mentioned what happened after you saw the text messages. Did she ever come back in and get her phone?" Cookie asked.

"Oh yeah, she did. Almost immediately after I took the picture of her screen she walked in and quickly grabbed her phone. She shot me the coldest look she's ever given me and then she walked right back out. By then, it was pretty much time for the wedding to start," Sheila responded.

"I just really have no words for all of this. I'm speechless. You know what? I haven't been completely honest with you either. That day of my wedding, I was so relieved when Brandon died. The funny thing is it was Chelsea's idea to even kill him. I went along with it though, because he literally made my life a living hell. We both thought he was dead until you said he called you. I guess she knew he was still alive all this time," Cookie uttered softly.

"Cookie, I know," Sheila said, crying.

"Wait. You know what?" Cookie asked cautiously.

"I know that you tried to kill Brandon. I may not be your blood sister, but we're close enough. I know when something's up and when I'm not getting the whole story. The day you told me everything that happened, I figured it out then. There was this rage in your eyes I had never seen before. There was a piece of you that also looked relieved though. I was happy for you that you had gotten rid of his ass. I just didn't know how to say it then," Sheila said.

"Ugh, I swear I can't get anything past you. I should have known that you had already figured it out," Cookie laughed.

"We have really been through a lot haven't we? I don't know about you, but I could really use a drink to take the edge off from all of this," Sheila added.

"You must have read my mind. Let's go, we can walk down to that daiquiri shop on Bourbon street and get some more of that bread pudding too. I've been craving that ever since we ate it Friday night," Cookie said.

"Look at you, Miss Thing, taking a walk on the wild side. Arrrggh," Sheila replied playfully, clawing her hand at Cookie.

"Yes, you look great. You can worry about getting into that wedding dress on Monday. This is our last night though, so we can't stay cooped up in the room," Cookie said.

"You don't have to tell me twice," Sheila responded as she and Cookie grabbed their purses and headed downstairs towards the front lobby of the hotel. They walked out into the street and the slightly humid night air greeted them with a cool breeze. There was zydeco music being played on the street, people dancing, the smell of delicious food and the idea of living the night life with no regrets.

Cookie and Sheila were only a few blocks away from Bourbon street, so they didn't have far to go before they reached the daiquiri shop. They stopped there first and each got 20 oz. drinks. Cookie got the Pina Coloda and Sheila got a Mango and Strawberry swirled daquiri. From there they only had about 10 minutes before they got to the restaurant to order the bread pudding.

Before they reached the restaurant, they passed the old voodoo fortune teller on the street. Cookie and Sheila tried not to make eye contact with her, but she made it a point to be noticed. "Hello there again, ladies. Hopefully you both have a calmer demeanor now, compared to the other night," the old woman said with a sarcastic sneer.

"Funny, ah yes. We're doing just fine. You have yourself a good night, ok?" Sheila answered quickly, walking away briskly and looking back for Cookie to follow suit.

"Yes, we're doing fine. Thank you. Have a good night," Cookie said.

"You as well. I'm not a total bitch like I came across the other night. For that I apologize. I see things clearly and I just tell it like it is, whether you like it or not. I think it was destiny for us to run into each other though, especially for you," the woman said, looking directly at Cookie.

"Oh and why is that?" Cookie replied with genuine intrigue. Sheila shot her a stern look and was clearly upset she was even entertaining a conversation with the woman.

"If you have a problem with me talking to your friend, you can go on ahead. I won't keep her long," she said to Sheila.

"No problem here," Sheila said with a forced smile. "We just have somewhere we're trying to get to, that's all. Take as long as you need".

"Well, I have something that I think you may need. Oh, my name is Ivy, by the way. I guess I could tell you that now," she said. Ivy pulled into her tattered satchel strapped across her shoulder and pulled out a small bag with a drawstring that looked like a mini potato sack. She placed the bag inside Cookie's hand.

Cookie squeezed the bag and could tell there was some kind of dirt or dust inside. Although she was intrigued to see its contents, she handed it back to Ivy. "Thanks, but I don't think I'll be needing whatever this is".

"Don't you want to at least know what it is?" Ivy asked.

"Ok, sure go ahead. What is it for?" Cookie said. By now, she was growing impatient with Ivy as well.

"It's to keep any evil spirits away. Line your doors with it at home. Even put a little of it in your car. It doesn't take much and this will supply you for a very long time. Here take it," Ivy said, opening the bag a little to show the contents the Cookie. Under the street light the dust looked like it had a purple hue.

"How exactly is this dust supposed to keep bad people away?" Cookie asked.

"You have a naivety that's really cute, chile. I didn't say bad people. I said bad spirits. A bad spirit can be in anyone, even if they are good people. This is a powerful thing and you must remember that those who you love may even be revealed as having bad spirits," Ivy replied.

"I'll go ahead and take it then, I guess," Cookie said, reluctantly holding out her hand.

"Are you crazy? You can't take this! Who knows what that stuff really is? Give me this. You told me you don't even believe in all of this anyway. We were just doing it for fun remember?" Sheila said, reaching for the small bag of purple tinted dust.

"You don't think she believes? I think she does," Ivy smiled.

"Sheila, it's ok. I don't think it's a big deal. I'll just hold on to it and see what happens, that's all," Cookie reassured her.

"Ok, suit yourself then," Sheila said.

"Well, one thing is for sure. Your friend is feisty, but she's a keeper. She has a good heart. This stuff doesn't lie," Ivy motioned to the dust. "She would have been itching so hard by now she wouldn't have been able to stand it," she laughed.

CHAPTER EIGHTEEN

While Cookie and Chelsea were driving on their way back to Dallas, little did they know they were exiting the place where Brandon moved to while he was in hiding all those years. During this time, he felt like a totally new man. He enjoyed frequent sexcapades with the creole women of New Orleans and those who were coming in town just to visit. Always one who favored the element of surprise, he changed his name and started a new life, complete with a drastic makeover. He shaved his head bald, grew out a thicker beard and became even more in shape than he already was.

Brandon was turned on in a sick, twisted way by Cookie almost flawlessly pulling off his murder. They committed the perfect murder, but they didn't plan for his perfect disappearance. He chose to live in New Orleans because of its mystery and influx of eccentric tourists. He fit right in without question. As time went on, he started stalking Cookie. First, it started off through stalking her social media accounts. However, she wised up after his supposed death and started blocking her accounts from public view, becoming more private.

He took a modest job and decreased his way of life down to a modest stature. In fact, he almost had forgiven Cookie and Chelsea for trying to kill him, until he found out about his brother's murder. He saw the story online one day by accident when he was surfing the Internet. Once he saw that it was Chelsea who killed him he became furious. He went on a search for her and made sporadic trips back to Chicago to find out where she was. He already figured out that Cookie was in Dallas by that point and he decided to focus on her later.

He then relocated to Dallas a few months before Cookie's wedding. The timing couldn't have been more perfect. At that time, his mind was still on Chelsea and he had no idea that Cookie was engaged. He soon found out who Ken was and made it a point to get hired on at the company that he worked for so that he could get close enough to him for him to let his guard down.

In the meantime, one night he found Chelsea by accident at a local gym when he was visiting Chicago again. She looked at him as if she knew who he was. He looked back at her with the most expressionless stare, totally unassuming. He didn't look anything like he did nearly ten years prior, but he knew that deep down she could tell it was him. She always was very intuitive, even more so than Cookie. It was a trait he deeply admired about her.

However, humans are one of the few creatures of the earth that habitually ignore their own instincts. Chelsea was just the same, as she came to the gym three more times that week, during the same time of the evening, always around 7:30 pm. He pulled in shortly after her and cut a small incision in her tires. She wasn't the type to shower at the gym at night, since she lived so close by. This worked to his advantage as he could easily tell when she was about to wrap up her workout.

He waited a couple of minutes as he saw her walking towards the door and then he followed her from his car. The road back to her house didn't involve any freeways and there wasn't much traffic out then, so he was confident she would just end up having a flat tire. Just as he predicted, a few blocks before she made it home, her tire went flat. She pulled over, put on her hazards and got out of the car, checking her surroundings before she used the flashlight on her phone to check out the tire. It was the front, driver's side tire and she didn't want to take a chance to keep driving it further down the road. Bill always taught his girls how to be self-sufficient, so although she was apprehensive about being stranded on the road at night, she proceeded to get the spare tire out of her trunk to change it.

Brandon pulled up slowly behind her and put on his hazard lights, parking right behind her car. "Oh, freaking great. Some weirdo pulling over to help me just like the dumb girls that get killed in the horror movies," Chelsea whispered to herself. She always favored more pessimistic thoughts, so she wouldn't be caught off guard. Brandon got out of the car and asked her if she needed any help.

"Hello, looks like you have some car trouble here. This is a pretty narrow street, not exactly the safest place to try to change a tire," Brandon said, looking down at the flat tire on her car.

"Yeah I guess not. Thanks for your help, but I think I can take it from here. I actually know how to change it myself," Chelsea said, hoping that would prompt this unknown man to go away. There was something strange about him that she couldn't quite put her finger on, but he made her feel incredibly uneasy.

"There's no way I could stand here and watch you do such a thing. That would be so rude of me. Here, let me help you with that," he said, reaching for the tire jack in her hand. Once he got a good grip on it, he slammed it to the ground, grabbed her wrist and turned her around so that he had her in a headlock with her back pressed against him.

"Let me go! Get your damn hands off me right now!" she screamed, hoping someone would hear her.

"Not so fast Chelsea. You are still the same loud firecracker you were years ago. Remember me? It's payback bitch," he said.

"Who is Chelsea? Wait….there's no way it could be you. We killed you. You're supposed to be dead!" Chelsea said, reaching back with her free hand and squeezing his balls. She stumped on his foot hard at the same time, as he almost fell to the pavement. All the while, he still had his burly arm wrapped around her neck.

"I'll let you make it for now. I figured you would try something like that. If you know me as well as you think you do, then you already know what I'm about to do next," he said, pulling a switch blade out of his back pocket and pressing it against her neck. She felt like she was about to black out. This had to be the end of her life.

"Please don't do this. I was only defending my sister. You know you deserved it. She was nothing but good to you, Brandon," Chelsea said.

"Hush, you killed my brother, so I'd say we're even. I know you'll just counteract that by saying it was an act of self-defense. Brian always was a bit of a nut case, so that just may be. But I think it's high time you and Cookie see how it feels to die and not have the luxury of well, living through it, like I did. You bitches ruined my life. Do you hear me? Ripped it to shreds.

Now you want me to show mercy on you? Is that what you want?" he said, rambling in an agitated tone.

"Brandon, I'm asking that you please don't do this. That was years ago. I'm sorry and we…" Chelsea said. Her sentence was cut off by him slapping her in the face.

"Now didn't I tell you to be quiet? Cookie's dead either way you slice it. I'm going to find her, which won't be hard since I work with her little fiancé now, and kill her. But the good news is you get to live, under one condition. I would much rather do this myself and keep my hands clean so to speak. As much as possible at least. If you help me, you'll live and she dies. If you don't help me, she dies and you get to die with her. Do we have a deal or not?"

Chelsea stood there in silence as tears began to race down her cheeks. She was usually able to get herself out of any situation, but she believed this time she had finally met her match. "Brandon, this shit is crazy. I'm not joining forces with you to kill my own sister," she said.

"Ok, well suit yourself. You just made the wrong choice," he said, yanking her head back towards him by her hair. He took the knife and slid it across her stomach. He must have broken her skin, because the pressure from the knife, mixed with her sweat, started to sting.

"Wait! Wait. Ok, I'll do it. I know a place that I get black market drugs from. Give me a couple of days to think and I'll let you know," Chelsea replied. She couldn't believe that she was now on the other side of the fence about to help her sister's supposedly dead ex-husband create a plan to kill her. She had to play it smart, if she wanted to save herself and Cookie.

"That's not how this works. I'm calling the shots. You have until tomorrow at noon to come up with a plan. We'll fine tune from there. Oh, and don't think about calling the cops. I've been watching you from a long time. I can make sure that you're erased even if I'm not around to physically do the job myself. Are we clear?" Brandon said. He felt an invigorating adrenaline rush having this much control over Chelsea. He knew he had her right where he wanted her.

"Ok, I'll send you the address to the place where we can meet then. They sell black market drugs of all kinds. I'm sure they'll have something that will work just perfectly for us. Now if you don't mind, I do have to get back to changing my tire," Chelsea said sarcastically. Although she was still fearful, she didn't think that he would try anything violent against her now since he was getting her help.

"Please, allow me. I'll change it for you. Chelsea, you're a smart woman. I was hoping you would choose to sacrifice your sister and not yourself too. After all, you're still here in Chicago and she's moved on with her life. She's far away from here living the American dream, while you pick up the pieces of a mess you helped her create. If that's not sisterly love, then damn it I don't know what is," he said, with a snickering smile.

"Ok, I really need to get going. So if you'll excuse me, I'll be making my way home," Chelsea said, after he finished changing the tire.

"Fair enough, I've kept you longer than I'm sure you've expected. Take a hot bath, pour yourself a good strong drink and make sure you think long and hard about how we're going to make this happen. I know you'll make the right decision," Brandon said, smiling and getting back in his car.

Chelsea got back in her car and barely made it home through the sea of tears flooding out of her eyes. She opened her garage door, pulled in and stayed in the car for over 30 minutes. She felt paralyzed and couldn't move a muscle. Her head was pounding and she replayed the last decade of her life. She thought about her being the one to even initially suggest that they should kill Brandon. Then she thought about the twisted victory she and Cookie felt when they realized he was dead.

She finally got out of the car and walked inside of her house. As much as she hated to admit it, Brandon did have a very good point. Here she was, still living in Chicago after all this time, looking after her parents without the help of her sibling, while Cookie moved to a new state and started a totally new life. She was happy for her sister and glad that she was finally able to get away from such an abusive situation. She would be lying if she said she fully knew everything her sister was going through.

As much as she tried to deny it, there was a piece of her that did resent Cookie. She did feel like she was the one being left behind to pick up the pieces and to top it off, Cookie found real love and Chelsea was still single. Granted, there were several men that she dated, some actually strong candidates for something serious. However, they all proved to be just smoking ashes over time.

She felt a wave of nausea come over her as she poured herself a shot of vodka. One shot turned into two shots and three turned into four. Chelsea felt powerless, but she couldn't spend the rest of the night wallowing in her sorrow. She had to think fast and just make a plan, regardless of whether or not she was actually going to follow through with it or secretly throw a wrench in it to save Cookie's life. She sat down on her couch for a few minutes and turned on the TV just to create some ambient noise to drown out all the competing thoughts running through her head. When that didn't work, she got up abruptly from the couch and took a shower. She kept on a few extra lights in the house just in case Brandon decided to pay her a surprise visit. She surely didn't want to be caught off guard a second time.

When she got out of the shower, she stared at herself in the mirror. Whenever she overcame a near brush with death or extremely adverse situations, she often looked at herself in the mirror at home. It was her way of digging into her mind and finding her inner strength. She exhaled deeply as she pulled her hair back in a ponytail and put on some jeans and a t-shirt from an old Lenny Kravitz concert she went to. She put on a hooded sweatshirt and took a trip to a place she had no business being.

The place was in the rough part of town and located in unassuming looking building. Being there was a bit nostalgic for her, especially considering she hadn't been back in over eight years. There was a front door that never opened; a side door with very heavily tinted glass. That door was the one she entered so many times she lost count. She tapped on the glass four times and until someone came up to the door.

"What's the word?" a man with a deep voice mumbled on the other side of the glass.

"Cloud 10," Chelsea responded, as she looked around on the street to see if anyone was watching. All those times before, she never felt afraid of being there, but this time she did. This was one of the few times she actually felt out of place being there. She was disappointed in herself for even stepping foot in the place again.

"Well look who finally decided to come on back home," Wayne said, as he let Chelsea in the door. No one ever answered the door without a gun and Wayne carried a glock 9mm, which complimented his tall and large stature.

"You're funny. I see things are still running in tip-top shape like the last time I was here. I came for something different this time though," she said.

"Well don't get too far ahead of yourself now. I don't think you exactly want to get back in the game starting out stronger than what you were used to. I heard you've been clean now. I'm proud of you. All of us don't get that chance. You're really blessed. Your parents and your sister really love you," Wayne said.

"Yeah I know. Listen, I can't stay long. I need a couple bottles of the hot sauce. That's all I need," she said.

"All you need? Yeah I'd say so. This is worse than that time you came in here looking for that stuff to paralyze somebody. Now you want to try this? I'd say you have a vendetta out for somebody. One you don't want them to ever come back from," Wayne said.

"I know. I figured this one would be pretty expensive, so I brought some extra cash just in case," she said.

"Yeah, you're looking at about $200 a bottle on these. Chelsea, I know it's your prerogative, but I'm concerned about you. Are you ok? You've never come in here and asked for anything remotely like this before," Wayne replied, with a perplexed look on his face.

"Wayne, I don't need the lecture right now. I can't really talk about it, but I have to do what I have to do to save my life," Chelsea said, with tears welled up in her eyes.

"Ok, you wait right here. I'm doing this against my better judgment, but I'll go get it for you," Wayne said, walking away to a dark room with black lighting illuminating from the entry way. He was gone for maybe ten minutes before he came back with what Chelsea asked for. While she waited, she looked around at everyone working inside and the desperate fiends in need of another fix. This was once a world she was all too familiar with. Somehow, she would rather still be that same woman she was several years ago than be there for the reason she was that night.

"I take it that you found it in your heart to get me what I need," Chelsea laughed as she saw Wayne come out of the room, with a brown package wrapped in butcher paper. It had a square shape, likely because he placed both bottles inside of the box.

"You just be careful with this. This is out of your league baby girl. I don't think you really know how powerful this stuff is. And if you get caught with it, I don't know you," Wayne laughed.

"I understand. I will keep you completely out of it. You know I wouldn't rat you out like that. Yeah, I heard about this one from a few people around the way. It's supposedly nothing to play with, which sounds like it will get the job done for what I need," Chelsea responded.

"Well it's good to see you and even though it's bad for business for us, it's good to see you clean too. I love you. Give me a hug. I can't tell you to stay out of trouble because that's exactly what that package is in your hand. Just promise me you'll stay off the 10:00 news," Wayne said.

"Will do, Wayne. It's good to see you too," Chelsea said, as Wayne walked her towards the door. She walked outside and on her way back to her car, she nearly stepped on a man with white stringy hair, gaunt features and tattered clothes who was laying by her car.

"Mam, I just need a few dollars. I need to get something inside of that place that you just left out of. I'm sure you understand," he said. The man looked mangy and troubled. Chelsea didn't have time for a soft heart right then and proceeded to quickly get in her car.

"I don't have anything to give you. I'm sorry. You probably need to not hang so closely to this area. It's very dangerous out here," she said, getting inside of her car.

The man jumped up from the ground, leaving his blanket behind and caught Chelsea's door before she was able to close it. "I need money. Anything you have is fine. I'll take it. But you have to give it to me," he said.

I don't have to give you shit. Get off of my car," she said, slamming her door and knocking the man to the ground. She pulled out of the parking lot quickly, looking in her rearview mirror to make sure no one saw where she was coming from.

CHAPTER NINETEEN

Ken called Cookie to warn her of what just transpired in their home. He knew she was up since she told him they were planning on coming back in the morning. The phone rang a few times before she finally answered. "Hey baby, well this a nice surprise. I'm sure you've already been up for a while. How are you?" Cookie asked. She and Sheila had knocked out about a fourth of their trip back by this point and had just stopped at a gas station to use the restroom.

"Well that's a bit of a loaded question. I'm ok, but we had someone break in the house this morning. The police are on their way here now," he said.

"Oh my God! What? Did this just happen?" Cookie asked.

"Yeah about 20 minutes ago. I was up cooking breakfast and was sitting in the living room, just watching TV. I heard someone rustling through the bushes and the next thing I knew, he started shooting through the house," Ken answered.

"I can't believe this. Who in the world would try to do that? Did he harm you?" Cookie asked. Sheila was driving and glanced over at Cookie several times by now, trying to figure out what was getting her so excited.

"I have no idea. He's dead though. I tried to just shoot him in the leg, but he kept coming for me. I didn't get hit though," Ken replied.

"Thank God. I'm so glad you're ok. I love you. I'll be there as fast as I can. We probably have another 5 hours or so before we get home," she said, with a concerned tone.

"It's ok, I just didn't want you to be alarmed when you got home. I love you too. The police have just got arrived. I gotta go babe," Ken said.

"Ok, bye baby," Cookie responded.

"Um, is everything ok? Sounded like Ken was really upset," Sheila asked.

"Yea, thankfully he is. Someone broke in our house this morning and was shooting at him. He um….he killed them, in self-defense," Cookie answered.

"Wow! I'm so glad he's ok! People are so crazy. I don't blame him. That's good for that bastard," Sheila said.

"Yeah who just breaks into someone's house and starts shooting?" Cookie sighed.

Meanwhile Ken was explaining to the police exactly what happened.

"You are very blessed sir. This could have turned out to be really ugly for you. Do you mind running down everything that happened?" the officer asked. He was a tall, slender man with dark hair and wide, broad shoulders. His name was Matt Williams.

"Yes, sure I uh was in the kitchen just making breakfast. I came here and started watching TV as I was eating. That's when I heard the first noise. It sounded like something was rustling in the bushes. It must have been him then. Shortly after is when I heard the first shot. Everything happened so quickly after that. I ran to go get my gun out of the closet. By that time several more shots rang out and that's when I opened fire on him in the leg. I was going to just stop there, but he shot at me again. That's when I shot him the last time in the head," Ken said.

"Ok sir, I know this is probably a lot for you to try to recount, especially with it all happening first thing in the morning. Is there anything else you can think of that you would like to add?" the other officer, whose name was Lorenzo Long, added in.

Ken took a long pause and figured he may as well add this piece in as well. "Well there is one thing. When the guy first came in the house I thought I heard him say, "Where is she?" I don't know exactly who "she" was supposed to be but it did worry me. My wife is on her way back from out of town. To be honest that scared me that he seemed to be looking for a woman and my wife just happened to be gone. I didn't really know what to make of that, though. He never mentioned a name," Ken said.

"Interesting. Well hopefully that has nothing to do with your wife. I'm sure you're glad that she wasn't inside the home when all of this happened," Officer Long replied.

"Yes, I'm very grateful that she wasn't here," Ken said.

"Well I think we have all we need here. Please let us know if you hear even the slightest disturbance. We'll be here right away," Officer Williams stated. Ken could see the man who broke into his home being wheeled in a body bag out of the door and into the ambulance.

When Cookie arrived at home a few hours later, Ken was just finishing up patching up their front door from the shots of the intruder. She couldn't wait to get home to check on him and felt so uneasy the rest of the trip home. Although she had a great (and somewhat frightening) time in New Orleans with Sheila, all of that seemed so far behind her now. Ken? Baby, I got here as soon as I could," Cookie said, dropping her bags at the door and going into the bedroom to find Ken. Before she could step in the room all the way, Ken greeted her with an extremely tight hug and a kiss.

"I'm good. I'm ok baby. I'm just glad you weren't here and out of the line of fire, that's all," Ken said. Cookie could tell he was disheveled and somewhat wool-gathered. For some reason, she didn't believe his uneasiness could be solely attributed to the shooting itself. Whatever the case, she hoped it would reveal itself soon.

"Thank God. I just can't believe this. I mean, who would do this? We don't bother anyone, but then again I guess a lot of innocent people get robbed every day," Cookie admitted. She walked back towards the front of the door, reached inside her purse for the small bag that Ivy gave her and sprinkled some of the dust along the base of the door. She kept moving and talking quickly, all the while spreading the dust along the floor and hoping Ken wouldn't notice.

"Yeah, it was so strange. It all happened so quickly, I can barely remember everything that happened. Baby, um, what are you putting down on the floor? That looks like some kind of purple dust. It may be a few bullet holes through the door, but I don't think we have to worry about any termites," Ken laughed.

"Ah, funny. I guess it does look a little weird for me to be doing this. It's just a little dust I got in New Orleans. Helps keep the bad spirits away. I figured it might actually come in handy in for times like this. Never can be too careful, you know?" Cookie responded nervously.

"No baby. I don't know. What's gotten into? And what is this purple dust? Don't tell me you and Sheila went into one of those voodoo shops on Bourbon Street. Those places are not good news," Ken said.

"It's a really long story and it's not so important right now. But I just think this will really help us. I'm just really afraid, that's all," Cookie admitted.

"Let's sit down. Tell me what happened. What did those people tell you there to make you believe you need to have this stuff?" Ken asked with genuine concern.

"She, her name is Ivy, told our fortunes. Sheila went first. She didn't really say anything bad about her. But when it came to me, she said I should be very cautious of my sister. She never said Chelsea's name but I knew she was talking about her. It was the creepiest thing ever. I was really shaken up about it. But it was my conversation with Sheila last night that really confirmed everything for me," Cookie said softly.

"Huh? What did she have to do with it? I don't understand," Ken asked, with a puzzled expression on his face.

"I know, it didn't make sense to me either when she first started telling me the story. Remember when she told me that everything wasn't over at the end of our wedding? Well, she was right in a way. Chelsea and Brandon had somehow reconnected while he was in hiding before he resurfaced. They were both plotting to kill me," she said.

"What? I can't believe this! Wait, I mean do you really know this for sure?" Ken asked.

"Yes, Sheila took a picture of Chelsea's phone when she left it unattended for a while. Chelsea had his name saved as "B" in her phone, but judging by the conversation, I'm pretty sure it was him she was talking to. It's so shocking but in a way it confirms all of the uneasy feelings I've had about her lately," Cookie responded. Ken sat there in silence for an uncomfortable amount of time before he spoke again.

"Cookie, there's something I need to tell you. I don't want to scare you with what I'm about to say. The guy that broke in today said, "Where is she?" At that point I had already shot him, but he didn't have to die. I had already shot him in the leg when he tried shooting at me again. But when he said that, I just shot him in the head. I thought he was looking for you. I couldn't take it, so I killed him. I can't lie, it felt so good to smoke his ass," Ken said.

"That is….um. Wow," Cookie said. She was at a loss for words as tears began to stream down her face. Ken reached out to hug and console her.

"Baby I'm not letting anything happen to you. You're my heart. I'm doing whatever I have to in order to keep you in my life," Ken said.

"I know you're going to protect me. I actually have no doubt about that. If I did, you proved it today. I'm just afraid. I don't know what's going on or what to believe anymore," she said.

"You can believe that I love you and I miss you. I'm so glad to feel you right now," Ken replied, kissing her deeply. He picked her up and sat her on his lap on the couch. He caressed the back of her neck and then laid her down on the couch as he started ripping her shirt off. He scooped her bra up over her head, without even unfastening it. He engulfed her ripe breasts and attempted to put both of them in his mouth at once. Cookie rose up and climbed on top of him, forcing him to lay down on the couch. Ken was turned on even more by her force, as he let her take control. She kissed and sucked on his bottom lip, as she slid down his grey sweat pants.

Cookie kept kissing Ken forcefully as she took him in her hand and slid him inside of her. She bounced up and down as the cuff of her behind slapped against his upper thighs. Ken let her ride for a few more moments until he used the strength of his legs to lay her back down on the couch and pulled out of her. She gave him a perplexed look, before she realized what he was doing. The next thing she knew, Ken was burying his face and scratching her with his beard all over her wet love land.

She wanted to show her appreciation for him being such a strong protector over her. As much as she wanted him to continue tasting her, she lifted up his face and kissed him. Then she pulled his sweat pants off all the way and got on her knees as she sat him down on the couch. She stopped just as he was about to climax and just stared at him. Ken stared back at her, panting violently.

"Please, just let me have my way right now," Cookie said, placing her finger over his mouth as she climbed back on top of him. Neither one of them could last long, as Cookie climaxed just a few seconds after Ken did.

"I love you," Ken whispered.

"I love you too. Thank you for protecting me. I'm just happy you're alive," Cookie responded, resting her head on Ken's shoulder as tears began to stream down her face.

CHAPTER TWENTY

Cookie walked into work on Monday morning with a rejuvenated spirit. Sure, her husband had just had a brush with death and she just learned that her own sister may have tried to kill her, according to Sheila. However, it was the best time to be alive. She reveled in the now and vowed to make the best of each moment that day. The first few hours sped by and when she looked at her phone, she had a text from Sheila that read, "Hey girl, just checking on you. Call me when you can. Hope everything is ok with Ken". Cookie decided she would just give Sheila a call back after work to fill her in on the way home.

There were also two unheard voicemails that she hadn't checked. She didn't remember missing any calls, but her reception was going in and out while she was in New Orleans. The first message was from her mother. "I hope you and Sheila have a great time on your trip. I didn't want anything special. I know you're fully grown now but a mother does reserve the right to still check in on her children, doesn't she? Anyway, I love you. Call when you can," Lisa said.

The second voice mail was from the most unexpected caller. The only person that would have surprised her more would have been Brandon himself, reincarnated for the second time. She played back the message and it said, "Hey there stranger. It's been a while. Just wanted to reach out to you to catch up. I have something I need to tell you. Nothing bad. But get back to me when you can Candy," Mike said.

Cookie hadn't heard from Mike since a couple years after Brandon died. It had been even longer than that since she had physically seen him. Her head felt light all of a sudden. Sure,

Mike was a great friend of hers, almost like a brother, but they rarely even talked anymore, besides holidays and birthdays. Ken knew of him and knew nearly everything about him. Awkward as it may have been, she was curious to hear what he had to tell her. She decided to step away for a minute and give him a call.

"Hello? I think I know this lady. I think her name is Pastry or something like that. I kinda forgot since she got her Ken doll and all. Oh, Cookie, that was it!" Mike said playfully.

"Wait a damn minute sir," Cookie laughed. "Last time I checked, phones work two ways. How have you been?"

"I guess you do have a good point. So that's why I'm calling you now. Seriously, it's great to hear your voice though. I'm doing well. Really well actually. I was calling because I'm actually moving back to Dallas soon for my job, and, I'll be getting engaged soon," he said.

"You've got to be kidding. That is so awesome that you'll be in Dallas now too! Wait, engaged? Look at you! You've been holding out on me. Well, who is the lucky lady? I need to meet her," Cookie asked.

"Her name is Kelly. You'll meet her soon enough. She'll be here in a couple months, but I'll be in Dallas before then. We should catch a happy hour or something. When she gets here, I'll propose then, right before the anniversary of our second date. I'll be in town this Friday. Are you free for a little bit then?" he asked.

"That should be fine. I know Ken has a work function that night, but I don't think he will mind. I'll ask him and let you know," Cookie responded.

"He's more than welcome to come too if he wants," Mike said.

"Well I'll definitely keep you posted. Congratulations again. I'm so very happy for you. Now we can actually keep up with each other since you'll be in Dallas with your soon-to-be wife. I have a meeting here in about 30 minutes, so I guess I should go, but I'll give you a call back tomorrow to confirm," Cookie added.

As Cookie drove home, she remembered the anxiety she once felt about having any male friends in past relationships. She was pretty sure Ken wouldn't mind her going to a happy hour with Mike, but she wanted to at least give her husband the courtesy of getting his approval.

Sure enough, she talked it over with Ken when he made it home and he had no issue with it. "I haven't heard you talk about Mike in forever. That's pretty cool that he and his wife will be here in Dallas soon," Ken said. He also had several female friends and she never felt threatened by any of them. Well, all except for maybe a couple of them.

"I know right. It will be nice. I'm just so shocked he's actually settling down. I thought that boy would never get married," she laughed. That was the extent of the conversation, no jealous undertones and insecurities peeking through. In fact, they even made love that night before they went to sleep.

****

"Well it's great to see you both again. Ken, I'd like to start with you today. Is there anything particularly pressing that you'd like to share?" Melissa said.

"There is one major thing. Last week a guy broke into our home while Cookie was out of town. He started shooting but that wasn't the worst part. At one point, he said, "Where is she?" I was just so enraged that I shot back of course in self-defense, but I wanted to make sure he was dead. I shot him right between the eyes," Ken said.

"Whoa! Okay! I'm so sorry to hear this and glad to know you're ok. Before we go any further though, have you told this same story to the police?" Melissa asked.

"Oh yes, they know about it. Come to find out it was just some crazy man that was trying to find his ex-wife that left him," Ken said.

"Cookie, well how did all of this make you feel?" Melissa asked as she turned her attention towards her.

"Well, what makes the story even crazier. I went on a girls' trip with my best friend that's getting married soon. Long story, she shared with me that my ex-husband Brandon and my sister were in cahoots to um...they're trying to kill me," Cookie said, with her voice shaking.

"Ok, well um this is truly a lot that the two of you have dealt with this past week. Cookie, do you have any reasons you can think of as to why anyone, let alone possibly your sister, would try to harm you?" Melissa asked.

"Not at all. I like to think of myself as a pretty nice person. I'm not judgmental. I'm helpful. I….the truth is, I'm afraid. I'm so afraid of my life. I've been having these premonitions about my sister even before my friend told me the secret she'd been holding in. The guy broke into our house over the weekend just took everything over the top," Cookie said.

"This may sound strange to ask this, but when was the last time you spoke with your sister?" Melissa asked. Ken had a perplexed look on his face as Cookie prepared to answer.

"Um, I guess probably a week or so. I don't understand. What does that have to do with anything?" Cookie asked, looking just as confused as Ken was.

"What I'm saying is get in her head. There's more than one way to skin a cat. Find out what makes her tick. Get to know her better, but don't be too obvious with it. Then again, you seem like a woman who doesn't back down against fear. You may even want to ask her straight out. Do it alone, if you do. If Ken is there, it will feel more like a threat," Melissa advised.

"I think I follow what you're saying. That sounds like a good idea. I can't lie, it's a scary thought but I think it's something that needs to be done," Cookie said, with a glossed over look in her eyes.

"Precisely. Trust me, as someone who has been in a similar situation of being in the dark about something for years, it's better to know and rip the band aid as soon as possible. Pacification doesn't take away the pain. It only masks it. Get to the bottom of it and find out the truth," Melissa responded.

"If you don't mind me asking, what was the similar situation that you've been in before? I just would like Cookie and me to have some kind of basis as to how to move forward with this," Ken asked, holding Cookie's hand on the couch.

"Well, I did set myself up for this one, didn't I? I guess I'm the one being questioned now. Nonetheless, this is all a part of the therapeutic process. I can't help anyone if I don't share a piece of myself along the way. My mother committed suicide years ago. I probably was five years old or so when it happened. I always lived with my grandmother because she wasn't able to look after me. She had an addiction. A drug addiction. I remember seeing her only three times my whole life. As I got older, I became more inquisitive, trying to find out the real answers as to who my mother was. I didn't find out she committed suicide until my 19th birthday," she said, with a stern expression, her composure collected and professional.

"I'm so sorry to hear that. I can only imagine how difficult that must have been," Cookie said.

"It's ok. The most difficult part was knowing but not knowing for all of those years. Deep down, I knew my mother wouldn't have just left me like that without ever seeing me again. I just got tired of the excuses my family dished out over the years. I couldn't miss what I never had. Although I am sad about my mother taking her own life, I never really knew her. My family hiding the truth for years was the true, deep hurt. That took years for me to get over. I'm saying all of this to say Cookie, start your healing process now before the scar comes," Melissa said.

"Maybe you're right. I'll reach out to her then and see what we can work out," Cookie responded.

"Sounds good. I think you and Ken are making some great strides already with getting in touch with your feelings. Hopefully, by next week you and your sister would have already talked and set something up," Melissa replied.

CHAPTER TWENTY ONE

Friday honestly came quicker than Cookie expected. She was excited about her meeting with Mike after work for happy hour, but she was also a little apprehensive about seeing her friend. She didn't let on to Ken that she used to have feelings for Mike. However, she could barely even admit it to herself. There had always been a sexual tension between her and Mike, but that was so long ago. She likely wouldn't even feel the same about him now.

Cookie pulled in to the restaurant right before 5:00 pm. Just as she suspected, Mike was already there. He picked the place, a new Mexican restaurant on the north side of town. He said they had great margaritas too. They both loved Mexican food and Cookie was looking forward to the great food and the company.

"Well, hello there Mr. How are you?" Cookie said, tapping Mike on the shoulder, excited to see her long lost friend.

"Hey Cookie! Wow, it has truly been forever. You look great. Keeping it tight for Ken I see," he laughed.

"Whatever. You are still crazy as ever, I see," Cookie responded.

"Well come on, let's have a seat. I think you're really going to love this place. I'm telling you, these margaritas are amazing. I was in town for a quick weekend a couple of weeks back and tried it. I immediately thought of you and that we could try it out the next time I saw you," Ken replied.

"Is that right? Well you have really good taste, so I trust your judgment," Cookie said. She and Ken continued small catch up talk until the waiter came to take their order. Cookie ordered some quesadillas and a strawberry lime swirl margarita. Ken ordered chips and queso for himself and Cookie to share, fajitas, and a Patron margarita.

"So, tell me what's been going on with you?" Ken said.

"I've been well. Just working and Ken has been really busy with his job, but we're planning on starting a family soon. Can you believe it? This old lady is ready for babies now," she laughed.

"Get out of here, you are far from old! You look better than most women in their twenties. There's nothing wrong with waiting a little bit later in life to have kids," he said.

"Enough about me though. I want to hear more about Kelly. I am so happy for you. I may need to get my questions out to grill her a bit," she laughed.

"Uh oh, let me hide her then," he grinned. "She's great. We actually met at a business conference at my old job. We met up for drinks one night and kept in touch, more on a friend level, at first. Then it evolved into something more romantic and we started going out. I'm telling you, she's the female version of me. I think you will really like her," he said.

"The female version of you? Can the world even handle such thing? That's awesome. I really can't wait to meet her. So when do you anticipate you would actually be married?" she asked.

"I'm thinking no longer than a year from now, for sure. I know she's probably going to want it, but we really don't need any big frocks and frills at this stage in our lives. I really just want to keep the costs down as much as possible so we can use that towards a great honeymoon. I just don't see the sense of a big wedding," Mike said.

"I'm totally with you on that. Ken and I really tried to keep our costs down too. That's one thing we were both on the same page about. The most important part was about us being married, not the wedding ceremony itself," she replied.

Cookie felt a slightly awkward feeling while talking to Mike but she couldn't quite put her finger on why. She just chalked it up to the fact that they hadn't seen each other since her wedding. She wasn't sure if he felt the same, but she tried to push the thought out of her mind. After all she was excited to see him again after so long.

"Ah yes, here they are," Mike said, as the waiter came to the table with the margaritas and the chips and queso. Cookie took a sip of the margarita and he could tell by the expression on her face that she liked it. The waiter came back in less than two minutes to drop off their entrees too.

"Damn. Now that's a good margarita. Wow, amazing. Not too sweet and just the right amount of liquor. Oh yeah, Ken and I will definitely be coming here. We'll have to do a double date together too. Great suggestion. Funny thing is I'm in this area occasionally and have never seen this place before," Cookie said.

"Yeah, that would be cool for all of us to meet up and come here," Mike replied, with a bit of a dazed look on his face.

"Everything ok? You look like you just dipped into the twilight zone for a minute," Cookie said.

"Oh yeah, I'm sorry. I guess I was hungrier than I thought. I didn't really eat a big lunch today, but I'm here with my girl Cookie, so I'm great," he smiled.

"Cool, well I'm definitely enjoying myself too and these drinks and the food are amazing. I love it," she said. They talked for another hour or so, until Cookie looked at her watch and said she should probably be heading home.

"This was great. It can't be this long before we see each other again. I really enjoyed you, Cookie. Can you believe we'll actually be in the same city again now?" he said.

"I know, right! I'm so happy about that. Now we have no excuses to wait literally years in between time when we see each other," Cookie responded.

"Exactly. Oh and this is my treat tonight too, so put that wallet away," Mike said.

"Oh, thank you so much. You don't have to do that," Cookie said. The waiter brought back their tickets and Ken offered to walk Cookie to her car. By this time the parking lot was full, but not in the area where they parked. Cookie was actually grateful for him walking her to her car, since the area where her car was parked was dimly lit.

"Well, Miss Lady, thank you for kicking my weekend off to a great start. I'll be catching up with you. Maybe we can do lunch sometime soon?" Mike said.

"Yes, we must. But you just make sure the future Mrs. gets settled in and acclimated to the city first, when she gets here," Cookie said.

"Mmmm, will do. That sounds like a plan then," Mike said, leaning towards Cookie to give her a hug goodbye now that they were at car. He pressed harder, leaned in and kissed her softly on the lips. Cookie let the kiss linger a couple of seconds longer than she should have. Fighting her urge to kiss him back, she slowly pulled him away.

"Whoa, um ok. Wow, that was a bit awkward. Very unexpected. Are you ok?" Cookie asked Mike. It was all she could say, although deep down she felt a great fire being lit inside of her. Truth be told, there had been much sexual tension between them for years. This was just the first time either one of them had acted upon it before.

"I'm sorry, I just couldn't hold it in any longer. I've always wanted to kiss you. I felt like there's always been this attraction between us that we've both held back on. I guess maybe I was wrong. Cookie, I'm so sorry," Mike said, now embarrassed, not for kissing a married woman and being in a relationship himself, but because she didn't seem to share his same sentiment.

"Mike, I would be lying if I said I was never attracted to you in the past. I'm married now though and you'll be married soon, too. I just can't do this. This isn't right," Cookie said.

"So you were attracted to me before, but not now. Is that what you're saying?" Mike asked, with a sly grin.

Cookie felt like one of those high school girls with her first big crush. She could feel her face turning red, as she tried to ask her true feelings. "Mike, what I'm saying is yes I think there has always been chemistry between us. For whatever reason, we were never able to be in a relationship, though. That wasn't meant to be for us. I should probably be getting home now. I had a great time. Thanks for walking me to my car," Cookie said.

"I understand. I really had a great time too. I know I shouldn't have done that, but I hope this doesn't make things strange and awkward between us now. You have a good night. Hopefully, I'll talk to you soon Cookie," he said, giving her a head nod and waiting until she got in her car before walking away.

"Mike, we will always be friends. Nothing will ever change that. Have a great night and be safe going home," she said.

The whole way home, Cookie couldn't stop thinking about the kiss with Mike. Everything happened so quickly and she was honestly trying to replay it all in her head. Had she given him any signs to say it was okay to kiss her? She just couldn't figure out what made him so bold as to do that tonight, especially since he was about to be engaged soon.

Although she may have thought about what it would be like to be in a relationship with Mike, she never wanted to actually cross that line. Their friendship meant far too much to her for them to possibly ruin it by ever being together. Then again, their pattern of singleness was never really on the same wavelength either. One of them was always married (only Cookie at this point) or either in a relationship. Whatever the case and what maybe could have been, she couldn't deny that there was something magical about that kiss.

Thankfully, Ken wasn't home yet when Cookie arrived. The alone time allowed Cookie to gather her wits about what just happened with Mike. She decided this was the perfect time to bite the bullet and reach out to Chelsea. She called her and Chelsea answered almost immediately, right after the first ring.

"Hello?" Chelsea said.

"Hey sis! How are you?" Cookie asked.

"I'm good, just about to head to the movies with a guy I just started dating. He's not here yet though. I still have about 20 minutes. What's up?" Chelsea asked.

"Look at you. Ok, I guess Mel is officially old news then," Cookie laughed.

"You already know it. He's been calling me still, but of course I haven't been answering," Chelsea laughed back.

"I don't blame you. He's such a loser. So tell me a little about the new guy. Who is he?" Cookie asked.

"You'll never guess who he is. Do you remember Trent from college? He was the transfer student that left after about a year. He used to always try to ask me out," Chelsea said.

"Oh yeah, I do remember him. You were so mean to that guy. He was pretty cute too, from what I recall," Cookie said.

"Yeah, well that's him. I guess you can say I've grown up a bit. I just don't think I was mature enough for him back then. You know I was chasing the bad boys. I ran into him at the grocery store last week. We've been talking a lot since then and this is actually our second date. I'm taking it slow though. I'm not ready to jump into another relationship right now. It's nothing serious," Chelsea replied.

"That's really cool. I don't remember him being a creeper. Sounds like he might be a good catch after all. Well, I don't want to keep you long. I was just calling to see how you were doing. Also, I think we should get together soon. What do you say I come to Chicago soon and we spend a weekend together?" Cookie asked.

"That sounds really good. We haven't done that in a while. Let's make it happen," Chelsea said.

"Great! I'm really looking forward to it," Cookie said.

"Cool, well I'll definitely give you a call tomorrow then and we can set up a time that works for both of us," Chelsea replied.

"Ok, sounds great. I'll let you get back to it then. Have fun on the date!" Cookie smiled. For a brief moment, she felt like she was talking to the sister she knew when she was younger, before any of the tension or secrets started.

"Ok I will do my best. Hey Cookie. Is everything ok?" Chelsea asked.

Cookie was a bit taken aback by Chelsea's question. She hoped that her true motives for wanting to visit her sister weren't that transparent. "Oh yeah, I'm fine. Just honestly missing my little sis. That's all. Thanks for asking though. I'm doing well," Cookie replied.

"Ok good, I'm glad to hear that. I've been missing you too. I know you're busy. You beat me to the punch actually because I was going to call you and see if we could set up some time too. I guess great minds and close sisters think alike, huh?" Chelsea laughed.

"Yes, they certainly do. I love you Chelsea," Cookie said.

"I love you too. Bye, Cookie," Chelsea replied, as she hung up the phone.

At that moment, it seemed unreal to Cookie that her sister would ever attempt to try to kill her. Although she couldn't fathom the thought of her sister harming her, she also couldn't deny what Sheila told her and even seeing the screen shots of the text messages herself. Nonetheless, she had to confront her sister face to face, even if it meant jeopardizing her own safety in the process.

CHAPTER TWENTY TWO

"Hey baby, what time do you think you'll be home this evening?" Bill asked Lisa. He was at home, while she was finishing up a women's event at church. She had been working hard all week to pull off all of the planning and coordinating for their big annual women's conference. Bill helped her wherever he could, but he wasn't nearly as crafty and creative as Lisa was. That was one of her specialties. Bill knew his place and stuck to carpentry, cooking and any kind of manual labor.

"Hey honey. Well, these ladies are having themselves a mighty good time. I believe we'll be done here around the next couple of hours, if they ever stop congregating when it's all over. Why? Is something going on?" Lisa asked.

"Oh no, I was just wondering. Is it ok for me to miss you?" Bill asked in a playfully sarcastic tone.

"Well of course. A lady does always yearn to be missed," she laughed.

"Alright then, well I'll let you get back to it. Don't worry about dinner tonight. I'll pick up something for us," Bill replied.

"Ok, thank you so much baby. I had the food here for lunch and as good as it was, I really would prefer not to see it for dinner," she laughed.

"I don't blame you. Well, I'll take care of the food and I'll see you soon. I love you," Bill said.

"And I love you even more. See you later babe," Lisa responded as she hung up the phone and attended back to manning the registration tables for the conference. She was double checking all of the gift bags for the women as they were getting ready to exit soon. The conference had about 30 minutes left to go and pretty soon, all of the women would be flooding the foyer, with their parting gifts in hand from the conference.

Lisa had just finished prepping all the bags and decided she better go to the restroom before the flood of women started to come on. As she went to stand, her head started swimming and she lost sight of colors for a moment. The lady sitting next to her at the table noticed and immediately asked if she was ok.

"Lisa? Are you alright? You looked a bit disoriented when you went to stand up," she said.

"Thanks, Stephanie. I'm fine, but I did feel a little woozy when I stood up. I probably just need to eat again. It's so hard for me to stop and eat at functions like this. I just need to go to the restroom for a minute and get a drink of water," Lisa responded.

"Ok, well be careful. I'm coming in there if I don't see you come out soon," Stephanie laughed.

"Uh oh, I guess I better hurry then," Lisa smiled back at Stephanie, as she headed towards the restroom.

Meanwhile, Stephanie went to go fix her a small plate of food that was waiting for her when she came back. "Ah, look at you. You didn't have to do that. See, I knew I was going to enjoy working with you. Seriously, thank you so much for the plate. Ooh, I should have just enough time to eat it too," Lisa said.

"Oh yeah, you'll be fine by the time they get out. I got myself a piece of cake. I didn't want to tempt you by getting you one too, so I figured I'd just take the dreadful task of devouring all of the evil calories for the both of us," Stephanie laughed.

"I'm so envious. I'm staying on my path though. I've lost a few pounds and I need to get off a few more," Lisa said.

"Congratulations. I guess I can't lose any eating this, huh?" Stephanie laughed.

The women started to pour out of the sanctuary as the conference ended. Lisa had literally just finished her plate of food, but Stephanie was still slowly nursing her cake. The ladies all beamed with smiles, some overcome with emotion as they wiped tears from their eyes. "That must have been a powerful word. Look at the expressions on their faces," Lisa told Stephanie.

"Exactly, I was just thinking the same thing. I've got to order the DVD of this. The only downside of working an event is you don't get to participate in it. But it's all for the Lord, so I'm satisfied knowing that, at least," she said.

Several women started walking up to the table to get their souvenir bags. There was one woman in particular that stood diagonal to the table against the wall, looking intently. Lisa caught glances with her a few times, but didn't recognize her. After more than a few looks, Lisa began to feel uncomfortable as the women stood there with a stoic expression on her face, leaning against the wall.

"Stephanie, don't look right now, but there's a woman over there that keeps staring at me. She's really making me uncomfortable. Maybe there's something wrong. I want to ask her if she needs help with something but she looks mean," Lisa said.

"I know exactly who you're talking about. In the long green dress? She just joined the church a couple of weeks ago I believe. I can't put my finger on it, but she's a strange bird I'll tell you that," Stephanie chuckled.

Just then, the unknown woman walked right up to the table as if she was being summoned by them. "Hello ladies, this is such a wonderful event today. Don't you think? I am totally in love with this church. Everyone here is so welcoming. There's a certain spirit.....moving. Can you feel it," she asked, raising her eyebrows.

"Yes, the Holy Spirit is definitely in this place. I don't believe we've met before. I'm Lisa. What's your name?" Lisa asked, extended her hand to the mysterious woman.

"You can call me Maria. I know who you are Mrs. Brighton," the woman said, never once directing much of her attention to Stephanie.

"Maria, well it's really nice to meet you. Who doesn't know Lisa? She's such a jewel," Stephanie chimed in.

"Yes, I would say so too. Although no good deed goes unseen, so do secrets," she replied softly.

"Excuse me? I'm not sure I understand what you mean," Lisa asked with a defensive look on her face. She was a quiet woman for the most part, but didn't take kindly to anyone trying to insinuate she had any sort of faulty character traits.

"That's between you and God. He knows. He just let me know. It's going to get dirty and it's going to be really ugly. Please cleanse your heart before it's too late. Before you lose something or someone you really love," the woman responded, leaning over to rub Lisa's shoulder.

Lisa jerked back as if the woman had punched her. "Please refrain from touching me. Maria, you enjoy the rest of your day. You can grab one of the bags on your way out," Lisa replied, with a look that could have burned straight through the woman. She was boiling inside. Stephanie could even tell she was starting to turn red.

"Ah yes, of course. Thank you ladies. You both have yourselves a fabulous evening," she said. She gave a sinister look at Lisa as she walked off.

"What in the world was that all about?" Stephanie asked.

"I have no idea. That lady is obviously bat shit crazy," Lisa concluded in a matter of fact tone.

"Lisa! We are still in the church you know" Stephanie replied.

"I'm so sorry. She really got me worked up. You know I don't normally even talk like that. I don't have any secrets. I have no idea what she's talking about," Lisa said.

"Judging by the look on your face, she left right on time. Come on, let's start breaking this table down so we can both get out of here," Stephanie replied.

"She was definitely pushing her limits. I'll say that. I agree though, let's start packing up so we can get out of here."

Lisa and Stephanie finished up their duties at the church and said their goodbyes as they both traveled to their respective homes. Lisa glanced down at her phone when she got in her car to see what time it was. 6:15 pm. She should be home shortly after 6:30 pm. She called Bill to let him know she was on her way back home. After she got off the phone, she decided to ride the rest of the way in silence. Inside her mind, she was confronted with her own blaring thoughts about what the strange woman at church told her. She didn't understand what kind of secret the lady was speaking of, let alone why she even had the audacity to say such a thing to her.

When Lisa walked through the door at home and saw Bill, all of her negative thoughts floated away. He took the bags from her hands and told her to have a seat at the dinner table once she changed into something more comfortable. "Mmmmm, it smells so good in here. Looks like you had a few tricks up your sleeve while I was out," Lisa.

"Maybe a couple," Bill said, kissing her on her cheek as he walked past her into the kitchen.

Bill came out with two glasses of Rosato, Lisa's favorite wine. He placed her glass in her hand and sat his down on the table across from her. When he returned again from the kitchen, he had two identical plates with a petite steak, homemade mashed potatoes and artichoke hearts.

"My goodness, this looks so delicious. I thought you were getting take out. Is there a special occasion that I forgot about?" Lisa said.

"As a matter of fact, there is. You're the special occasion. I know you've been really busy with the conference, so I just want to celebrate your accomplishment. Plus, I'm glad to finally get my wife back," Bill laughed.

"Thank you so much, honey. After all these years, you still know how to make my heart melt. I love you so much," she said, with tears forming at the corners of her eyes.

"Of course, you're welcome baby. You deserve it," Bill said.

"This food is absolutely delicious and I love how you included my favorite wine too," she said.

"Thank you. I was trying to time it just right. That's why I called you right before I thought you might be leaving church," Bill said.

Lisa felt so relieved and relaxed. Their marriage together had its ups and down like anyone else's. They were not perfect by any means, but Bill always knew how to make her feel special. That was one of the traits she loved most about him. She took a deep breath, sipped some more of the wine and exhaled the cares of the day away as she enjoyed her unexpected romantic dinner with Bill.

Meanwhile, Chelsea was just leaving the grocery store. The sky was just starting to turn a mixture of light purple and deep blue, as the night began to set in. She pushed her basket to the car and purposely parked far away so that she could get some extra exercise in. She kept feeling like someone was walking behind her, but no one was there, every time she turned around. She brushed it off and chalked it up to her being paranoid.

She opened her car to place her groceries inside and looked back up to find bright headlines shining through her windshield. She squinted so she could get a better look at the car and immediately she had a pretty big hunch as to who it was. This was just the most amazing timing ever. Mel. She really wasn't up for any of his shit. She suspected he was probably upset because she hadn't answered any of his recent calls or texts. He jumped out of the car, dressed in sweat pants and a t-shirt. Mel looked like someone who was trying to recover from a bad breakup. A piece of her celebrated inside.

"Mel, if this is the part when you try to win me back, please give it up. It's not happening," Chelsea told him coldly.

"Hi Chelsea. I know you've been ignoring my calls and I can't say I really blame you for it. I messed up. I messed up in a horrible way. I know I did. She meant nothing to me and I haven't even spoken to her since. I'm done with all of that and I want you back. I need you," Mel said.

"I really loved you. I did. It takes a lot for me to feel that way about a man. Somehow, you tore my wall down. It's amazing how in a matter of just a few minutes it went all the way back up. I can't do this. I have to go," she said.

"No! I won't let you get away this time. I want to make it up to you. I want to be there to and be the father I'm supposed to be to our unborn child," he pleaded.

"Mel, there is no child anymore. I had an abortion last week," Chelsea said coldly.

"What! How could you do that? Why would you even go through with that and not tell me? You said you were going to let me know when you made your final decision," he said, with a very confused and angry look on his face.

"Well I figured since you decided to go fuck some other bitch and not tell me until you got caught up, that was no situation to raise a baby in. I think that's good reason enough, don't you?" she said.

"You can be so cold-hearted sometimes. Chelsea I want to be back with you. I've changed: I love you, I promise. I'll help you with the rest of your groceries and I'll let you get back to your evening," Mel said.

"That won't be necessary. I got it, but thanks. I suggest you get in your car and leave now. I've exhausted all of the energy I'm going to spend on this. Have a good life," Chelsea said, as she placed the last few bags of groceries in her car, got inside and slammed the door.

CHAPTER TWENTY THREE

"Hey Cookie. How is my beautiful sister doing?" Chelsea asked.

"Well this is a nice surprise. I'm doing well. How about you?" Cookie asked. She wasn't expecting to hear from her sister again so soon, especially since they just talked a few days ago. Maybe she was calling her to set up a time when they could see each other. Although Chelsea threw it in Cookie's face a few times over the years that she hardly ever saw her family anymore, she rarely took initiative to change that.

"I'm ok. I ran into that bastard Mel Sunday at the grocery store. He was talking about getting back together and of course I shut him down. I went ahead and told him about the abortion too. I figured then was the best time to tell him. I'm so done with his sorry ass," Chelsea said.

"Do you think there's a chance he really could be sorry? I mean, maybe he's changed, I don't know. I really had high hopes for him. He was such a nice guy, but scratch what I just said. His dumb ass cheated though, so I agree. Let his ass go. He's not worth the headache," Cookie replied.

"My thoughts exactly. Damn loser. I'm sorry, I just started going on about his lame ass. That was rude. How is your day going?" Chelsea said.

"It's been going by fast, but I can't complain. Today has been going well so far. I'm alive, I'm well and I'm talking to the best sister ever. What more could I ask for?" Cookie said.

"Aw, aren't you sweet? I was thinking about our last conversation and I actually have some downtime from work in the next couple of weeks. I was thinking maybe we could plan something about three weeks out from now. Is that too soon for you?" Chelsea said.

"Let me check my calendar. I'm looking now and actually three weeks from now looks perfect. Let me talk it over with Ken tonight, but it looks like I'll probably be seeing you in three weeks," Cookie replied.

"Perfect. Well, talk it over with the hubby and just let me know when you can. I'm looking forward to it. I know you're busy over there and I have a meeting coming up here shortly myself, so I'll let you get back to it. I love you Cookie," she said.

"I love you too. I'll let you know tomorrow for sure about the trip too," Cookie said.

"Cool, sounds like a plan. Talk to you later," Chelsea responded.

Cookie tried to shake her nervous feelings the rest of the day while she was at work. No matter how hard she tried, people seemed to see straight through her. A few people asked if she was ok. One of her employees even told her that she seemed to be in another world. The truth is, she was. She couldn't imagine Chelsea actually confessing to her plot to kill her, let alone the two of them being able to move forward after that.

Later that night, Cookie ran the conversation she had with Chelsea by Ken. She didn't want to just dump all of her fears and troubles on him, so she decided she would soften the blow by preparing him a nice dinner. She made some scallops and shrimp, with fresh sautéed spinach and rice pilaf. Ken had been talking about craving seafood lately and she thought this would be a great time to surprise him. By the time he got home, she was just finishing up the rice and putting a coat of dill butter over the scallops.

"Is that the most handsome man I know walking through the door?" Cookie asked.

"Only if that's my beautiful queen talking to me. Today was a beast at work baby. Mmmm, it smells so good in here. What is that you're whipping up?" Ken asked, putting his bag down and leaning in to kiss Cookie.

"Not so fast, sir. No peaking. I've prepared something I think you'll like but I want it to be a surprise. So if you don't mind, go get undressed and put on those grey sweatpants I like. Feel free to leave your shirt off too," Cookie smiled.

"Ok boss, I kinda like it when you tell me what to do," Ken smirked as he went to the bedroom to change clothes.

Cookie exhaled deeply as she finished setting their plates. Ken walked back into the living room a few minutes later, wearing exactly what Cookie requested, grey sweatpants and no shirt.

"Well, well, if I knew it was that easy I would have requested a lot of other things. Umph, you take your sexy self a seat in this chair right here," Cookie said. She walked up to him and placed a chilled glass of wine on the table. As she turned back around to go into the kitchen again, she knew Ken would comment on what she was wearing.

"Wait a minute now. Not the boy shorts too. You trying to start something tonight?" Ken smiled.

"I'm just keeping it a little spicy that's all," Cookie said, taking off her apron, revealing a midriff T-shirt and placing their plates on the table.

"What? You are something else. You remembered I've been talking about wanting some shrimp and scallops lately," Ken said, with his eyes lighting up.

"Yes, I remembered. I hope you enjoy it baby," Cookie replied.

Cookie and Ken prayed over their food and started talking about each other's day. Ken immediately dived into the food and Cookie could tell he was enjoying it. Ken started off by asking Cookie how her day was as he took quick breaths between bites of food.

"There's more in there baby. I think someone was a little hungry," Cookie laughed.

"Oh, I guess I was a little hungrier than I thought," he replied with a smile.

"It's ok, seeing you enjoy this food like this really makes my whole day. Today was busy but all in all I can't complain. It was pretty smooth, for the most part," Cookie answered.

"Oh ok. Well I'm glad that wasn't anything too eventful that shook up your day. Have you heard anything back from your sister?" Ken asked.

"Damn, I really can't hide anything from you. I hate it sometimes, but it's also one of the things I really, truly love about you. Well, you found me out. I need your opinion on something," Cookie said.

"Ok, sure what's that baby? I only know you so well because I love you. I'd like to think that I pay attention to everything about you," Ken replied.

"You are unbelievable. I love you. Well, I talked to Chelsea today. She called me while I was at work. Long story short, she suggested that I come there sometime in the next three weeks. She sounded really excited, relaxed and back to her old self honestly. I feel a little silly now even after what Sheila told me. I guess I'm just nervous about going now. I wasn't expecting to have to face it this soon," she said.

"Wow, that is a lot. I must admit, I wasn't expecting her to call you back this quickly about it either. I think it's natural for you to be afraid. Hell, truth be told, I'm nervous about you going by yourself. I know you have to find out the truth, though. Plus, I don't think that she'll actually try anything crazy," Ken said.

"Ok, thank you so much baby. I've been really anxious about the whole thing ever since I talked to her earlier. I'll just give her a call tomorrow and let her know I'll be there," Cookie said.

Cookie and Ken made more small talk about the happenings of the rest of their days respectively, but something was different. Each of them now carried an uneasiness that they couldn't talk away. The feeling just was and existed in the atmosphere. They decided to watch a little TV on the couch together to take their minds off of the serious conversation they just had. Cookie was more exhauseted than she realized, as she fell asleep nearly 30 minutes into them watching reruns of some of their favorite sitcoms.

Ken lied awake most of the night watching Cookie as she slept. She was still as beautiful, if not even more so than the first day he met her. He couldn't fathom anyone harming his heartbeat. If Chelsea did try anything suspicious with Cookie while she was back in Chicago, he would kill her himself.

CHAPTER TWENTY FOUR

"Well, I don't know about you two, but it feels like we were literally just here yesterday. The last week has really flown by. I've been anxiously awaiting today. Cookie, I know the last time we talked, you were going to reach out to your sister to set up a time to visit her soon. How did that go?" Melissa asked.

"I did actually talk to her and we discussed me coming up there just to hang out. The next day she called back and said I should come sometime in the next three weeks, so basically two weeks from now. I wasn't ready for it. Honestly, I was afraid," Cookie said.

"I see, that's totally understandable, especially considering the reason you're going to see her. Don't be dismayed by your heart, though. You have to find out the truth. Living in the truth is so freeing. Trust me, I know. Ken, how does all of this make you feel, if you don't mind me asking?" Melissa replied.

"I'm afraid to be honest. I want to go with her to protect her. I can't take anything happening to my baby. No way. I love Chelsea as my sister in law, but I'll take her out if she hurts my wife," he said.

Cookie shot a glance over to Ken. Although she was a little oft put by his response, she loved it. She was thrilled that Ken was so protective over her. He was the only man that truly knew how to make her feel loved like she should be. In some regards, she still wasn't fully used to that feeling.

"I like that. A man who stands up for his wife. I don't think anyone could ever blame you for that," Melissa said, catching herself as not to slip into unprofessional territory. She wanted to stand up and shout, "Amen"! However, they were talking about Cookie's sister, so she didn't want to be rude.

"I love you Ken," Cookie said softly grabbing his hand.

"Cookie, do you have any pictures of you and your sister together from your wedding?" Melissa asked.

Cookie had a puzzled look on her face as she pulled her phone out of her purse. "Yeah I'm sure I have one somewhere here in my phone. Why do you ask?"

"Find that picture and remember it. Every time you get weak thinking about asking your sister whether or not she tried to kill you, look at the picture. Let it be a reminder to you that if your friend is right, you may not have even been alive to take that picture with her," Melissa said.

"Hmmm, I guess that is a really good point. Oh, I found one here. This is actually a really nice one. Probably one of the best pictures we've ever taken," Cookie said, as she turned her phone to show the screen to Melissa.

"Oh, yes that is nice. Very nice. She looks so familiar. Hmmm, interesting," Melissa said, not fully able to hide her expression of surprise as she saw the picture. She tried to fix her face quickly as not to alarm Cookie, but it was already too late.

"Is everything ok? You look a little flustered," Cookie said.

"Me? Oh no, I'm fine. I honestly was just taken aback a bit after seeing your sister on that picture. She looks very familiar. I just can't remember exactly where," Melissa answered. She started to ask Cookie what her sister's name was, but thought that might be a little too evasive. Plus, the full photo just flashed back in her mind and she remembered reading the tag of "Chelsea Brighton".

"Oh ok, well you know they say everyone has a twin. Maybe it's someone else you know that she really resembles," Cookie said.

"Yeah, that's true. I'm sure that's got to be it. I'd also like to ask you to forgive me if I seemed too pushy about you going to visit your sister and finding out the truth. I encourage all of my clients to do things that rip the band-aid off. Always get to the root of the problem and that's where your healing will be. I've lost a lot of friends, hell even my ex-husband, because of it. After the sting wears off, you'll sleep much better at night and have less stress," Melissa said.

"No, I'm actually glad that you suggested it. I'm a little, well we both are, somewhat apprehensive about it but it's a great idea. I'm going to do it and follow through with it come hell or high water," Cookie said, looking over at Ken to catch his facial expression. His face read that he was supportive but would still erase Chelsea if she tried to harm his wife.

The three of them went on talking and traded different stories during the conversation. This time, it felt more like chatting with an old friend to Cookie, more so than a therapy session. Maybe that was Melissa's intent. However, Cookie felt a hunch that possibly she was enjoying the conversation too. Melissa kept talking until she realized the session had gone over 10 minutes past the cut off time.

"Wow, I guess time really does fly when you're having fun. As much as I would love to continue conversing with you both, we have reached our limit for this session. I look forward to seeing you both next week. Please take care and have a great evening and rest of the week," Melissa.

"Thanks Melissa. You have a great week too. We appreciate your time," Ken said.

"Yes, thank you so much, Melissa. Have a good one," Cookie said, as they walked out of her office.

Melissa had less than 20 minutes before her last client for the evening arrived. In the meantime, she decided to go over to her computer and do some digging on Cookie's sister, Chelsea. She looked all too familiar to her and not in a way that's a regular acquaintance. She had to be someone who was somehow woven into her life. She just couldn't figure out how.

She started looking through her Facebook profile first, which offered little help. Chelsea had most of it blocked to those who were not her friends. As she kept looking though, she found an old Tumblr page that was listed under the name @UnderTheC. After looking through a few of the photos, she was convinced it was the same woman. The page didn't show any new activity within the last two years. However, the content that was there was a bit disturbing. There was one with her in a dimly lit room of red lights and candles. She stared seductively through the camera as if she was piercing straight through her viewers. There was also a blog post entitled "Why Some People Should Just Die" with a top 10 list of annoying things people do that irritate her. She looked up and the clock said 6:28, so she closed out the search window and made a mental note to come back to it later.

Meanwhile, Cookie and Ken were discussing how they thought the session went on their way home. "Well, how do you feel about everything now after talking to Melissa about the trip," Ken asked.

"I don't know. I was just thinking about that. I'm still a little nervous, but I guess more at ease about it now to be able to talk it out more. What about you?" she asked.

"Honestly, I thought it was a little creepy the way she reacted when she saw the picture of you and Chelsea together. Her face looked so flushed like she had seen a ghost or something. She tried to hurry up and hide it though. I just don't know about this trip anymore. It all just seems to be so much," Ken revealed.

"So you don't want me to go anymore? I know, I take that back. I get it. I know you're just being protective of me. I love you for that. I though the whole picture was strange to me too. I really wasn't expecting her to react like that. I'm sure between now and next week, she'll figure out where she knows Chelsea from," Cookie said.

"You're right. It's not that I'm forbidding you from going. This is just a lot to confront your sister with. What if the whole story was misconstrued and it didn't even happen the way Sheila thought it did?" Ken said.

"I don't know. With all that I've seen there's got to be some truth to it. I just don't know anymore. I do see your point though. I don't want you regretting this decision either," Cookie said.

"As long as you come back to me in one piece and she doesn't try anything on you, then everything is all good," Ken said.

"I will. I promise baby. I promise," Cookie replied.

As soon as they got home, Sheila called her. Although she was a little drained from the day, she welcomed the distraction from her friend. She was almost positive she was calling her to talk about something regarding the wedding.

"Hello sweetie. How are you?" Cookie answered the phone.

"Oh wow, this is a nice surprise. I was almost half expecting not to get you. I don't want to hold you long, but I was thinking of a really nice dress for you for the wedding.. I found a few variations of it online. I'll send you the pictures. I think you'll like it," Sheila said, excitement beaming in her voice.

"What? Somebody is making progress. I would love to see the dresses. Please send them over! Have you and Sean already set a date too?"

"We're narrowing it down. Right now, it's looking like early October. I'll definitely keep you posted as soon as we decide. Tell Ken I said hello and thanks for letting me steal his wife for a minute. I know how you two like to be in the evenings," Sheila laughed.

"Oh shut up girl. Look who's talking. If your walls could talk too, I'm sure they would have plenty to say. I love you," Cookie said.

"I love you too Cookie. Talk to you soon," Sheila said, as she hung up the phone.

"I take it that was your partner in crime," Ken smiled.

"Yes, you know it babe. She is something else. She said she's going to send me some pictures of the dress she would like for me to wear. I hope it's something I look good in, because if not, I'd hate to gently burst her bubble. You know I will, but with tact," Cookie laughed.

"Baby, you could come down the aisle in a potato sack and you would be the finest thing in the place," Ken said, with a seductive grin.

"Aw, hush now. Look at you. You always know the right thing to say," Cookie said, wrapping her arms around his shoulder.

Cookie was so grateful for Ken. She closed her eyes and rested her head at the top of his chest. He may not have been perfect, but he was as close to perfection as she could have ever asked for or deserved. He squeezed her tightly with his strong arms around her waist. Cookie couldn't fathom sharing her life with anyone else. Selfishly, she just hoped that Ken didn't have a closet full of skeletons like she did.

CHAPTER TWENTY FIVE

There were only two days left until Cookie boarded the plane to Chicago to see her sister. Her insides were turning cartwheels but she knew it was something she had to do. Melissa was right that this trip would help give her some closure. She looked at her watch and it was already 5:10 pm. The day was moving along way quicker than she expected or wanted. Ken would probably be home within the next hour or so.

Cookie didn't exactly feel like cooking so she ordered some Chinese takeout. She decided to text Ken first to make sure he'd be home in time when the food got there. Right after she placed her food order, Spicy Beef and Broccoli for Ken and General Tso Chicken for herself, her phone rang. As fate would have it, the caller was Mike. She really didn't have time for him right then. Plus, their last encounter was awkward; she really didn't want to have to deal with it. She answered the phone anyway, against her better judgment.

"Hey…um Mike?" Cookie said.

"Well don't sound so disappointed to hear from me," Mike said, in an uncomfortably humorous tone.

"Oh it's not that at all. Just been a long day and waiting for Ken to get home soon. What's going on? How is Kelly?" Cookie asked.

"She's ok. She's supposed to be here in the next couple of weeks actually," Mike said.

"Oh that's great. Hey Mike, I'm really not being funny when I say this. The last time we saw each other was really inappropriate. I don't really know where to go now from there," Cookie said.

"I know. I get it. I really do. I apologize again. I meant to call you earlier in the day to tell you this. Cookie, I don't know if you've ever felt the same way about me but I have always loved you. I watched you be mistreated by different men for years. I was your shoulder you could cry on. I was your brother that couldn't move past the friend zone," Mike said.

"Wow, this is really a lot to hit me with all at once. Look, Mike I won't lie to you. There was a time that I really felt a strong attraction to you. I always wondered what would happen with us in a relationship, but never wanted to ruin our friendship over that. Trust me, I wasn't just trying to stick you into any friend zone," Cookie said, looking out of the window checking to make sure Ken hadn't pulled in yet.

"Cookie, I love you. I am in love with you. You're the one woman I've truly loved. Do you not see that?" Mike asked.

"Mike, we can't do this. We shouldn't be having this conversation. What about your fiancé? You're about to get married. Whatever we could have had back then it's over now. Don't you love Kelly?" Cookie asked in a confused tone.

"You really don't get it. Yes, I love Kelly. But is she you? Hell no. I had to move on. You finally found the love of your life with Ken and I had to do something. I knew that was the end for us at that point. I kissed you that night because I was being selfish. I just wanted to go for it and I knew that would probably be my only chance to have a piece of you," Mike said.

"Well I understand and I love you too, but it has to be on a friend level. I still want us to be close and hang out, but what happened the other night cannot go down again," Cookie replied.

"I'm really sorry to disrespect you and your marriage. Ken is a very blessed man to have you. I know he'll probably be home soon, so I should probably let you go. You take care Cookie. Hope to talk to you soon," Mike said.

"Ok, yeah I probably should go. You take care too Ken and look forward to talking to you soon," Cookie said. As she hung up the phone she really hoped she would have a few more minutes to pull herself together before Ken came home. She would never betray his trust, but there was a certain fire that rose inside of her hearing Mike's confirmation of love for her. However, she had to tuck that heat away to never be released or tampered with.

A few minutes later, Cookie saw headlights pulling into the driveway. She thought it was Ken, but it was actually the delivery man for the food. After she paid for her and Ken's dinner, she placed it in the microwave to keep warm until he got there. Ken's timing was perfect, as he pulled in a couple of minutes after she brought the food in.

"Hey baby, got stuck at work a little longer than I planned. How is my love?" he said, putting his bags down and kissing her on the cheek.

"Sorry you had to stay at work late. You do have perfect timing for dinner though. I really didn't feel like cooking tonight so I just ordered some takeout from the Chinese place we like. I hope that's ok," she said.

"Of course baby. I don't expect you to work hard every day and come in here whipping up food like Top Chef every night. You know, maybe just three or four nights out of the week," he laughed, letting her know he was joking.

"Well I am so glad to be married to a man who isn't stuck in the last century. I love you. Now, this food that I didn't slave over smells too good not to eat. Let's go get changed and dig in," Cookie smiled.

"I'm starving. Let's do it babe," Ken said.

"Oh yeah, we sure can later," Cookie replied playfully.

"Mmmm, can I give you two eggrolls tonight?" Ken said.

"You are such a freak. I guess I knew that from the beginning. I'm stuck with you now," Cookie joked back.

"Somehow, I don't think that's such a bad thing," Ken joked.

Meanwhile, Sheila and Sean were discussing options on getting a new home. They were trying to time everything just right to where they could move into a home together right after the wedding. Neither one of them was looking forward to the stress of planning a wedding and shopping for a new home at the same time. However, they both knew it was the most financially sound thing to do.

"How about I just give Ryan a call right now and leave him a message?" Sean asked.

"Yeah, I think that would be good. I know he had those two strong leads on the houses near downtown, but I would really love to stay on the north side of town if possible. We both work over here. We agreed the school districts will be better too if we have kids. Plus, this area is booming. Our property value would skyrocket in just a few years. It just makes the most sense," Sheila said.

"Oh I totally agree with you baby. Hold on I'm calling him now," Sean said.

Ryan's phone rang a few times before going to voice mail. Sean waited patiently, hoping Ryan would pick up, but he didn't. His voice mail prompt made him sound much more articulate than he actually was in person. "You have reached the voice mail of Ryan Kenton with Supreme Realtors. I sincerely regret missing your call, but if you would be so kind as to leave your name, number and a brief message, I'll be sure to get back to you as soon as I can. Goodbye". The dreaded beep followed as Sean left his message.

"Hey, Ryan. It's Sean here, just calling again. Not sure if you got my last message or not. Sheila and I have really discussed all of the options we have on the table and although the downtown homes do sound really tempting, we prefer to be on the north side of town. There was one we spoke about that was slightly below our threshold that just opened up. That's the one that's our top contender. So, let us know when we can check that one out. The address for it is 1411 Fulton Street. Talk to you soon," Sean said as he hung up the phone.

"If I haven't told you lately, thanks so much for staying on top of everything with the house baby. Even with trying to make sure that we have a low profile wedding, there still seems to be so much to do. I love you," Sheila said, giving Sean a kiss.

"I love you too baby. I don't mind at all. The more stress I can take off of you right now, the better. I know you have everything mapped out in your head for how you want the wedding to go. We really should look into getting a wedding coordinator soon. Isn't that the kind of thing they do anyway? Help take off some of the load for the bride?" Sean suggested.

"I already have a couple people in mind. But baby, you know I do this for a living. Planning events is my thing. I'm sorry, you're right though. I guess I was just being caught up in my feelings a little bit. I'll make the decision on who it will be this week, I promise," Sheila said.

"I know you can do a bang up job by yourself and better than any wedding coordinator. I'm just looking out for your well-being. Besides, I need you to save all of that energy for the honeymoon," Sean said.

"Mmmm, ok I won't argue with that. I like your thinking," Sheila smiled.

Sean's phone rang and it was Ryan calling him back. "Hello Ryan," Sean said in a friendly, yet stern tone.

"Sean, I'm great man just busy as ever. How are you? I'm so sorry I haven't gotten back to you before now. I did get your message and I totally understand about you and Sheila's preference to stay on the north side of town. I will be honest, we'll have fewer options there, but I do get that you have to go where your heart is," Ryan said.

"Yes, I left the address on your voicemail too. We were hoping that we could get a chance to see that one soon. From the pictures, it looks really nice. We even drove by there the other day to check it out," Sean said.

"Wait. You drove to that house already?" Ryan asked in a defensive tone.

"Yes, we did. Is there a problem with that?" Sean asked. One of the things Sheila really loved about Sean was his quiet, yet strong demeanor. She was always such a firecracker, but Sean was not a pushover by any means. He had a way about him that was polite but clear that he meant business. He also had no problem telling anyone when he was upset about something. Sheila could tell by his response that the conversation was on the verge of going sour at any minute.

"Please don't take that the wrong way. Of course, you can stop by any house that we discuss on your own. However, I just want to be able to present it in the best light. If that's the home you're seriously interested in though, we can definitely take a formal tour of it," Ryan responded in an apologetic voice.

"Ok, that sounds good. Just let us know when we can go take a look and we'll be there," Sean replied.

"Sure, I'm looking at my calendar now. How about this coming Thursday? Does that work for you and Sheila?" he asked.

"I'm pretty sure that will work for us. I know I can make it happen. Let me ask Sheila now if you don't mind holding for a moment," Sean said.

"Of course, please. Go ahead," Ryan said.

"Hey baby, are you free this Thursday to go look at the house?"
Sean asked Sheila.

"I sure am. Thank goodness. I'm so glad we're getting a chance
to look at it. The time we go may be an issue, but I can make it
work," she said.

"Hey Ryan, I'm back. Thursday works for both of us. What time
were you thinking?" Sean asked.

"How about 6:30pm? If that works for you, we can do a walk
through and if you still like it, then we can move from there,"
Ryan said nervously.

"6:30 it is. We look forward to seeing you then. Oh, and Ryan, I
just thought I'd ask this while it was fresh on my mind; Is there
something strange with this house that we should know about?
You seem a little uneasy every time we have a conversation
about it," Sean asked. He and Sheila both noticed how Ryan
always seemed to dodge the conversation of them checking out
the house. Sean was actually surprised Ryan followed through
this time with a date for them to view it.

"Strange? Well that's a way to put it. I wouldn't exactly say
strange. I'll just say that the house has a bit of a violent history,
that's all. Then again, I guess every home has that to some
extent, now doesn't it?" Ryan replied.

CHAPTER TWENTY SIX

"Look at you! I am loving this new hair. You look fabulous girl. When did you get the new do?" Cookie gleamed as Chelsea picked her up from the airport. She never felt so much like a stranger towards her own sister in her whole life. She had to push through her anxiety and remember the reason why she was there in the first place.

"Thank you sweetie. It's so good to see you. We are going to have a great time! I just got my hair done a couple of days ago. I had to try something new. I was getting tired of the same old look," Chelsea replied, with a sincere and bright smile. Despite her uneasiness, Cookie really did love her sister's hair. It was styled in an asymmetrical bob with a deep plum coloring that almost looked black.

"It's really good to see you, too. I hadn't told mom and dad that I would be here just yet. They knew I was going to be here this week, though, because I did talk to dad earlier this week. How is he really doing?" Cookie asked.

"I know they will be just beaming with joy to know their oldest daughter is in town today. But for now, I'm keeping you all to myself. Dad is still dad. I will say he seems to genuinely be doing much better though. He's so cute. You can tell he's actually trying to limit his physical activity now, which is so hard for him," Chelsea replied.

"You got it. I'm so ready to hang out. We'll just tell em I'm here in the morning. In regards to dad, hey that's progress that at least he's attempting to slow down. I never thought I would see that day. I don't think any of us did," Cookie said.

"I know, right. I hope you have an appetite worked up. There's a new seafood house that just opened here a few weeks ago. It is amazing. I've already been there twice. What do you say we stop there first?" Chelsea said.

"That's fine with me. I'm actually just now starting to get hungry too. I had a smoothie early this morning and then a yogurt parfait at the airport terminal, but that felt like just a drop in the bucket," Cookie confessed.

"Well sounds like we're on our way there then. I'm telling you it's delicious. How is my favorite brother-in-law doing?" Chelsea asked.

"Your favorite? Girl, he's your *only* brother in law. He's doing well, just working like crazy. I love him though. He's been such a breath of fresh air. I've just now gotten out of the mindset of thinking that the ceiling is going to break. I'm just trying to live in the moment, you know? Day by day," Cookie said. She felt like she could have kicked herself in the ass right after she spoke. She felt so wrong saying how good Ken was knowing her sister just had an abortion and broken up with Mel at almost the same time.

"I'm really happy for you. I am. After all you've been through, if no one else deserves to find true love, you definitely do," Chelsea said, placing her hand on Cookie's arm and squeezing her hand.

"You helped me though when times were really hard. I'll never ever forget that. I literally wouldn't have survived without you. You are truly my ride or die sister. Hmmm, we've done some crazy shit together," Cookie laughed.

"Yeah we sure have. Wait a minute. Is that Mel's car? I really am not in the mood to see that bastard again. Oh well though, if he's here, he's here. He may not actually try to talk to me if he sees you're with me. He'll be too afraid he'll get some acid thrown in his face by both of us," Chelsea joked.

Cookie let out a forced laugh as Chelsea found a parking spot that was to her liking. Did she really just reference throwing acid in someone's face? Then again, it was Chelsea so she couldn't really expect much different. Ever since they were teenagers, she had been a firecracker with a slick mouth. She was never afraid to back it up either.

"This place looks really nice. Judging by all of the people here, it must be really good. I can't wait," Cookie said.

"Me either," Chelsea said as they were greeted by a waiter as soon as they walked through the door. Neither one of them were expecting to be seated so quickly, but they welcomed the nice surprise.

"Ladies, we are so glad you decided to dine with us this afternoon. If you will allow me to go over our daily specials and then I can take your drink and appetizer orders, if you wish," the young man whose name tag read 'Frank' said.

"I'll have water and a Shirley temple," Cookie said.

"I'll have water as well, with a sweet tea please," Chelsea replied.

"Alright, I have two waters, a Shirley temple and a sweet tea for you two lovely ladies. Would you like to get any appetizers as well?" Frank asked.

"Oh sure, let's see. How about the loaded potato skins?" Chelsea asked.

"Yes, great choice. That's one of my favorites here. I'll get those potato skins in and have your drinks out in a couple minutes," Frank said.

"Great. Thank you so much, Frank," Chelsea replied.

"Yes, thank you," Cookie chimed in.

Just then Cookie's phone rang. She looked down and saw that it was her and Ken's counselor Melissa. Cookie contemplated answering the phone, especially since Melissa had never actually called either of them on their cell phone. She knew she was on the trip now, which was even odder that she would call.

"Girl, you look like you've seen a ghost. I take it that's not Ken," Chelsea laughed. "Go ahead and pick it up".

"Oh no, that's ok that's just a counselor that Ken and I started seeing. I'm surprised she's calling me, though. If she leaves a voicemail, I'll just give her a call back later," Cookie smiled nervously.

"Go ahead. See, your phone just went off. She probably left a message now. I need to go to the restroom anyway. Take your time sis. I'll be right back," Chelsea said.

"Ok I'll just call her right back to see what she wants. I won't be long, I promise," Cookie responded.

"Cool, don't sweat it. Oh, and when I get back I need to know why in the world you and Ken are seeing a counselor too. You're not slick. You don't get to just slide that one past me without me asking any questions," Chelsea said.

"I'll be happy to tell you when you get back. Believe me, I don't think anything gets past you," Cookie answered back in a playful, yet serious tone.

Chelsea walked away towards the restroom. Cookie spotted the restroom when they walked in and she waited a couple of seconds to turn around to make sure Chelsea had her back to her. She quickly checked her voicemail and heard Melissa's message.

"Cookie, this is Melissa. I know you're on your trip right now and I'm actually glad I got your voicemail. I found out some information that I think you'll be interested in finding out. Just contact me when you get back. It's nothing that needs any attention at the moment. We'll chat when you get back. Take care," Melissa said.

What kind of information could she be talking about? Cookie could only assume that Melissa was speaking of something in regards to Chelsea. Her curiosity was getting the best of her now and she had to call back. She dialed Melissa's number and she answered on the second ring.

"Cookie? Hi, I'm so sorry. This is not even professional for me to call you like this. Please forgive me. I do have some information for you about her. I think you'll want to know this. Let's have lunch when you get back," Melissa said.

"Hi Melissa. You're no bother at all. I'm just here at a restaurant with my sister, waiting for her to get back from the restroom.

I'm totally interested. We can see when we're both available as soon as I get back," Cookie said.

"Sure thing. Ok well, have a great time and remember the picture," Melissa said.

"I will. That actually just made me laugh," Cookie said.

"Well I'm glad to hear that. You take care now," Melissa responded.

"Ok, I will. Oh, Melissa, thank you. I really appreciate everything you've done. Seriously," Cookie said.

"Anytime," Melissa responded before hanging up the phone. The timing was perfect as Chelsea was just coming back to the table.

"Was everything ok with the shrink lady?" Chelsea asked.

"She's not a shrink, girl. She's a counselor. I debated for a while if it was even a good idea. I brought it up to Ken and he didn't have a problem with it. I think after the miscarriage I just really needed a professional to help me sort out everything in my head," Cookie said.

"I understand. I mean, I don't think that kind of thing could ever be for me, but, whatever works is what you should do," Chelsea replied.

"I used to think like that too. I'm telling you though, it has really helped me confront things in my life and just even open up to myself more. She's not creepy either. She's very down to earth," Cookie said.

Just before Cookie was afraid their conversation was about to go sour, Frank arrived at the table with their drinks and the potato skins. "Alright ladies, here are your drinks and the appetizer. I can take your entrée orders now or I can come back in a couple minutes, if you still need more time," he said.

"Actually I think we're ready. Well at least I am, if you are Chelsea," Cookie said.

"Yes, I'm ready too. We can go ahead and order," Chelsea chimed in.

"Ok, great. What can I get for you ladies this afternoon?" Frank asked.

"I'll have the shrimp scampi with the jumbo lump crakes and a Caesar salad," Cookie said.

"Great choice, that's definitely a customer favorite here. How about for you, mam?" Frank asked.

"I'll take the shrimp, chicken and Andouille sausage pasta with a side of sautéed spinach," Chelsea said.

Frank recapped both of their orders and topped off their drinks before briskly walking back towards the kitchen. Cookie was scanning the thoughts in her head and decided now wasn't the best time to even allude to her dreaded conversation with Chelsea. Thankfully, they had more of a pleasant conversation catching up on what had been going on in their lives recently, including a hilarious rant about Mel being proof that there were no good men out there for her.

"Don't jinx yourself like that. Mel was a good guy I think. He just made some dumb, really dumb ass choices. Did I mention he made some dumb ass choices? I must admit, he had me fooled," Cookie said.

"Hell, he had my ass fooled too evidently. What a waste. I haven't told this to anyone but I've actually contemplated taking him back. Can you believe that? Ugh, I must be getting old," Chelsea laughed.

"Old? Hey, watch it now," Cookie laughed.

"Oh yeah, I forgot just that quick that you are older than me," Chelsea joked.

"Seriously though, if you take him back, do it with a clear conscious. At the end of the day, it's your life and your decision that you have to be happy with. Just know that your sister is here to support you with whatever you decide," Cookie said.

"I didn't say I was going back. I just contemplated it that's all. Although I do understand what you're saying. I love you for that. I really do appreciate it," Chelsea said.

"Hey, you don't have to prove anything to me. I just want you to be happy, that's all. That's alright, though. He just made room for the amazing man that's going to come sweep you off your feet," Cookie said.

Just as Cookie and Chelsea were finishing up the potato skins, Frank was already making his way back to the table with their entrees. "If the rest of the food is anything like these potato skins, then I don't know what I'm going to do with myself. These are so delicious," Cookie said.

As Frank picked up their appetizer plates and sat down their entrees, Cookie noticed two lobster tails on the tray as well. "Oh and the lobster tail is on me. You just have to try it with their butter sauce. You are absolutely going to love it," Chelsea said.

"Look at you being sneaky. When did you even order this?" Cookie asked.

"When you were returning your call and I went to the restroom. Thanks, Frank. I think she's really surprised," Chelsea laughed.

"Yes, I would say so as well. I hope you ladies enjoy the food," Frank said.

"This food is better than sex. Well, not really but you get the point," Cookie laughed.

"I tried to tell you. What do you say we catch a movie tonight? You can pick. Whatever you want to see. We usually have the same taste in movies anyway," Chelsea said.

"Hmmm, ok let me think. What is out right now that's good? Oh, I think there are a couple of comedies that came out today, actually. Maybe we can check out one of those?" Cookie suggested.

"Yes, that sounds perfect. I could use a good laugh. We can go to the theater right up the street from here. It's on the way home too. They just upgraded that theater a few weeks ago. They have these amazing recliner chairs now. I'm telling you, they are so comfortable," Chelsea said.

"Hey, well it sounds like a plan," Cookie responded. They finished all of their food and were too full to even think about dessert at the moment. Frank brought their checks out soon after and Chelsea quickly took Cookie's bill to pay for it.

"I know I have to move quickly with you," Chelsea joked.

"Thank you. You didn't have to do that. How about I pay for the movies then?" Cookie asked.

"Ok, that sounds like a deal," Chelsea smiled. They headed back towards Chelsea's car and traveled down the highway to get to the movie theater. When they arrived there, Cookie was hit with a wave of nostalgia. She remembered coming to the theater a few times during the summer when she was home from college. The place still looked presentable, even somewhat better than what she remembered. She could tell they took time to put in some worthy upgrades. They looked at the show times and found a movie that started in the next 20 minutes.

Chelsea chose some seats for them near the top of the theater. Although they were both full, they decided to get a medium-sized bag of popcorn, with two slurpees a piece. Chelsea's was white cherry and Cookie's was blue raspberry. Those guided two hours were great with Chelsea. They both laughed through the entire film and Cookie was just glad she didn't have to worry about how she was going to frame up her confrontation with Chelsea. However, it was just a movie. Reality sunk back in as soon as the credits rolled.

As Cookie and Chelsea were on their way to Chelsea's house, Cookie started replaying her conversation with Melissa back in her head. Chelsea could sense the tension in the air and tried to pick her sister's mind. "You're so quiet over there. You would have thought we just saw a scary movie or something. Are you ok?" Chelsea asked.

"Oh yeah. I'm sorry. I'm good, I promise. I'm just taking in the moments you know. I'm really trying to practice just living in the now. Enjoying life as it happens. I'm so glad I came here. I think we both really needed this time," Cookie said.

"I agree, we did. You know, if this was 10 years ago, I would say we could go home now, change clothes and get back out for a wild night on the town. But I can't snap back as quickly as I used to. So what do you say we just sit up and have some drinks in our pajamas, while we listen to some music?" Chelsea suggested.

"Girl, who are you telling? I totally understand that. I'm so not about the party life anymore. I go out to a club once in a blue moon now, if ever. PJs and drinks sound excellent to me," Cookie laughed. About 15 minutes later, they pulled into Chelsea's driveway. She punched the remote on her sun visor to let up the garage door. She kept looking back in her rearview mirror as she could vaguely make out someone walking on the sidewalk behind the car.

"Chelsea, is everything ok? Who is that guy walking behind the car? Is it someone you know?" Cookie asked.

"Some old creep that's always walking around here at night. I've told the police about it, but every time they come out here, he's gone. He's weird; I swear he disappears and then just pops up again, out of nowhere. I don't trust this guy. Let me hurry up and let this garage down," she said, as they pulled inside.

"I'm with you on that. We don't need any encounters with weirdos tonight," Cookie said, looking in the rearview mirror as the garage went down. She couldn't make out the man's face since it was dark outside but there was something about his silhouette that seemed familiar. She tried to cast the thought out of her head, despite her eerie feeling about the man. She had enough unsavory thoughts running through her head already. She definitely didn't need to add anymore.

"Of course, please make yourself at home sweetie. I spruced up the place a bit, since I knew you were coming. There are fresh sheets on the bed in the guest room too. I tried out a new fabric softener that smells so good. I just love washing clothes, just to inhale it," Chelsea said.

"Oh, you didn't have to do all of that for me. Look at you being so hospitable. Honestly, I really do appreciate it. Thank you so much," Cookie said. Although she found it odd that Chelsea was offering for her to sleep in the guest bedroom instead of the room with her, she thanked God for it. This is one time she definitely felt more comfortable sleeping in a separate room.

"Of course sis. What do you say we go get changed up and I can make us some amaretto sours, for old time's sake?" Chelsea said.

Cookie was hoping she would get to taste her sister's amaretto sour because she made the best ones she had ever had to this day. However, she wasn't too trusting of her sister alone in the kitchen, unattended. She had to think quickly as not to alarm Chelsea or get her thinking that Cookie was up to something. "Yes, you know I was going to request your amaretto sours. How about we make them together this time? I've always wanted to learn how you make them taste so good," Cookie asked.

"Oh, well yes, that would actually be fantastic. I guess I can let you in on my secret ingredient. Sure, well, I'll go jump in the shower and change into my comfy clothes. There's some soap and towels up there in the guest bedroom," Chelsea said. Cookie could see the surprise on her face that she asked her to make the drinks with her this time. Nonetheless, she didn't seem too suspicious about it, just surprised. Cookie was at least proud of herself for thinking so quickly on her feet. Even though Chelsea was her sister, she really didn't even trust leaving a glass of water unattended in her presence right now.

"Thank you. A shower actually sounds so good right now. I'll be back downstairs in a little bit," Cookie said. As soon as Cookie was able to close the bedroom door, she decided to give Ken a call. She texted him earlier to let him know she made it, but she desperately needed to hear his voice as well. He answered just before she thought that it would go to voicemail.

"Hey baby. How are you? Everything going well with your sister?" Ken said, in a concerned tone.

"Oh yes, everything is fine baby. Thank you so much. We've actually been having a really good time. I'm about to take a quick shower and then we're going to hang out downstairs and have some girl talk," she said.

"Okay, that sounds good. You call me at any time if something goes wrong. I mean it," Ken said.

"I know you do. That's why I love you so much. I'm still a little nervous, but I have to do this. I think it will just help me move on with everything," she said. Cookie turned her attention towards the bedroom door as she heard the floor creaking just outside of it.

"Well, have fun and remember why you're there baby. I love you," Ken responded.

"I love you too, baby. I'll talk to you tomorrow," she said. After she hung up the phone, she tip-toed towards the bedroom door to see if she could still hear anything coming from the other side. She was convinced she was just being paranoid and took off her clothes to step into the shower. The water was so hot she had to step back quickly to avoid being scalded. She turned the dial back so the water would cool down a bit. Cookie stood there for a couple of minutes and inhaled the smell of the water, the steam and the demons that still haunted her, after so many years. She was finally ready to confront them head on, even if one of them happened to be inside of her sister.

Cookie made her way downstairs after getting dressed and putting on her sweatpants and a crop top T-shirt. Chelsea was already downstairs, pulling the liquor out of the cabinet in the kitchen. Dammit. She took a little too long. However, she couldn't be so paranoid the whole time she was there. Caution was okay, but she couldn't even stand herself for being so concerned with her sister's every move.

"Girl that water was hot! It felt so good though. I'm so ready for these drinks. It's been so long since we've had a chance to hang out like this, without it being an obligation or an event. It feels good just to be in your presence for fun," Cookie said.

"I know, right. I totally agree with you. I haven't felt this relaxed in a long time. Come in here and I can show you how to make those drinks," Chelsea said.

"Well, I don't mind if I do," Cookie replied, quickly making her way into the kitchen.

Chelsea started explaining how she made her amazing amaretto sours and Cookie was all ears. She was actually starting to let her guard down a bit. As Chelsea began to explain how she made the drink, she felt a little silly. So far it didn't exclude anything she already knew.

"Alright, so now that we've done all of that, we add this – my secret weapon," Chelsea snickered. Cookie waited to see what her sister was pulling out. It was a small battle of vanilla extract. She added just a splash and then topped it off with a sprinkle of cinnamon.

"All these years and I never knew what you added to it," Cookie laughed.

"Yep, that's all it is. I love it. It really turns it up a notch. I have some chips in the cabinet and some salsa in the refrigerator too if you want to grab some," Chelsea said.

"Oh yeah that sounds good. I'm just too excited that now I can make these amaretto sours at home. Mmmm, this is so good. It tastes just like I remembered," Cookie smiled.

"Cookie, I've known you all my life and I can sense when something is wrong with my sister. Is there something on your mind that you want to talk about?" Chelsea asked in a concerned, yet unbothered voice. Her demeanor couldn't be more cool and calm. In a strange way, it seemed as if she was daring Cookie to really speak what was on her mind. Cookie didn't expect the conversation to segue way into this so quickly, but it was her perfect opportunity to go with it.

"Hmmm, well there is something that I've been meaning to talk to you about. I got wind of some news that was really unsettling to me; something that I would think you are honestly incapable of. In fact, I still think you are. I just can't swallow this one whole," Cookie said.

"Well there's no better way to shoot than from the hip. Spill it. What exactly do you mean?" Chelsea asked, turning her position on the couch with a defensive expression on her face.

"Chelsea, I found out that on my wedding day, you were in cahoots with Brandon to murder me. I just can't believe it. I won't believe it. I had to ask you though, straight to your face," Cookie said.

"Oh I get it," Chelsea laughed, placing her drink on the coffee table in front of her. "So is this what you came all the way home to ask me? 'Miss Prim and Proper, and Pretty and Perfect'. Huh? Was this your whole motive for us "hanging out" as you call it?"

"Chelsea, come on now. Of course I wanted to see you. That doesn't change what I found out, though. Plus, you didn't answer the question. Did you or did you not have anything to do with Brandon coming back for me?" Cookie asked with a stern expression, not backing down in the least bit from her sister.

"Well, if you must know, yes. I did," Chelsea said. There was a long paused that filled every space of the room as Chelsea witnessed Cookie's face turn to stone.

"What did you just say? Are you telling me that you actually tried to kill me? This is some bullshit. I should have never come here," Cookie said, jumping up from the couch.

"Cookie, wait! I know this is a lot to take in right now and it's really fucked up. I get it. Please, just let me tell you what happened," Chelsea said.

"Chelsea, I really don't see how you're going to be able to talk yourself out of this one. But since I'm obviously stuck here for the time being, go ahead and spill it. I'm all ears. Please tell me your side of the story," Cookie said.

"Oh and I have a pretty good hunch as to who even told you this to begin with. I heard Sheila had gotten engaged. I never really cared for her ass anyway, but I digress. I was leaving the gym one night when that crazy ass Brandon was following me. I didn't realize it and of course I didn't even think he was alive. I had a flat tire and he pulled into an alley behind me. He put a knife to my neck and said he was going to make both of us pay. He told me the only way I was going to stay alive was to help him kill you," Chelsea said.

Cookie took a moment to absorb what Chelsea just told her before she decided to respond. "Well, if this is true, why in the world didn't you just tell me?"

"I couldn't bring that to you. It was right before your wedding and my job was just to make sure that psycho didn't follow through with anything crazy. He originally wanted to shoot you and I said that would be too messy; too brutal. I suggested that we just put something in your drink instead. Do you remember when you thought you knocked your glass over at the reception, right after the toast?" Chelsea asked.

"Oh yeah, I do remember that. I was so embarrassed and felt like such a klutz," Cookie said.

"Well there was no need to feel like that. I made you think you did it, but that was actually me. I knew he wouldn't be able to see it from where he was sitting, since I was standing so close to you," Chelsea said.

"Oh my God. So you really were trying to protect me? This makes sense.... it's just so much take in," Cookie said.

"You don't have to say it makes sense because I know it's crazy. I had to agree to him that I would help kill you and then just throw a wrench in it, so we could both live. It was a major gamble and the most frightening thing I had ever done in my life. But it was worth it. When he died, I was more relieved than anyone could have ever known," Chelsea said, exhaling deeply as she grabbed her cup again and took a long gulp of the amaretto sour.

"I guess I didn't really realize how it would have impacted you back then. Then again, I didn't know all of this either. This is such a weight lifted. I just had to know! I needed to ask you what happened so that I could be relieved," Cookie said.

"Yep, well now you know. That's how it happened. I'm glad it's all out in the open and we have that behind us now. Cookie, you're my sister and I would never do anything to hurt you," Chelsea said.

"I know. It's just that finding out everything was such a shock to me. I felt paralyzed when I heard it," Cookie said. Although Chelsea had already guessed Sheila was the one that made Cookie aware of the plan to kill her, she never confirmed whether or not that was how she got the information.

Cookie and Chelsea stayed up talking for another couple of hours or so before both of them started getting too sleepy to stay awake. "Whoa, my eyes are getting so heavy. I guess I really can't hang as hard as I used to," Cookie laughed.

"You and me both. Trust me, you are not alone. I'm struggling to stay awake too. What do you say we call it a night for now and start this party over again in the morning?" Chelsea said.

"I think I like that idea. Then we can get to see mom and dad sometime in the afternoon too," Cookie said.

"Of course, yes we'll go see them, go to the outlet to do a little shopping and of course, eat. I think there are some new museums that opened here recently too. Maybe we can check some of those out too," Chelsea replied.

"Oh really? That sounds really good. Yes, we should definitely do that," Cookie responded.

Both ladies headed upstairs towards their respective rooms for the night to get ready for bed. "Goodnight Cookie. Sleep tight, sweetie. Snuggle up so the monsters will stay away," Chelsea said.

"You remember that? Mom was smart when she used to tell us that. It made sure we stayed in the bed the whole night. We weren't getting unwrapped for anything," Cookie laughed.

"Yeah, those were the good ole days when we didn't have a care in the world. Hey, I really appreciate you listening to my side of the story tonight, too. That really means a lot," Chelsea said.

CHAPTER TWENTY SEVEN

"Ok, here we are. This is the house you both have wanted to have a look at. As you can see it needs some work. I know you two aren't really looking for a big project like this, but the house actually does have a lot of potential. There's a beautiful fireplace here, the crown molding is still intact. There's a spacious backyard too. Two stories like you both wanted with a guest room downstairs, as well as another two bedrooms upstairs," Ryan said.

"I love the layout. This is pretty much what we talked about babe," Sean said turning to Sheila to read her expression.

"You're right. I do see a little work that needs to be done, but nothing really major. This is beautiful and it's a great first home. The floorplan is even conducive to us having a child. I like it. I really like it," Sheila said.

"Well, the lady of the house is pleased. I think we're leaning even more towards this one Ryan," Sean said.

"I definitely know about that all too well. A happy wife is a happy life for sure. Ok, well, if you both insist we can start moving forward in the process. Just make sure you get to look around at everything really well," Ryan said.

"Wait, are you married Ryan? I didn't think that you were," Sheila said, noticing there was no ring on his finger.

"Oh, I'm actually not. I was, but recently divorced now. So, I'm living life as a single man again," he said, with a tinge of disappointment in his voice.

"I didn't know that either. I'm sorry to hear that," Sean chimed in.

"Oh, it's ok. I'm getting over it. Just wasn't meant to be, that's all," Ryan replied nonchalantly.

They continued looking through all parts of the house and neither one of them had any major complaints. However, Sheila did mention how hideous the paint color in the bathroom was, but that was an easy fix. Ryan wasn't exactly short with them, but he did make sure they wrapped up the look-through within the next 10 minutes. They all said their goodbyes and Ryan gave his word to follow up with them on the house.

When Sheila and Sean got in the car, something still didn't seem right to her. "I'm sorry but I just can't shake this. There is something up with this house. There's gotta be a reason why he's so apprehensive about our interest in it. Don't you think? I'm going to look up this address; can't believe we didn't think of that sooner," Sheila said.

"I don't know baby. I don't get it either. He does seem overly protective about this house. How are we going to find out anything that may have happened within, around or involving this house?" Sean said in a doubtful tone.

"Look, I found it. I just searched the address and here it is on the second page of the search results. I'll be damned," Sheila said.

"What happened? What did you find?" Sean asked.

"This link says, "Sudden Brawl Shuts Down Christmas Party". Wow, ok I'm reading this now and basically the house belonged to some woman named Brenda Russell. The article doesn't mention whether or not she's married or has any children. Check this out though. Melissa Kenton, the wife of Ryan Kenton, attacked her with a knife at the Christmas party. There are pictures of all three of them here too. That's why he doesn't want us in this house. That dirty bastard. I bet he cheated on his wife and that's why they got a divorce," Sheila responded.

"Wow, that sounds like something out of a movie. I can't believe it. As much as I don't want to believe it, that story does sound like a fight over some bizarre love triangle. I'm glad at least we have some context around why he was being so secretive about the house. How does that make you feel about it now?" he asked.

"I say we should still go for it. The article doesn't say the woman died or anything so we shouldn't have to worry about any weird spirits. Of course, we won't mention it to him, but I think we may have just found our new home," Sheila said with a smile.

"Yep, our new home with a violent backstory to it," Sean laughed.

Meanwhile, Cookie was waiting at the airport for her flight to board back to Dallas. Overall, she had a great trip and even felt more at ease about Chelsea now. Although the story seemed so far-fetched that Chelsea had to side with Brandon in order to spare her life and essentially spare Cookie's too, anything dealing with Brandon was complicated. She was glad to have also seen her parents and spend some time with them. Plus, she picked up a couple things from the outlet she and Chelsea went to and even got something there for Ken.

She decided to give him a call while she was waiting on her flight to board. "Hey baby. I was just thinking about you. I was going to call you in a few minutes. I'm glad you're on your way back and everything is ok. I love you," he said.

"I love you too. Oh, I can't believe I almost forgot to tell you this. I know I've been keeping you informed of everything that happened on the trip. You won't believe who called me shortly after I got here," Cookie said.

"Who is that?" Ken said, sounding very intrigued.

"Melissa, our counselor. She left me a message and I called her right back when Chelsea and I got to the restaurant. She was calling to tell me something about Chelsea. She said she wants to meet with me, to tell me in person. The whole conversation was strange because she kept everything so vague," Cookie said.

"Wow, what do you think she's going to tell you about Chelsea? This is all becoming too much," Ken replied.

"I know, tell me about it. I don't know what she has to say, but I'm definitely curious about it now. Oh wait, baby I they just called for us to board. I'm going to grab my things and be ready to go. I cannot wait to see you," Cookie said.

"Ok baby, you be careful. Text me before you take off. I can't wait to see you either. I'll be there waiting for you when you land. I love you," Ken said.

"I love you too. Bye baby," Cookie said, hanging up the phone. When she finally sat down, she realized the plane was less empty than she expected. She was grateful to have the seat next to her empty. She took a selfie and puckered up her lips as if she was kissing Ken. "Love u much sweetie," she texted him and put her phone in her lap.

Cookie didn't realize how much the excitement of the last few days had really exhausted her. She sent a quick text to Chelsea and her parents to let them know she was on the flight and then laid her head back on the seat. She kept the window open because she always liked to look outside at the view of the plane. The last thing she remembered was looking down at all the trees below and how they reminded her of a detailed landscaping blueprint model.

She could feel her conscious mind battling with her unconscious thoughts while she was asleep. Just as she feared, she had a strange dream that gave her quite a headache when she finally did wake up 30 minutes before the flight landing. In her dream, she was all alone in what appeared to be a damp, dark warehouse with one spotlight shining on the chair she sat in. Water dripped on her shoulder from the ceiling, as her hands were tied behind her back in the chair. Her legs felt numb like she had been previously sedated. She looked down to find her feet constrained to the legs of the chair as well, with a thick, frayed rope.

There were laughs filling the room that came from all directions. The voice sounded familiar but she couldn't quite make out who it was. Then all of a sudden it hit her; Chelsea. She was the voice Cookie heard laughing in the room. There weren't any windows or doors that she could easily see. Yet, the sinister laughs sounded like they were coming from right outside of the confines where she was being held. Why wasn't her sister trying to save her? Maybe she didn't want to and this was some sort of sick, twisted torture she was putting Cookie through.

Cookie began to sit in the chair and cry uncontrollably. Her face felt oily and sweaty, an indicator that she had been in the room alone for quite some time. She couldn't find a way out, despite surveying the entire room for an escape. She started to feel dizzy as she noticed a gray and red snake slithering from the far left corner of the room in front of her. She couldn't fathom how the snake could have even gotten inside of the room or why it decided to just now start moving (if it had already been there). As it continued to writhe its way towards her, she noticed it was at least 10 feet in length and extremely wide. This was it. This was how her life was going to end, with no one ever knowing what happened to her.

The snake stopped moving about a foot away from the chair where she sat. It stood up in the air, now eye level with Cookie. There was still plenty of room left in its tail. The snake started moving its torso and hissing at Cookie. She was now looking it square in its eyes. She let out a sigh of fear and it jumped straight towards her face. She could see the fangs moving too quickly for her to turn her head in time. That's when she woke up.

Cookie whispered a silent prayer of relief once she awoke and realized her nightmare was not a reality. Several of the passengers around her were also sleeping. She looked out of the window at the orange tinted sky. The beginning of the sunset was a beautiful picture from up so high and a nice distraction from her frightening dream. When she finally landed, she checked her phone and noticed there were four unread text messages.

The first message that she read came from Chelsea. "Be safe. Love you much," it read. Her mother and father sent the second and third texts. Her mother said, "Let us know when you make it. I love you!" and her father's text said "Safe travels to my princess. Let me know when you land." The last message was from Ken. He was letting her know that he was already at the airport waiting on her.

Cookie picked up her luggage fairly quickly from baggage claim and turned around to see Ken walking towards her. She always missed him whenever one of them was away for more than a couple of days, but this time she really missed him more than ever. She needed to feel his embrace, inhale his scent and look into his warm eyes.

"Mmmm, well who is this beautiful lady? Do you mind if I take you home? Let me get those bags for you," Ken whispered in Cookie's ear as he gave her a tight gripped hug.

"You are so silly. I love you and I am so glad to see you," Cookie said. They walked towards the car and Cookie asked him how his day was going.

"Oh it's been pretty good. Went to the gym, finished up a couple of reports for work and then came here to pick you up baby. Nothing major on this end. How was your flight in?" Ken asked.

"I had the craziest dream when I fell asleep on the plane. Other than that, it was a smooth flight, especially since I was knocked out for the majority of it," she laughed.

When they got in the car, Cookie called her parents and Chelsea to let them all know she landed safely. She kept the conversations short and sweet so she could have more time with Ken. Still in the back of her mind was an urgent feeling to call Melissa. She had to get to her soon to find out what she wanted to tell her about Chelsea.

"Hey baby, do you mind if I call Melissa really quick? I'm just dying to know what she has to tell me about Chelsea. I'll check with her and see when she's able to meet," Cookie said.

"Of course not. I actually was going to ask you if you already secured a time to meet with her. I think you should. I'm also very curious to see what she's going to tell you," Ken said.

Cookie dialed Melissa's number and waited in anticipation for her to answer. Right before Cookie thought she would have to leave her a message, Melissa picked up.

"Hello?" Melissa answered.

"Hi Melissa. This is Cookie. I'm back in Dallas now and thought I'd give you a call to find out when we can meet. Did I catch you at a bad time?" Cookie asked.

"Oh, not at all. This is perfect and actually you just saved me from watching some mindless TV that I didn't need to be looking at anyway. Yes, I do have some information about your sister that I think you will find helpful to know. I will warn you though, it's pretty serious. I just would rather lay all of this out with you in person," Melissa said.

"I'm actually a little nervous about it, but yes of course I'll meet you to find out what it is. When is a good time?" Cookie asked timidly.

"How about this Tuesday afternoon? If you have the time, we can meet for lunch and I can tell you then," Melissa responded.

"Ok, Tuesday afternoon it is then. I'll be there. I guess we can coordinate exactly where between now and tomorrow," Cookie said.

"Yes, that sounds perfect. Hey, I'm really going against the grain of my professionalism here by sharing this with you. However, I feel compelled to tell you. In other words, I can't be traced back to this," Melissa said sternly.

"Um ok, well I'm not going to share it with anyone besides Ken. I understand though and I do appreciate you even bringing it to my attention. Is there anything I should bring with me or do beforehand?" Cookie asked.

"Just bring yourself and an open mind. That's all you'll need," Melissa replied. Now Cookie was feeling even more apprehensive about meeting with Melissa and more importantly, extremely concerned with what it would mean regarding her future relationship with Chelsea.

CHAPTER TWENTY EIGHT

Cookie arrived at the café where she and Melissa agreed to meet on Tuesday afternoon. She could barely focus at work, due to the anxiety building up about their meeting. She glanced down at her watch and it was 1:50pm, ten minutes before their set meeting time. When the waitress came to the table, she requested two waters and said she would wait for Melissa to place any other orders.

A couple of minutes later, Melissa walked through the door and quickly spotted Cookie. They hugged and greeted each other as Melissa immediately asked Cookie how her trip with Chelsea was.

"Well, believe it or not, she did admit to it. The weird thing though is she said she had to agree to do it in order to save both of us. According to her, she was never going to go through with it and she purposely threw a wrench in it. If you had met my ex-husband, he was capable of anything so I was actually crazy enough to believe her," Cookie said.

"Hmmm, that's interesting. Well at least she did admit to it. I think that's a positive step towards your healing. Hopefully that gave you some kind of closure to the situation," Melissa spoke to her, in a less professional tone than she did during their counseling sessions.

"Yes, I do feel somewhat relieved. But, there's still a piece of me that feels a bit uneasy. I can't put my finger on it, but something still isn't right," Cookie confessed.

"That's totally understandable. Honestly, if I were in your shoes, I would feel the same way too. Listen, I don't want to take up too much of your time, so I should probably get right to the reason why I wanted you to meet me here," Melissa said.

"Ok. Well I'm ready to hear it. I've been wracking my brain for the last few days trying to figure out what it might be," Cookie said.

The waiter came back to the table to get their orders, right before Melissa was about to reveal her information about Chelsea. Cookie ordered a chicken pesto panini with a side Caesar salad and Melissa ordered a grilled chicken Thai salad, with a small cup of home-style chicken noodle soup.

"Cookie, has your mom ever mentioned a woman named Sandy to you before?" Melissa asked.

"Yes, that's actually my aunt's name. She's deceased now. She died when I was about 5 years old, I believe. I can't even say I remember her. I just remember the stories about her. My mother used to always tell my sister and I that Sandy was a troubled woman and she made some bad decisions. She loved her sister, but I got the impression they were total opposites," Cookie said.

"Hmmm, well Sandy was my mother. Funny thing is I didn't get much more information about her than you did. Sandy, your aunt, is actually Chelsea's mother," Melissa said.

"What?! Excuse me. This is going too far. Come on now. My mom had Chelsea. We are blood sisters. She looks just like my dad and my mom," Cookie exclaimed, now getting upset at what Melissa was telling her.

"Here, take a look at these. These are the only two pictures I have of my mother. See a striking resemblance to anyone?" Melissa asked.

Cookie took the pictures from Melissa and was shocked to see how much Sandy looked like her mother. They could have practically been twins from the photos. Despite Cookie not wanting to accept what she was hearing, there had to be some validity to Melissa's story.

"Wow! Okay, I do admit that they look a lot alike. I never got to meet my aunt. I've only seen a few photos, but this does look like her, just more like my mother than I remembered. I just don't get it. So, you mean to tell me that my sister Chelsea is not my sister after all, but your sister?" Cookie asked, with a perplexed look on her face.

"Yes, that's precisely what I'm telling you. Of course I couldn't go back now and ask her, but I did get confirmation from a very close family friend of my mother. She always tried to help her get clean. My mother was strung out on drugs and she just wasn't fit to raise two girls. We were split up. I was raised by the friend I was just telling you about, who is the only mother I've known. Her name is Elaina. Your sister, Chelsea, was given to your mother and your family. Can you believe I've never even met her before? The world is really a small, absurd place isn't it?" Melissa asked, with tears welling up in her eyes.

By this time, their food had come to the table but neither one of them could really work up the appetite to enjoy it. "This is so much to comprehend. I don't even know what I'm supposed to do with this information," Cookie said.

"I know you may not believe me, but I'm telling you this is the truth. The best thing you can do is keep this in your back pocket. I'm pretty sure your sister doesn't know because your mom would have told you too," Melissa said.

"I guess everybody has a damn secret that someone doesn't know about. I never would have thought that my mom, of all people, would keep something like this from me," Cookie said.

"Baby, everybody has a deep, dark secret. If you don't think so, just keep on living. I'm not talking bad about your mother so please don't think that," Melissa said.

"Well, thank you for telling me this. I guess Ken and I will still see you this week?" Cookie said, with a dazed look in her eyes.

"Sure, yes we are definitely still on. Oh, I almost forgot. I found a really strange page that your sister has on Tumblr. I was actually pretty disturbed by it. Go and check it out when you have a chance. The user name is @UnderTheC. I think it will give you a little more insight as to what's going on in her head," Melissa said.

"Oh, so she's my sister again now, huh?" Cookie said.

"Touche. If she's anything like you, I know she's quick on her feet. Just be careful Cookie," Melissa said. Just then, Cookie heard her voicemail alert on her phone go off. She looked down and saw she had a missed call but never heard her phone rang. She decided she would just wait until she got in the car to find out what the message said.

Melissa and Cookie wrapped up their lunch and paid the waiter, before parting ways. "I know this wasn't easy meeting me here, especially not knowing what I had to tell you. I really appreciate your openness. If you ever need to talk about this, feel free to call me, even if it's outside of our counseling sessions," Melissa said.

"That sounds good. I truly do appreciate that, more than you know. Don't be surprised when I take you up on it," Cookie smiled. The two ladies hugged and left in opposite directions towards their cars.

Cookie let out a sigh of relief as she slumped down into to her car. She was about to drive off, but then she remembered that she still needed to check her voicemails. Just as she picked up her phone, her dad was calling her at the same time.

"Daddy? This is a nice surprise. How are you doing?" Cookie asked. She was honestly glad to hear from her father. Going home really made her realize just how much she missed it. Although she enjoyed her life in Dallas, she wanted to be closer to her parents and even Chelsea.

"Cookie. My baby," Bill said. He could hardly mouth the words and Cookie quickly changed gears. She could tell something was seriously wrong with her father.

"Daddy? What's wrong? Where's mom? Are you feeling sick again?" she asked. She tried to calm herself down and not ask so many questions. There was complete silence on the other end for a few seconds. Finally, her father spoke again.

"I wish it was me this time. I wish it was me. Cookie, Lisa….I lost my heart. I lost my heart. Cookie, your mother passed. She went to go take a nap and she's gone now. In her sleep," Bill said, his voice cracking uncontrollably. Her insides felt like acid eating away at themselves. There was nothing she could do and she refused to get any more bad news. This was totally unexpected.

"Passed?! Daddy, what do you mean passed? She's dead. No, she's still here. I just saw her. We just talked a few days ago. No!!!" Cookie screamed into the phone.

"You're my oldest, so I wanted to tell you first. I don't have any idea how I'm going to tell your sister," he said.

"I would call and tell her, but um…I uh, think she would probably take it better coming from you," she said, feeling a pounding sensation forming at the back of her head.

"I know. I know. Well the doctor's coming back so I have to go now. I'm going to call Chelsea in a couple minutes. I love you," he said.

"I love you too, daddy," Cookie replied as she hung up the phone. She literally felt paralyzed as she sat in her car. There was no way she was fit for going back to work. She tried what she knew best and that was holding everything together. She quickly dialed her assistant and told her that she wasn't going to make it back in to work. She needed her to run their 4:00pm meeting and she shared that her mother had just passed. She nearly made it through the whole conversation but then broke down before hanging up the phone.

Ken still didn't know. She felt horrible that she tried to cover things at work before calling Ken to let him know about her mother. She pulled out of the parking lot and tried to concentrate on driving while calling Ken. She placed her Bluetooth inside of her ear before she entered the highway. She wasn't going back to work, but she didn't feel like going home alone right then either.

"Hello? Hey baby, what's up?" Ken answered in a bit of a hurried voice.

"Ken, I just heard some really bad news. It's about my mother. She passed. She's gone. My um….my dad just called and told me. She died in her sleep, just like an angel. I just can't take any more bad news. There must be something I did to deserve this. I just don't understand it. I'm so sorry. I know you're at work. I just don't know what to do," Cookie sobbed uncontrollably.

"Baby, I'm so sorry. I can't believe it. You just saw her. I just saw her a few weeks ago. We will get through this, baby. She's smiling down on you now. Like you said, she's your angel and she's going to be able to follow you everywhere now to watch over you," Ken assured her. He tried to offer soothing words, but even his own voice was shaking as he was trying to offer comfort to his wife. Lisa had been like a mother to him, beyond just being his mother-in-law. She really drew to him and he liked it, especially since both of his parents were gone.

"I'm going to uh go ahead and go home now. I'll start looking up some flights. I'll see you later when you get home. I love you so much. Thank you for being there for me. I don't ever want to wear that out," Cookie said.

"What do you mean? Baby, I love you. I'm here forever. I'm wrapping up here now at work and I too should be home soon. We're in this together. Remember that," Ken said.

"I know. Believe me; you have proven it to me time and time again. Ok, baby. I'll see you when you get home then. I love you too," Cookie hung up the phone and continued to drive down the highway. She couldn't even feel her hands on the steering wheel.

As she was driving, she started reflecting over her life and just how many unfortunate things had happened in such quick succession. When she first moved to Dallas, she thought the she was leaving her past behind her for good. Ken was a God-send and she felt like he genuinely loved her. However, she couldn't shake the fact that she still felt guilty for running away and making a new life for herself. Now, her mother was dead and she would never be able to feel her hugs, have dinner with her or even ignore her phone calls when she was upset with her.

Cookie cried uncontrollably until she could barely see the road in front of her. She initially thought to exit at the next street, but decided to pull over on the shoulder of the highway instead. There weren't too many cars passing by at this time of day and it was one time she hoped no one would try to come to her rescue, thinking she had car trouble. There was no reason for her to exist anymore; at least that was the way she saw it. Everything she touched had a dark cloud hovering over it. She didn't deserve to continue on and Ken definitely didn't deserve all of the baggage that being married to her came along with.

She looked over the freeway as cars passed beneath her. The tears still continually flowed down her face. Her eyes soon began to burn and her chest felt like a bag of bricks was sitting on it. She climbed on top of the ledge and prepared to do the unthinkable.

CHAPTER TWENTY NINE

Bill's first night without Lisa was heart-wrenching. He survived many things in his life, but telling his daughters that their mother died and the harsh reality of losing the love of his life was more than he could handle. He was never a heavy drinker, but he downed a fifth of an old bottle of whiskey they had kept for years. He was exhausted, yet still unable to go to sleep. Bill stayed up the entire night and barely got two hours of sleep by the next afternoon.

He forced himself to get out of the bed for a brief moment. He took the whiskey in his hand and finished the last swig left in the bottle. Through each empty room of the house, he half expected Lisa to appear or pop out of a closet like her death was some sort of twisted joke. He would have given anything to hold her face. He saw his cell phone on the edge of the bed in the guest room; the same room that used to be Cookie's. He picked up the phone and there was only 15% battery left.

Bill's daughters both took the news of their mother's passing very differently. Cookie was immediately distraught but she was always the stronger of the two sisters. Chelsea was more in shock and sounded like she needed more time to process the reality. Her hard outer persona is what made tragic things in her life harder to resolve and digest. However, Bill felt an urgent need to check on Cookie.

He dialed her number, as the phone rang and eventually went to Cookie's voicemail. Cookie barely heard her cell phone ringing in her pocket as the cars were whizzing by on the road below. She looked behind her and there wasn't a car in sight. By the looks of it, she had gotten her wish and no one would probably even witness what she was about to do.

She pushed back off of the barrier separating her from life and death. She reached inside her pocket and pulled out her phone. Fate works in mysterious ways because she thought she left her phone inside the car. In fact, her intent was to not have her phone on her at all. She saw the missed call was from her father.

Cookie slowly walked back to her car as she dialed her father back. He picked up on the first ring.

"Cookie? Baby, you crossed my mind and I wanted to check on you. I know things are really hazy right now, but we will get through this. We're strong. You're strong. Ok?" he said.

"Yes, you're right Daddy. I was actually just having a weak moment before you called. You always know the right thing to say. Thank you so much. I don't feel so strong right now, but I'm trying to push through it. I know you are too," Cookie responded.

"I'm dealing with it. We all have our different ways of coping. Where are you right now? There was a strong wind in the background earlier, like you were going through some kind of tunnel or something," he said with concern.

"Oh I'm sorry about that. It's pretty windy here outside in Dallas. You know how this weather is. No real seasons here. I love you so much daddy. I haven't talked to Chelsea yet. How did she take the news?" Cookie asked.

"Well, you know your sister baby. She deals with things in her own way. When I told her she seemed numb about it and then she broke down towards the end of our conversation. You may want to give her a call, if you haven't already. You two are sisters and will really need to lean on each other during this time. I'm concerned about both of you. Well, your dad is going to start stirring around here at the house and try to do something with myself. I actually feel a little better now that I hear your voice. It's like having a piece of your mother back," Bill said.

"I know what you mean. That's how I feel when hearing your voice too and I'll reach out to Chelsea to check on her. I should have already done that by now I guess. I love you daddy," Cookie said.

"I love you too," Bill responded.

****

The evening of Lisa's wake, everyone seemed to be moving in a cloud of haze. Cookie was trying her best to be strong for her sister and her father and then breaking down with Ken whenever they were alone. Ken was saddened in his own way about Lisa's death but didn't dare show any weakness, to be strong for Cookie. Bill was still drinking every day, not enough to get drunk but just enough to take the sting off of his reality. The sting was only lessened a hair, as he still felt the emptiness from his wife being gone.

Chelsea had reverted back to her old habits. The family all had dinner the night before, but she left early, saying that she had a headache and wanted to turn in early for the night. Instead, she went to her old stomping grounds to pick up another package to make her feel better. She knew she would regret breaking her steadfast path of sobriety in the morning, but she could only live in the now. Her pain was too great to bear right then.

"I knew you would be back," Al said he when opened the door.

"Whatever man. I'm not in the mood for any shit today. I just need a little bit. The smallest bag you have will be fine. I just need something to get me through tomorrow, that's all," Chelsea said. She showed up to the building in some jeans, sneakers and a slightly oversized t-shirt with some sunglasses on. Her purse was draped across her shoulder and fell right at her hip.

"Still as feisty as ever. I'll get it for you soon enough. You know, I always did think you were pretty sexy. That ass is looking nice and round in those jeans too. What do you say we work out some other form of payment?" he said, with a devilish grin.

"Mmm, another arrangement. That could maybe work. Open your mouth for me," Chelsea said.

"What kinda freaky shit are you into?" he said, reluctantly opening his mouth.

"This is the kinda freaky shit I'm into," Chelsea said, whipping out a gun from her purse and pointing it at his forehead. "Did I tell you to close your mouth? Open it. Open it right now! Yeah, just like that. Now you go back there and get me what I need. How about the payment is I spare your sorry ass life? I ain't got anything to lose right now and I will blow your brains out, right here, right now. You got that?" Chelsea said, looking around to see if anyone could see what was going on, but still focusing her attention and the gun in her hand on the man in front of her.

"Yeah, just get that gun out of my face. Damn. I'll be right back," he said.

"That's more like it," she mumbled.

He came back quickly with the bag and Chelsea threw some money at him for payment. "Crazy bitch. Go on and get out of here," he said.

"It's always the little puppies that have the most bark with no bite. Go on and play now. I've been called worse by worse. You have yourself a good day, little man," Chelsea said, looking down at his crotch before turning around heading to her car. She kept her gun out in case he decided to try anything slick when she turned her back on him.

As soon as Chelsea got in her car, she placed her gun in her lap and drove quickly out of the parking lot. She cried all the way home and could feel her face trembling as she finally pulled into her driveway. She got out of the car and immediately started unraveling the brown paper package on her kitchen counter. She smashed the white heaven up and then proceeded to snort a couple of lines of it. She just needed to feel the hit to ease her mind; at least that was how she justified it to herself.

Her head started swimming and she suddenly felt as if her body was levitating inside of itself. She felt like she was watching herself lift off from the ground and she loved it. Chelsea hadn't felt like this in a while. Just then she heard her phone ring and it sounded like a blaring marching band. She looked over at it and saw Cookie's face. She tried to answer, but couldn't reach the phone in time. This high was different than what she felt before; more potent and euphoric. She poured herself a glass of water hoping that would lessen the overwhelming warmth building up inside of her. Her decision turned out to be a bad idea, but there was no turning back now. She slumped to the floor before she was able to get the water up to her mouth, as she laid sprawled out on the kitchen floor.

Meanwhile, Cookie and Ken were on their way to spend the night with Bill. He wanted Chelsea to spend the night there too, but he could tell she wanted to be alone. Cookie left a voicemail on Chelsea's phone and decided to drive by her house, just to see if there were any signs that she was at home. The journey there was a bit of a detour, but Chelsea only lived about 15 minutes away from her their parents' house.

Cookie parked the car a couple of houses down and walked up the street to see Chelsea's living room light on. Her car was parked outside of her garage, which was a bit strange for her. However, she was just glad to know her sister was safe and sound at home. She started to go knock on the door and tell her to make the sacrifice to spend the night with them tonight, but she didn't have the energy for a potential argument. Ken was walking closely behind her, since it was now dark outside.

"You see anything?" he asked.

"Yeah, well other than her car being out here, her light is on inside. I guess she's ok. We can go ahead and go now," Cookie said.

No sooner than they turned around, did a thin Caucasian man with stringy black and gray hair meet them face to face. Cookie was stunned and silent, while Ken immediately went on the defensive.

"Excuse you? Can we help you with something?" Ken asked.

"Hmph. No, but I can help you. I'm assuming you're looking for the lady that lives a couple of houses down. Do yourselves a favor and leave her alone," the man said.

"What are you talking about? She's my sister," Cookie said, realizing she probably shouldn't have revealed that information to a total stranger. The more she looked at him, she could see some familiar traces. She had seen him somewhere before. That's when it clicked. He was the man that took them to the hotel from the accident when they were there a while back. He seemed even creepier now.

"I'm sorry to hear that. Then I must offer my condolences. I heard your mother passed. I'm so very sorry. I only met her a couple of times, but she was a very sweet woman," he said solemnly.

"I remember you. You're the guy that dropped us off at the hotel when we had the accident," Cookie said.

"Wow, he sure is. Look man, I don't know how we ran into you again, but you have a good night. We'll be on our way now," Ken asked.

"I don't want any trouble, I just want to tell you to get as far away as you can from that woman. She's no good. She has a dark soul and she'll drag you to hell with her. I've witnessed her doing some very ugly things. You two have yourselves a lovely evening now," he said, walking away.

CHAPTER THIRTY

The day that Bill, Cookie, Chelsea and Ken were dreading had finally come. Everyone was walking around with a somber demeanor. Chelsea barely made it there on time. Little did they know, she was still recovering from her relapse the night before.

"Alright everyone. The family car will be here soon. Let's make sure we're all ready to go. Your mother would be proud. You two look so beautiful. Ken, you don't look half bad yourself," Bill said. He was trying his best to still be the patriarch of the family and hold everything together. A few minutes later, the family car did actually arrive and reality sunk in a little deeper as they walked outside the front door.

When they finally arrived at the church, they were pleasantly surprised to see people were already there. Cookie and Chelsea shed tears at different times and even together at some points. Cookie felt so weak and was not able to hold it together and be the bigger sister right then. Ken supported her and doted on her every request. He felt awkward and just tried to help wherever he could, but mainly stay out of the way. Meanwhile, Bill was holding up very well. His strength was in tact, but the pain was definitely present in his eyes.

"Cookie, do you see how many people are here? Your mother was really loved. That should make you feel good," Ken said.

Cookie turned around to see what Ken was talking about. She was in a twilight zone and hadn't paid much attention to who else was there. She gasped as she looked behind her. "Wow, you're right. Yeah, this does make me proud," she whispered, dabbing her eyes with tissue.

"Yeah, they say that you preach your own funeral. Mom really lived a life of sacrifice and greatness," Chelsea chimed in. The rest of the service was somber, yet uplifting as more and more people poured in. The resolutions were comforting, yet bittersweet since Lisa wasn't present to hear them in person. Everyone started to hold it together until the end of the funeral, right before the casket was closed. That was the final confirmation that Bill had lost the love of his life and Chelsea and Cookie had lost their mother.

Ken acted as one of the active pallbearers and he had a hard time keeping his composure together, especially when he saw Cookie. Sheila and Sean sat closely behind Cookie and she could feel Sheila rubbing her back. Sean was holding on to Sheila, as she herself was beginning to feel weak at the thought of her best friend's mother being gone. Although she knew she was not Chelsea's favorite person, she tried showing her an outward expression of condolences. Chelsea was not receptive at all and did just enough to show her gratitude for Sheila's presence.

"Thank you Sheila. The family truly appreciates your support. We're strong and we'll be ok," Chelsea responded and flashed Sheila a forced smile.

"The family?" Sheila thought to herself. She was so pissed at the underlying sarcasm of Chelsea's response that she almost forgot how grief stricken she was. That crazy bitch. She was determined not to let Chelsea get under her skin because that's exactly what she wanted.

"Yes, you are. All of you have always been strong. Sean and I are here if you need anything," Sheila said. Sean gripped her shoulder to offer support and also give her a silent reminder to keep her cool.

When everyone finally arrived at the burial site, Bill stayed in the family car. He didn't want to get out and no matter how everyone tried, he stayed put. Chelsea turned back to the car, as Cookie stood behind her to try to get their father out of the car. "Daddy, come on. I know it's hard. I really do. But mom is going to be here with us forever in spirit. We're just saying goodbye to her shell," she said. This was the strangest feeling for Chelsea and Cookie because usually it was their father playing this type of role, not them.

"Chelsea, I can't baby. As much as I would like to get out of this car, I can't do it. My mind just won't let me. I know this is the final goodbye and I guess I just really don't want to accept it," Bill replied. Chelsea stood back and sighed, backing away from the car. Cookie walked up closer to the car and rubbed Chelsea on the back. She walked up a little closer to speak to her dad.

"Hey daddy, do you know that you are the strongest man I know? Well, of course you have to share that title with Ken now," she laughed. "Seriously though, I know it's hard. I can't even say I know how you feel because although Chelsea and I lost our mother, you lost the love of your life. I'd be lying if I said I totally understood that. Don't you think that mom would be so proud that you made the sacrifice to stand for her today?" Cookie asked, with tears streaming down her face.

Bill smiled through his tears, before answering Cookie. Chelsea looked on in the background, waiting to see if he would actually get out of the car. "I know you're right. That's the last thing I want is to disappoint my baby. I never want that. Come on, let's go and pay our respects to your mother just the way she would want it," Bill said. Bill smiled at Chelsea and wrapped his arms around her waist as he walked with both of his daughters towards the burial site. She wouldn't dare show it, but Chelsea was seething with jealousy yet again. Cookie swooped in and saved the day. Her words to her father were not enough, but Cookie's were.

She was so damn sick of living in her sister's shadow. The impact of her sister always being treated as the favorite was beginning to take its toll on Chelsea. However, she was still able to hide her frustrations, up to this point.

CHAPTER THIRTY ONE

The next afternoon, everyone was still in a bit of a fog but not as much as they were yesterday. Bill called Ken earlier that morning and Cookie was surprised that she didn't hear from her father first. Ken was honestly just as shocked as Cookie was, as he answered the phone.

"Hello, Bill? You have good timing. Cookie and I were about to call you soon to check on you and see if you needed anything," Ken said.

"Well actually you've got perfect timing too then. I guess I'm doing ok as I can be. I was thinking I never get a chance to hang out with my son alone. I know you and Cookie will be heading back soon, so what do you say we give the girls some bonding time and we shoot a game of pool this evening?" Bill asked.

"Sure, that sounds great. I haven't played pool in a while. I'm looking forward to it then. How about 6:00 pm? I'll check with Cookie," Ken responded, with a pleasantly surprised look on his face.

"Ok, well just keep me posted. I'll be here. Hopefully you have some skills to bring to the table," Bill laughed. Behind his laugh, Ken could still hear he was in great pain.

"Let's just say I'll keep the game interesting," Ken laughed. Cookie looked on intently, waiting to find out what her father was talking to Ken about.

"He has some confidence. I like that. Means my girl is in safe hands. I always knew that she was with you. I guess I'll talk to you later then," Bill said.

"Ok, I will give you a call soon then and fill you in on the details," Ken said.

"Sounds like a plan. Oh and tell Cookie that there are some things of their mother's here that they may want. Maybe they can sort it out here at the house. I already told Chelsea right before I called you," Bill stated.

"I'll be sure to tell Cookie. I'm sure she'll be so happy to have some of her things at home with us," Ken said. Bill and Ken hung up with each other and Cookie immediately started asking questions.

"Baby, did my father just sign you up to do something? I'm so sorry if he did. You can say no," she asked.

"Well, he actually invited me out to play pool tonight. I told him around 6:00 pm would probably be good. Plus, he said there are some things of your mother's that you and Chelsea may want to sort through. He didn't say exactly what it was, though," Ken said.

"Look at you. I've seen you play pool before. Don't tell me my dad is going to get played by my husband, the pool shark. Although, I'm sure he'll be able to hold his own. Can I just go with you instead of staying with Chelsea? I'm sorry. That's not even like me to be clingy like that. I just don't know how it's going to be when I'm alone with Chelsea again. What do you think?" Cookie asked.

"I know it's probably going to feel awkward. Believe it or not, I really think the story she told you is the truth. Chelsea may get angry with you at times. But do I think she would intentionally try to harm you or take your life? No. Besides, this may be a good time for both of you to get some bonding in. You know if I felt differently, I would tell you. I really think it's going to be ok though," he said.

"Well, you sound pretty sure so I guess I should be too. You're right. I'm just....I have to be just overreacting," Cookie said.

****

Chelsea looked down at her watch at the red light. It was 3:45 pm. She was a couple of minutes away from pulling in to her parents' driveway. She felt a lump in her throat form as she realized that the house she grew up in was now her father's house. Her mother would never step foot in it again. She exhaled deeply before she turned off her ignition and got out of the car.

Bill already opened the door before Chelsea got a chance to knock and put her key in. "Hey, my baby girl. I'm so glad to see you. I love you. You look beautiful. I see so much of Lisa when I look in your eyes," he said.

"Thank you, daddy. I love you too. I think for now, I'm just going to psyche myself out and say that mom is away on a really relaxing trip. That's how I have to think of it right now to be okay," Chelsea replied, holding back tears and hugging Bill.

"I know. I'm pretty much doing the same too. It's definitely going to take some time to get used to, although I don't think we'll ever really get used to it. I have a few of your mother's things. I figured you and Cookie could sort through them later.

Ken and I are actually meeting up to play pool this evening," Bill smiled.

"Oh nice, don't beat him too bad then. Sounds like fun and you deserve to get out and do something different. That will give Cookie and I some bonding time too," Chelsea responded.

"Good, well that's what I was thinking. You and your sister are going to need each other during this time. I really wish she would come back home and live here sometimes, especially now. Come on, let me show you where some of your mother's things are. These are a few things that I thought your mother would be honored for you and Cookie to take," Bill said.

He handed her several bags filled with clothes, pictures, keepsakes and jewelry from Lisa. Chelsea was overwhelmed as she quickly glanced through the contents of each bag. "I guess I should play fair and maybe give Cookie a chance to look through some of this too. I think I will take a look at this one though, before she gets here," Chelsea smiled.

"Oh yes, I remember that one all too well. Your mother kept that one like Fort Knox, even from me. I think she had some old papers in there or something. I learned at an early age from my father that whatever secrets a woman is keeping, it's best to just leave them alone. He said open secrets are sometimes better left unconfirmed. Well, baby I'm getting a little light headed. I think I need to go lie down for a bit. I need to get some rest before my big pool game tonight," he laughed.

"Alright daddy. Go ahead and get your rest. Cookie called me on the way here. She and Ken shouldn't be here until around 5:00

anyway. So, you'll be able to get a good nap in. I can wake you up in about an hour, if that's fine," Chelsea said.

"Would you please? Thanks so much, baby. I'll see you in a little bit then," Bill said, walking towards the bedroom. Even in agony, Chelsea was amazed at how much spunk her father still had.

Chelsea moved the bags next to the couch and turned on the TV in the living room. She surfed through the channels until she found something lighthearted and comical. Anything that would take her mind off of the pain would help. She sat there and watched TV for nearly twenty minutes before she couldn't take it anymore. She picked up the beautiful ceramic pink mauve colored box and held it in her lap.

She shook the box and could hear some things rustling inside of it. There was paper mainly, but a few small solid items too. The box was dense, made of good quality. The finish had a marbled look and the shape of the box was slightly rectangular. Chelsea decided to get up from the couch and get something to drink from the refrigerator. She glanced back down at the box and decided to take it with her. Somehow, she felt a little silly packing around her mother's box under her arm, but on the other hand, she loved how it made her feel closer to her.

She opened the refrigerator door to find some juice, with the box tucked under her left armpit. Then, she turned around to find a half empty bottle of wine. She looked closer to see that it was her mom's favorite. The sight of the wine crippled her emotions more than she thought it would. Before she knew it she dropped the box and its contents were now displayed on the floor. The shattered box pieces were indicative of her mental state; broken, crumbled and smashed.

Chelsea peaked around the corner and down the hallway to check on her father. He must have been sleeping pretty hard because he didn't move an inch. She was relieved that she hadn't woken him up with the loud noise of the box breaking. Her attention was redirected at cleaning up the mess on the floor. She swept up the pieces of the box and then picked up all of the things that belonged inside of it. There were a couple of necklaces, a pair of pearl earrings, but mostly cards and various papers. She couldn't make out the handwriting on most of the letters and cards, but there was one in particular that looked just like her mother's handwriting.

I am so angry right now at my sister for this. I love her, I do. But there is no way that Bill and I are ready for another child. Our marriage is already on the rocks and I don't know that we can withstand this. Plus, Candice is so young. How would she feel when she gets older? I could almost take Bill cheating on me and getting some other woman pregnant, than I could carrying the weight and responsibility of this.

But I do love Chelsea. She has the brightest, most intense eyes. She's beautiful and she looks like she could be more of my child anyway. I will love her and care for her as if she were my own. I will put all of my efforts and energy into making sure that she grows up to be the opposite of what her mother was. With God's help and Bill's, we will make this work.

Chelsea could feel her face turning red and her heated tears were streaming down her face. The note didn't have a date on it, just her mother's words. How could she have kept this from her all her life? How could her father have kept it from her? Did Cookie know? She couldn't understand how her whole life was a lie and everyone seemed to know it but her. Once again, she had been betrayed and lied to. This time, the lie was in the worst way imaginable.

She quickly picked up the contents of the box and threw away its broken pieces. Cookie should be there within the next 10 minutes, so she knew it was nearing the time to go wake up her dad. She walked softly into the bedroom and spotted a nearly empty bottle of Jack Daniels on the nightstand. She guessed that everyone had their own way of coping, some with worse mechanisms than others.

"Hey Daddy, I think it's time for you to wake up from your nap. Cookie and Ken should be here any minute. I have a little bad news. I accidentally broke the pretty box mom had, but at least the stuff inside was salvaged," Chelsea said, lightly tapping her dad on the shoulder. She raised up her other hand to show him what she found in the box. She kept the note written by her mother tucked away in her pocket.

"Oh no, I'm so sorry baby. Well, at least you were able to keep the inside of the box intact. Find anything interesting in there?" he asked.

Chelsea swallowed the uncomfortable lump forming in her throat. She contemplated answering his question honestly for a split second, but of course, she lied. "Oh yeah, some really cool earrings, a necklace and some old cards and papers".

"That's good you found something nice. That was a hard sleep, I tell you. I had this crazy dream. There was some dragon breathing fire and all of this glass shattering. The heat felt so real. It was like a fire over me while I was sleeping or something. Let's just say I'm glad it was just a dream and not reality," he said. The doorbell rang and there was a quick knock on the door. Cookie always rang the doorbell first and then knocked before she put her key in.

"Well, I am certainly glad that was just a dream too. I think you're getting up just in time. Sounds like that's your darling coming through the door now," Chelsea smiled cheaply.

"Well, last time I checked I had two darlings. Now I have the pleasure of having them both here together at one time. How about that?" Bill smiled.

"Sounds great to me. I'm sure Cookie would agree," Chelsea said.

"Hello? Hey, there you are. Chelsea, I love that top. Orange always was a beautiful color on you," Cookie said.

"Thank you sis. You are so sweet," Chelsea said, reaching out to give Cookie a hug.

"Hey daddy, I came to bring you pool partner for the night to you. Make sure to go easy on him now," she said, smiling back at Ken.

"Well, I'm sure the man can hold his own. But yes, I will definitely keep in mind to let him down easy," Bill laughed.

"Touche. I'll do my best to keep up a good fight, at least," Ken joked back with Bill and greeted Chelsea with a tight hug. Cookie loved how he wasn't afraid to speak to her father head on. Even Brandon couldn't stand up to her father quite as well as Ken could. That was one of her favorite qualities about him.

"Alright, I'm ready now. We can let the ladies have their time together and get the pool game started. Come on son," Bill said, parting Ken on the shoulder.

"Ok babe, we'll see you later tonight," Ken said goodbye to Cookie, kissing her on the forehead.

"Have fun you too. Be safe out there," Cookie said, kissing Ken back and giving him a hug around his waist.

"Yes, we need a play by play when you return. We want to know all the details," Chelsea chimed in.

"Yes, we will definitely be sure to do that then. We'll even send pictures," Bill replied.

Cookie shut the door and locked it behind them as she walked towards Chelsea to join her on the couch. Right before she took a seat, she noticed the bag of her mother's things next to the couch. Her eyes then directed to the stack of cards, papers and jewelry placed on the coffee table.

"What's all this? Are these things dad said belonged to mom?" Cookie asked.

"Yeah there were a few loose things in the bags, but I figured we could look at them both together and just split some of the things we liked," Chelsea suggested.

"That sounds good to me. Wow, I um....You know what? Do you remember those pecan pies mom used to make from scratch?

To this day, I've never tasted a pecan pie so delicious. I could really go for one of those pies right about now. How about you?" Cookie said, fight back tears.

"How could I forget those pies? Yes, they were truly amazing. I loved those too, but I think my absolute favorite thing that she made were those apple cobblers. My goodness. She was a slick one too. I never really got the full recipe. I couldn't figure out how to make it taste like hers if I tried," Chelsea said.

"How are you feeling about everything?" Cookie asked.

"Honestly, it's so much for me that I can't even fully process it right now. I just tell myself she's away on a trip or something. I'm still thinking of her in the present tense and still half expecting her to call me every day. It's so weird. It hurts. How about for you?" Chelsea asked.

"It's pretty much the same for me too. I think with you being here, you're more in touch with reality about it than I am. When I go back home, it will be easy to tell myself that it's just a time in between visits before I see mom again. I'm sorry, I wasn't trying to create a somber mood. I was just curious to see how you were dealing with it all," Cookie responded.

"Oh no, it's ok. I get it and honestly, I'm glad you asked; makes me feel like I'm not alone. Ugh, I forgot to charge this phone last night. I'll be right back. I'm just going to the car to grab my charger," Chelsea said, standing up and grabbing her coat.

"Ok cool, I'll be right here," Cookie said. She started looking through some of her bags as Chelsea went to the car. She immediately saw some things that she recognized and she fought back tears as she could smell the scent of her mother inside of the bags.

"Hey, I'm back now. How about I make us some drinks? It's not like we're going somewhere anytime soon. What do you think?" Chelsea asked, with a wide grin spread across her face.

"Oh sure, that sounds great. You know I'm always ready for your amaretto sours. Funny thing is I've tried to make my own since you showed me how to make them last time. They taste nothing like yours. I guess you have that magic touch. Even Ken had to admit that he liked yours better," Cookie laughed.

"Oh I'm sure you're just being a little hard on yourself. I was actually thinking of trying something different today though. I have this new app that gives you all of these different kinds of cocktails. Are you in the mood for a little surprise?" Chelsea asked.

"Ah, a walk on the wild side. Sure, I'm down for it. Sounds good to me," Cookie replied, leaning back on the couch and grabbing the remote.

"Cool, now let's just hope there's enough stocked in the liquor cabinet and the refrigerator for me to make it. Anything good on TV?" Chelsea asked.

"Not much yet, but I'm looking. Oh wait! Look, one of our favorites, *Miss Congeniality*. I haven't seen this in forever," Cookie said.

"Oh yeah, leave it on there. That movie is so hilarious. I laugh like it's my first time seeing it even to this day. I think we both could use a good, hearty laugh right about now anyway," Chelsea said, her voice trailing off.

"Yeah, ain't that the truth," Cookie sighed.

Within a few minutes, Chelsea came from the kitchen into the living room with two drinks in her hand. She handed one of the drinks to Cookie and placed the other one on the coffee table. "Now I'll be right back. Don't get started without me. I just need to go to the restroom, but I have a feeling you'll like this one," Chelsea said with a cheerful smile.

Cookie stared at the drink in her hand for a few moments. She could smell a hint of pineapple, but that was the only thing she could really make out. She fought the urge to take a sip and wait until Chelsea returned.

"Alright, I'm ready now. We can start looking through some of mom's things, if you want," Chelsea said.

"Sure, now is as good a time as ever," Cookie said, picking up the bags from the side of the couch. "Ouch! Ugh, what is this?" Cookie removed a piece of hard, mauve colored material from the bottom of the bag. She looked at it closely and then glanced down at her arm. She was relieved there was just a deep scratch there but no blood.

"Oh no, I'm sorry. That's probably my fault. Mom had this really pretty box that was in one of the bags. I accidentally dropped it when dad was taking a nap earlier. I tried to quietly pick up all of the pieces, but I must have missed one," Chelsea said.

"I see. What was inside of the box?" Cookie asked.

"Just this stuff right here," Chelsea replied, pointing to the cards and jewelry laid out on the table.

"Hey at least we got to see what was inside it. Let me taste my drink first, before the ice dilutes it," Cookie said, taking a generous taste of the drink.

"So, what do you think?" Chelsea smiled, taking an even bigger drink than Cookie did. Before Cookie had a chance to answer, Chelsea started coughing uncontrollably and her face started turning red. She grabbed at her throat and tried to motion for Cookie to help her, since she could barely speak.

"Do you really want to know what I think? I think you better finish the rest of that drink. I knew that story you told me was bullshit. Right now, I have more than enough reason to not trust anything you say. Finish the drink right now, dammit!"

"Cookie, I love you. I'm so sorry. I just couldn't…." Chelsea said, her voice fading and eyes rolling back in her head.

Cookie stood above her and pulled out a small gun from her the back of her pants. "Sorry won't work this time baby sis. I gotta look out for me. Now you're going to finish this drink or say your prayers before I blow your brains out all over this floor. Don't tempt me. I'll do it," Cookie said.

Chelsea looked inside her sister's eyes and witnessed a rage she had never seen before. Cookie still stood over her with the gun pointed at her head. She grabbed the drink and gulped the rest of it down as tears streamed down her face. Shortly after, her body began to convulse wildly. Chelsea put up a strong fight but it wasn't enough to save her life. Her body fell lifelessly to the floor, with her head turned to the side. Foam began to form at the corner of her mouth.

Cookie smiled and cried simultaneously as she watched her sister take her last breath. She was devastated that she was dead, but also relieved that she no longer had to live in fear wondering what she was going to do next. She stood there in silence, looking around the room then back at Chelsea on the floor. She half expected her to move and try to get up again; but she never did.

She pulled her cell phone out of her pocket and dialed 911. As she waited for dispatch to answer, her heart felt like it was going to explode. Never in her life, had she felt this nervous and conflicted before.

"Hello? 911. How may I direct your call?" a woman answered.

"Um, yes I need someone to come here right away. My sister, she's…I'm not sure if she's dead but she's passed out for sure. She's shaking uncontrollably. I just need you to get here fast please," Cookie cried hysterically.

"Yes mam. Can you please tell us where you're located and we'll get someone there right away," she said.

"Ok yes I'm at 6102 Phoenix Lift Lane. Please send someone quickly. I don't know what to do," Cookie replied. As soon as she hung up the phone with 911, she made the dreaded call to Ken to tell him and her father what happened. She knew she had done the right thing. Otherwise, Chelsea would have killed her. At least that's what she had to start telling herself to be able to sleep at night.

EPILOGUE

"Baby, I know you're nervous about these results but you have to get some rest. I'm concerned about you. You stayed up pretty much all night yesterday too," Ken said.

"I know, thank you baby. I'm trying. I really am, I promise. I'll just feel so much better after I know how that toxicology report comes back tomorrow. I'm telling you, she put something in that drink. Even the way she looked at me as I was drinking it. I know she was banking on me not thinking to switch them around while she went to the restroom. I just kept getting this weird feeling, you know?" she said.

"I get it. You had to do what you had to do. It was either her or you and you know who I'm going to pick," Ken said, holding her with his arm wrapped around her as she laid her head on his chest. Cookie could finally feel herself fading to sleep as the last thing she remembered was Ken rubbing her shoulder and kissing her on the forehead.

The next morning seemed to move in slow motion. Her appointment with the toxicologist was at 11:00 am and she was sitting in the passenger side as Ken drove. She glanced down at her watch. 10:46 am. A few minutes later, she and Ken pulled into the parking garage and walked towards the building to meet the toxicologist.

They took the elevator up to the fourth floor and walked towards the office to hear the results of what could have been in Chelsea's system that ended her life. Cookie and Ken were greeted by a warm receptionist as they entered the office. Ironically, the name on her badge was Chelsey.

"Hello, how may I help you today?" Chelsey asked.

"Hello. My husband and I have an appointment with Dr. Bederman at 11:00 am today," Cookie responded.

"Sure, he's actually ready to see you now. I can escort you back to his office. Let me just give him a buzz," Chelsey said.

"Ok sure, that will be great. Thank you so much," Cookie said.

"Of course. You're welcome. Dr. Bederman, your 11:00 am is here. I'll go ahead and bring them back," Chelsey said. She motioned for Cookie and Ken to come through the door and she took them back to Dr. Bederman's office.

"Hello Candice and Ken. Great to see you. I know losing a loved one can be a really difficult time, but hopefully today will help bring some closure to both of you for the situation," he said.

"Yes, of course. That's what we're hoping for," Cookie said.

"Well, I don't want to belabor this any longer than it has to be. will say that our findings were interesting and honestly unexpected, based on the series of events. Have you ever heard of a street drug called hot sauce?" Dr. Bederman said.

"I don't think I have. What is that?" Cookie asked, looking at Ken. He looked just as confused as she was at the mention of the drug.

"Ok, well in laymen's terms, it's extremely powerful. Many people mix it in with drinks and it's very lethal. It only takes a teaspoon or two to end someone's life. This drug was found on your sister's possession at the time of her death. She had a small bottle that had been opened, but obviously not used; at least not in the drink she made for you or herself the day she died. Perhaps some of it spilled without her knowing. That I'm not sure of. However, no one carries that kind of drug around unless they're planning on using it if you catch my drift," Dr. Bederman said.

"I don't get it. What are you saying she died of then?" Cookie asked, extremely fearful now of what really happened to Chelsea.

"Candice, I'm so sorry to break this news to you but what your sister died of was an overdose. A heroin overdose," Dr. Bederman said.